BIOMASS
Rewind

by

Terry Persun

Biomass Series, Book 1

Biomass: Rewind

Contact Information: info@thewildrosepress.com

Cover Art by *Jennifer Greeff*

The Wild Rose Press, Inc.
PO Box 708
Adams Basin, NY 14410-0708
Visit us at www.thewildrosepress.com

Publishing History
First Edition, 2022
Trade Paperback ISBN 978-1-5092-3888-0
Digital ISBN 978-1-5092-3889-7

Biomass Series, Book 1
Published in the United States of America

Roger yelled from the rear, "Let's go, let's go."

I jumped up and ran, bursting through the underbrush toward the buggy. Josh brushed past me. I halted and looked back. Karen stood still. Bill, wide-eyed, wouldn't leave her side, all the while trying to coax her forward with one arm around her back and one gripping her bicep.

Roger wildly slashed at the brush to get around them.

"Oh, shit," Josh said and pointed into the trees.

Four howlers perched on branches near Bill, Karen, and Roger. Somehow my mind took over. "Get out of there!"

Praise for Terry Persun

"Terry Persun's *Biomass: Rewind* has everything I love in a novel: fully fleshed characters, thought-provoking science, and a story that grips you by the throat until the last page...while still leaving you wanting more. If Orson Scott Card and Isaac Asimov had collaborated on a novel, it might look something like this book. Highly recommended!"

~James Rollins,
#1 New York Times bestseller
of The Last Odyssey

*

"I love a book that makes me think about what makes us human. From the opening, bone-rattling descent to a new world, Terry Persun takes us on a twisting journey of discovery that reminds us that friends can be enemies, enemies can be friends, and "intelligent" isn't the same as "most intelligent.""

~Eric Witchey,
author of Littlest Death,
winner of the International Book Award

Dedication

For Catherine, Nicole, Mark, and Terry.
And Val Mathews for her editing skills.

Chapter 1

Dropped

It all started with twelve of us stuffed into a landing pod, plummeting violently toward the planet we were to colonize. I gripped the seat arms, excited and terrified at the same time. We were layered into the pod, one mated pair angled above the next, each with different instrument panels in front of us. My paired partner, Missy, controlled the data stream.

I couldn't see any of the other pairs. Missy and I had been loaded first. Everyone had a purpose, mostly scientific in nature—except me. My job was the least technical and most expendable. I hadn't been told that but knew it intuitively. All I was to do was document events, attitudes, emotions, personalities—seemingly whatever I liked.

The pod rattled and bounced. I heard the others spouting out information, orders.

We could all die. That much I gathered.

I reached for Missy's hand.

"Concentrate on the details," she said over my com unit.

She was right.

At that moment, we were heading for the second planet from the sun of a small solar system where there were five planets. It was the only one that remained in a habitable orbit during its entire travels around its sun. Two of the other planets spent short times in the habitable zone but much more time outside of it. I didn't know whether Argentina had made drops to any of the other planets, or if she would, but I was glad I was going to this one.

I focused on the vibrating video monitors in front of me. I kept thinking, wow, it looks a lot like Earth, even though I'd never seen Earth.

My download included all kinds of memory tags of Earth experiences I never actually had. It's a strange concept to consider and a stranger one to live. And I wanted to live. It was a compulsion, an instinct. I liked the freedom of physical movement now that I had it. The only other option was to be folded back into Argentina. Even the thought sent chills up my spine.

Our landing was as rough as the drop through the atmosphere, only with a quick stomach-churning roll and hard stop at the end. I slammed against the side console and felt something squishy happen in my arm as if something leaked out. I decided to have Doc look it over once we were settled. In the meantime, we began setup immediately upon landing. The time went by quickly, and suddenly it was several hours later.

As for the planet, it has a magnetic pole that is somewhat out of alignment from what Earth had. Because of that, we used two forms of direction, solar and magnetic. I set all my log and audio controls to register time and date, from the time of touchdown, based on planetary specs.

We set up a tent camp at the edge of a field of tall grass. The fifty-plus acre field sloped toward a river a mile and a half away. Underbrush and some trees also ran along the far side of the river.

Thick-trunked conifers with scale-like leaves and seed cones, as well as other strange trees interspersed with the conifers, stood along two sides of our camp. The other trees were leafy at that time of year, or in this hemisphere anyway.

The sky was a brilliant and friendly blue, and clouds filled with evaporated water as we worked. We named the planet Beauty, based on our first impressions.

Each tent enclosure was square and incorporated a sleeping compartment, small working area, latrine, and lab space, which was unique for each tent based on who the occupants were. The infirmary was separated from the other tents so that Marie—who we called Doc— didn't have to sleep and live with a contaminated person. I went to see Doc and have her check my bruised arm. Bill, our electrical engineer, was already there.

"Not you, too," Doc said. "You must be the fourth one." She was busy getting her tent in order, so she checked me out quickly and proclaimed my arm was only bruised and that it would be fine. "Bill got the worst of the drop. He's bruised all along his side and arm."

During setup, Donna, our botanist, was eager to traipse into the woods a few hundred feet and collect samples but got a rash from some plant she touched. Doc didn't appear to be concerned.

While Donna was gone, I tried to help her paired partner, our biologist Chip, set up their tent, but he snapped at me to get out of his way.

It was a long day, and before our late all-hands

debriefing, Chip came over and slapped me on the shoulder. "Sorry for yelling at you. Emotions were running high, and I was afraid I'd be the last to finish. Couldn't let that happen."

"I didn't want to get in the way," I said.

"No hard feelings then?"

"None."

He looked over at Missy. "You get what you needed, too, I hope."

"I did," she said.

Chip had his foot on a chair and loomed over us as though waiting for one of us to say something else. I placed a hand on Missy's knee and stared at Chip for a moment until he turned away. Then the meeting started, and he found a seat.

Our strategic team leader, Angie, stood and asked everyone to quiet down. She made a little speech about being colonists, being chosen, being the right team for this job—very motivational. Afterward, she went around the room and asked for reports. Everything appeared to go well, and we were dismissed to go back to our tents for some sleep.

Only a few hours into the night, we were awakened by long, low howls coming from the river—our first indication of life on the planet. Soon after the noise started, Josh, our chemist, yelled from just outside our tent. "Wake up, you guys! Angie wants everyone on deck—Donna's rash has spread."

****

All beings are robots. A redefinition puts everything in the universe under a single perspective. Some beings are electronic in nature, some electromechanical, some chemical. In the distant past, completely mechanical robots had to be manually manipulated by another type of robot, but that has little relevance here. Whether you call the study of electrical charges in biological systems electrobiology or bioelectronic doesn't matter. Either can be incorporated into a mechanical system and produce a bioelectromechanical device. Terms. Science. Intelligence often gets in its own way. Together or apart, the elements mentioned produce, on some level, the fourth element: magnetism. Pulled together into a system, they are magical.

(Deployment Date: AA52374.17)
—Argentina

Chapter 2

Night

Missy and I were the last ones to get to the infirmary. Donna lay inside an oxygen tent with almost all her exposed skin covered in reddish-pink welts.

Worry had drained Chip's face of color. He paced the floor near her body.

Doc gave orders to Sam, her paired partner and lab tech, as they took samples and ran them through various simulators. "There was a strange odor coming off her skin when I took the sample," she said.

"What are you talking about?" Chip asked.

Before Doc could answer, I pulled Chip aside and asked about the evening. He looked at me intermittently as he shot worried glances back toward Donna. Their attachment seemed as tight as my attachment to Missy, and I wondered if that was as good an idea as I originally imagined it to be. Her incapacitation rendered Chip almost useless when he ought to be helpful. Trying to make conversation, I asked, "Have you noticed any rash on your body? Might it be spreading?"

"No. Doc had me strip down when we first got here to make sure."

"You were sleeping together?"

"Yeah. We even practiced sex. We weren't worried. Then a few hours later, this." He swung away from me and leaned over Donna, staring into her sleeping face.

From the other side of the room, Sam yelled, "Got it."

"Hit me, Sweety," Doc said with a big smile.

"A virus from one of the cones she collected. Biological, not botanical. The plant didn't carry the virus—Donna will be able to tell for sure later—but was left behind in dung. Had she gotten the cone from the tree and not the ground, this might not have happened, although who can be sure?"

Bill had just finished securing an energy fence and looked anxious. "Now that we know what's going on, can I check the fence?" A bead of sweat emerged over his brow. Ellen had a hand on his shoulder as though trying to keep him calm, but it wasn't working. "Well?" He didn't wait for an answer. He just rushed out.

Donna moaned in her sleep.

Chip raised his head, eyes wide in question.

"Don't worry so much," Doc said. "These things are going to happen. She'll be fine."

The cone sat in a dish on the lab bench. Everyone standing around in the same room seemed like a bad idea to me, but no one appeared to be concerned. I'm not the doctor, so I just did my job. I took notes to document everything, including the scraping of their feet over the tent bottom. I felt less useful than the others, all of whom had specific scientific duties. For example, Doc and Sam discussed alternatives for care and brought Josh into the mix to create something inside one of the simulators. Missy used an interface to gather data while they worked. It was all some kind of teamwork I didn't understand. Everyone involved looked serious and calm.

Except for Chip.

I stepped close to him and tried to keep his mind off of the situation. I simultaneously monitored the emotional responses of the others the best I could and got some of that down even while talking with Chip.

An alarm horn rang out, and I jumped. Roger, our tactical leader, rushed from the tent.

Angie raised her hand and said, "Stay calm."

Soon afterward, Roger came back. "Bill, testing the fence," he said. "Everything is fine. We're all safe."

An hour later, Doc and Sam sprayed something all over Donna's body—even with her clothes on—rolling her over and spraying her other side. Most everyone was asked to leave, thank goodness, which emptied the infirmary. I asked Doc why everyone had been called in to begin with. "Wasn't it possible that we'd all get infected?"

"We knew it wouldn't spread," she said. "We had already determined that after checking Chip out. Anyway, the team needed to witness how dangerous the planet could be if we aren't careful." She tightened her lips and glanced over to our strategic leader. "Angie's idea really. She wants everyone to be more cautious. Just because the planet looks beautiful and safe, doesn't mean it is."

"Those howls earlier," I said.

"Precisely," Angie answered for Doc.

"It's important that everyone know what could happen," Roger said from behind me. "We can't have people wandering off alone or acting as though this is Earth. Hell, none of us have even been to Earth, so just because this looks similar doesn't mean it's safe. Earth wasn't safe."

Angie stared at Roger as he spoke. "What he said."

"You hear those sounds?" He addressed Chip, who nodded. "That's danger waiting to find us, and it's your job to help keep us safe. I don't appreciate how frazzled you got tonight. You've got to buck up under pressure."

"Yes, sir," Chip said.

"You two look pretty calm," I said to our leaders.

"Someone has to be," Donna said from behind them.

Doc turned around, and we all walked closer. Chip appeared the most relieved. The rash had faded, even in such a short time.

"Topical," Doc said. "Nonetheless, it spread quickly."

"I can create a solution to add to our body-wash," Sam said, "that will keep us safe from this happening again."

"Our antibodies will kick in as well." Doc glanced around to be sure everyone heard.

"Why didn't I get it?" Chip asked, much calmer now that Donna was alert. She propped herself up on her elbows.

"Direct contact with the little buggers," Doc said. "Donna must have washed after setup, removing the chances of you getting it."

"Everyone should wash their hands regularly after I include my solution," Sam said.

Angie nodded toward me, meaning that I could go, but I waited until Missy was through so we could leave together. Once outside, the howling sent chills up my spine again. The sounds weren't close, though. Missy pulled my arm around her and shivered, not, I suspect, from the chill in the air.

****

The magic created by adding magnetism to the bioelectromechanical elements—however they are mixed and matched—makes humans. I use the term human *loosely because all things have these same qualities. In fact, if you delve deeply enough into the science, it becomes apparent that everything is interrelated; it's all one thing. Animals, plants, atmospheres can be included, but I'm going much too deeply. What I'll be expressing here are what are called bios, or biomass, even though the beings, human or otherwise, incorporate so much more than mere biology. Once built, the biomasses referred to as humans are based on their original Earth origins.*

—Argentina

Chapter 3

Observations

Sam had been up all night working with Josh to prepare enough solution for all the containers of body-wash in the camp. Doc created a drug to inoculate us for future run-ins with the stuff and to build our immune systems as we went. The right team can do anything. The next morning, all three looked tired sitting together in the cafeteria.

Donna walked in looking strong and vibrant. Chip's complexion had fleshed out. They held hands and sat together. The rest of the crew mingled in groups of three or four. I walked over and congratulated Donna on her quick recovery.

"How'd *you* sleep?" Roger asked me after joining the group. "Whatever is making those howls got louder and seemed to be coming from down near the river, right outside your tent pretty much."

"A mile or so away," I reminded him.

"Still. How long's it take to walk a mile? Or run?"

"Donna's situation had us all up late, but Missy and I managed to doze off and sleep through until a little while ago." I wasn't sure if Roger wanted to worry me or keep me prepared. He didn't say.

"Not me," Missy corrected.

"Me either." Ellen stood next to her. Quite a crowd

grew around Donna.

"Surprised you did, Carl—" Roger pointed toward Missy. "—if she didn't."

I shrugged. If Missy were awake and worried, why didn't she wake me? Why didn't I notice? I'd do anything to protect her. I'd be more aware the next time. I turned toward Missy to apologize when she made a quick shake of her head, letting me know it wasn't necessary.

Breakfast smelled like bacon and eggs, although I'm not sure how I knew that. Like most meals, it was premade, synthetic for the most part, and buffet style. We took turns creating the buffet, and Bill and Ellen had done the job that morning. After a high-protein breakfast, Angie stood in front of the team. "We made it through the night, and everyone got to see that this is not familiar territory. Donna's serious skin irritation and those howls all night long should remind us that we're not alone here. Beauty is a strange, new planet. We're intruders. Chip named our neighbors river howlers—" She raised a transparent cup of orange juice. "—our second named item. I hope you get this down, Carl. The first was the allergic reaction Donna got to whatever it was she touched. Doc called them brushwelts."

I raised my hand. "River howlers and brushwelts." Neither were very inventive, but at least they didn't name things after themselves. Either way, I was realizing that our new home wasn't getting the creative attention it deserved.

Angie nodded toward Doc and Donna before continuing. "As you're out in small groups today, I want you to be careful and stay close to one another.

Return on time. Any team that's late will have a party sent out to find them immediately. Don't make us worry. Roger is going to prep every team before it leaves. Doc and Sam, and Roger and I are staying behind for medical assistance if it's needed and to plan ahead for our colonization."

I wondered if anyone else loved the idea of creating a home here as I did. The whole concept that this small team of scientists would be documenting and categorizing—and naming—everything on this planet was thrilling. Amazing. From now on, this was our home.

Home. The idea was so much larger than I originally had thought.

We had a lot to do that second day. Teams of four were to leave for two hours, while the rest of the team collected local samples and performed diagnostics on the ground we had chosen as home base. This process would repeat twice during the day, with an hour between each outing for exchanging information and sharing samples. Twelve hours or so, back and forth.

Missy and I joined Josh and his mate, Karen, our meteorologist. I started calling us the science-lite team. The science-heavy team was made up of Chip and Donna, biology and botany, and Bill and Ellen, electronics and mechanics. It was easy to fit four of us and some light evaluation and collection equipment into one buggy. I have to say, it was pretty great being the first ones out, too. We suited up in protective exploration gear and were off through the field toward the river.

As a meteorologist, Karen placed sensors around, sometimes on the ground, sometimes at the end of a stake she pounded into the ground. Later she planned to locate sensors in the trees, but not on this trip.

We traveled through the field, exploring its upper perimeter and its center. Karen observed, recorded, photographed, and drew pictures of the clouds, took note of wind direction and force, and a lot of other things I was totally oblivious of. Karen appeared so intent on her job, as did Josh, that Missy and I were a little left out of things. Well, me more than Missy. She continually appeared to be logging data that one of the others would offer her.

I asked questions, stood back, observed, and jotted down whatever I liked. For example, how Josh and Karen looked at each other every once in a while, lovingly, like Missy and I do. Paired as we were, it was starting to appear as though our connections were an important part of our colonization.

The field grass swayed with the breeze and was a light tan color, yellower for new growth. A thick stalk lifted from the ground and spread into three long, slender leaves, while a plume of what would eventually be either a flower or seeds jutted through the center. That part looked to be a darker brown. We all wore gloves, of course, and I wandered around with my hand out, imagining how soft the grass might feel on my bare hand. The blades didn't catch on my clothing at all.

Josh, trying not to cross-contaminate his collection while bagging samples, used up a whole bag of thin medical gloves while collecting everything imaginable. With a small chemical kit, he tested rocks and soil—he also knew a lot about geology. Early in our research, we refrained from using long-range wireless signals of any kind because we didn't know how they might affect the wildlife, of which we'd seen none so far. After a few days here, we'd incorporate some local radio signals. That was the plan.

Prior to our journey, Roger ran through how to handle an emergency confrontation with an animal that threatened us. Surround the offender and use our weapons only if absolutely necessary. Weapons. We all wore laser pistols, which can be set from low energy to high energy for everything from what we call pinching to killing. He also explained about backing away slowly and getting into our buggies, not to get aggressive, to keep our eyes on the thing while one designated person glanced around for additional danger. It reinforced our training prior to our drop.

The closer to the river we got, the more edgy and cautious the others acted. The fact that the river howlers hadn't kept me awake the night before must have helped me remain less worried. Plus, I figured they'd stay away from a group of strangers and not attack, even though I had no basis for that thought.

We did run into, if I can say that, insects of some kind. They were eight-legged like spiders, but they had wings and a single antennae, or stinger as Josh suggested. They landed on us but didn't appear to do anything else. There were also some beetle-like things that crawled out from under a rock near where Karen pounded one of her stakes into the ground.

Using tweezers and spoon-like utensils, Josh bagged as many different things as he could. "I suspect Chip and Donna will find a lot of the same things we have even though they're going to hike into the woods." He held up a sealed bag of yet another hard-shelled eight-legged something.

I pulled a pair of low-range binoculars from my suit and scanned the river and the heavy brush and trees on the other side. Not much to see. The water didn't have a strong current, which was good since we'd eventually want to traverse it. Thick brownish brush with lighter-colored leaves swayed in the breeze. Nothing moved about, not even in the trees, but we knew there were animals close by. They were either afraid of us or nocturnal.

Before we left the area, Josh changed his gloves and one of the flying insects landed on his hand. He brought his hand up close and observed the insect. "I think that thing's an antennae, not a stinger. It's poking around on my hand but isn't puncturing." Then he shook his hand and yelled, "Whoa."

"What is it?" I rushed over and so did Karen.

"Be careful." She took his hand in hers. "What happened?"

Josh laughed. "Nothing. Just scared me. All of a sudden, its little head started leaning closer to my hand and I thought it was going to bite or something. But that's ridiculous. A mouth that small couldn't wrap its jaws around my hand."

He shook his head at his own nervousness and then slipped on another glove. It was time to leave, so we piled into the vehicle and, with Josh driving, crept up the hill and back into camp.

"It's amazing to be here," Missy said. "We are so lucky."

Karen agreed. "We're lucky to be alive. Sometimes this whole place, Argentina, the universe, everything downloaded, and everything learned, feels unreal. Not that I don't understand the concepts, but the actuality of it all." She shook her head as though her own thoughts were beyond her.

I was intrigued. "How do you mean unreal?"

She turned around, and I saw absolute wonder in her eyes. "We were *made*—" She wrinkled up her face and narrowed her eyes. "—made. Yet we're here. Not only can we see everything around us, but we can hear the sound of the wind through the trees, smell the dirt and loam under our feet. We're expected to procreate, yet that's not how *we* got here. Doesn't that feel strange to you?"

It did seem strange, but I didn't say that at the time.

"I like the procreation part," Josh said with a large grin on his face.

Karen's face flushed and so did Missy's.

While driving back to camp, Josh scratched his hand, but I didn't put it together for several more hours.

****

It is important that colonists begin to explore and experience the planet they must colonize as soon as possible. Experience helps to move them from being strictly scientists measuring and taking samples, into integrating directly with the planet itself. Integration adds more risk, but that is a necessary hurdle in successful colonization.

—Argentina

Chapter 4

Biologics

The second crew returned with twice as many samples as we had brought back. We helped out in the labs wherever we could during the hour between their return and our second excursion. Missy seemed as busy as any of the scientists, collecting and organizing data into a singular database. Team members interacted as though they had two different personalities—the scientist while working and the individual when not working. Most of the time, we worked together, seriously, robotically.

While they were actively researching and studying, I wandered the camp, observing and taking notes. Signs of exploration were everywhere, such as holes in the ground, areas where the grass had been cut short, a stake or pipe sticking up with some type of instrument strapped to it. The equipment hummed slightly and had its own odor, familiar because it smelled like all the equipment we brought with us, metallic—at least that's what came to mind. Sometimes an antenna stuck out the top of an instrument, and sometimes wires spiraled down its length and entered the ground. I found Karen sitting on the ground at the edge of camp near my tent and facing the field, looking toward the river. As I approached, she leaned back on her elbows with her face toward the sky.

"Do you mind?" I asked.

She jumped with surprise before turning to look at me.

"You know if I were a river howler, you would have been eaten!"

She gave a little chuckle. "They'd have to cross through the fence first. But if they could do that, it would have been worth it."

"Why do you say that?"

"I was caught up, mesmerized by these clouds." She didn't elaborate, just turned back toward them. A stake and a few tools lay haphazard near her discarded gloves. Her fingers wrapped around a pair of needle-nose pliers.

"What is it about them?"

"They move. They change shape. They change color." She swung her head around and with the most delightful expression said, "Think of how they've been here for hundreds and thousands of years. How they've seen this whole world."

"Well, not those clouds. Those particular ones."

She sat up and spread her arms toward the sky. "On a grander scale? We don't know yet where the water goes once it starts to flow. I know we can look at the maps and identify the oceans. We can study the terrain. But I—" She let her arms flop to her sides, and she shrugged. "—I don't think Josh gets it either."

I observed the sky for a moment, allowing the quiet to fall between us with only the occasional tapping or distant voices talking in the background. "The more I watch them, the more I see what you're saying. Imagine what these particular clouds can see right now, what they might know that we don't. They're probably wondering where the birds are, just like us."

"Or why the river howlers aren't in the field grazing, if that's what they do," she said.

"Or hunting. Although, I'm glad that's not the case."

We both laughed.

"What amazes me," I said, "is that I've never seen real clouds until now, yet my memories have, and that makes it feel normal…but not normal. New, but not new."

Karen rolled to her side and then to her stomach and pushed back onto her knees, facing me. "We'd better get back. We have to go out in a few more minutes. Roger's going to want to prep us again." She rolled her eyes.

I walked with her and thought about her eye-rolling. She didn't like the preps, especially from Roger, I suspected. Hers was my first encounter with such an emotion here. I don't think I'd been bored since the drop, but she was bored by Roger.

Before we left for our afternoon trip, we were told that we didn't have to worry about the field grass. It was safe to touch and probably to eat, according to Donna. "We're pretty excited to find out what its flower or fruit might look like," she said with a grand look on her face. "And taste like. But don't try eating it just yet. And just be sure to put your gloves back on so you're totally covered when you enter the woods."

"Is it dangerous?" Everyone's eyes turned to me. I felt embarrassed for asking. My face filled with blood and my stomach tightened.

Angie piped up. "*Always* consider it dangerous. We

can't let our guards down."

No one said it, but I'm sure we were all wondering if we'd run into a river howler in the woods. Regardless, the woods offered a lot more items to gather than what we found in the field. Josh, who helped to catalog all the samples collected so far, knew he could identify any repeated specimens. The other team had already taken photos of bugs, plants, and rocks and handed them to Missy and Josh. I guess Karen and I weren't expected to worry so much about it. I don't know about Karen, but I liked being instructed about what to look for. I wanted to be involved, so while Missy drove the short distance through the field toward the northern woods, I leaned over Josh's shoulder to familiarize myself with the photos.

Once we stopped, Missy took each of our recorders and touched them together to transfer the photos.

"I guess I could have done that," Josh said.

"Your explanations were helpful," Missy said. "I was listening."

"Okay, gloves off." Karen jumped out and rushed toward the front of the buggy. She made a show of removing her gloves, shoving them into her belt, and then running her hand through the very top of the field grass. At camp a lot of what was left were stalks—out here, it was different. She gleamed. "Oh, it's so soft."

I tried. The grass felt almost like it wasn't even there. I gripped a stalk and pulled it out by the roots. Donna had already done that at camp, but I couldn't help myself. Yellowish tendrils swirled downward. Dirt, moister than expected, clumped to its roots.

Josh was quick with a bag and scissors. He came

toward me—"Let's clip and bag that."—and I held it up.

"Wouldn't Donna have what she needs?" Karen asked. "All those holes in the ground at camp."

"It's not in the photos," Josh said, his eyebrows raised, "so I'm going to assume not. The soil could have different qualities as it gets closer to the woods. Or a change happens once it's been trampled." He snapped a picture with his recorder.

"Maybe," Karen said before she turned, and we were on our way again.

Josh got a machete from the buggy's tool compartment and cleared a skinny path through some knee-high underbrush. The first few swipes were slow. He stopped and picked up samples and slipped them into bags that Karen held up. He reached and plucked a few small, round berries from a bush and bagged them too. By the time we were in the woods, we had already bagged six things, and we were only getting started.

The air quality changed the moment we entered the tree line. A heavy moistness settled around us. Visibility had been reduced considerably, and although it reminded me of living on Argentina, it was also the opposite. Instead of comforting and secure in the dim light, I felt vulnerable and exposed. I felt watched. The others acted tentatively as well. Karen continually glanced into the trees overhead. Missy turned her head quickly whenever she heard the slightest sound. Josh appeared to be the most on-task. Idle time was something we didn't have during the few months we trained on Argentina.

To my right, Karen jumped and pointed into a tree over Josh's head. A small, fuzzy, big-eyed round thing hung diagonally along the tree, its head turned toward Josh. It held there motionless as though it had just woken up to find these strange beings coming toward it. No one said a word, but Missy had the sense to take a picture. As soon as a light flash happened, the thing rushed up and around the tree.

"Wow," Josh said.

"It's not gone, you know." I slowly closed the gap between Josh and me, my heart beating faster than I'd like to admit.

"I wonder if it was feeding," Josh said.

"Or sleeping," Karen said. "That's what I think. It looked as surprised as we were."

"I'm going to walk around this tree," Josh said. "Missy, you take another photo or two of it as it comes around. This could be the biggest discovery of the day." He took a wide berth while slowly walking, looping around the tree, staring at the height about where the animal hung originally.

I pulled my laser pistol in case it was aggressive.

Josh made his way completely around the tree. "It must be hiding in the crook of one of those branches, or it scurried along one limb and into another tree and got away. Either way, that was the coolest thing. From now on, Karen and Carl, you two keep your eyes on the canopy while Missy and I collect from the ground. I have a feeling we'll see more of those. Or something else. And we want to get pictures."

A short while later, Josh and Missy were way ahead of us. Since we weren't watching the ground, we moved more slowly. Karen stopped and pointed. The same fuzzy, big-eyed round thing, or one like it, perched in a branch eating a leaf. Its raccoon-like front paws had fingers, and its rear paws seemed to have claws that held to the branch. It was the size of a large squirrel but much fatter. And its fur had a yellowish tint to it. Karen must have turned off the flash on her recorder and held the camera still long enough to get a clean shot. I did the same. The fuzzy thing didn't seem to care.

After we both took photos, I glanced over and Karen was looking at me. We both shrugged at the same time. We didn't know what to do next, stay or leave? Finally, Karen said in an intense whisper, "Josh. Missy."

Josh perked up and waved his hand toward Missy to get her attention. He couldn't hide his excitement. The moment he came into view of the thing, it turned, let out the scariest screech I've ever heard, and leaped toward Josh. He swung his arm out and smacked it to the ground. It ran up the next tree and was gone.

"Holy shit." Josh's face glowed with elation.

"I got it," Karen yelled, "just as it was halfway through the air." She rushed over, and everyone leaned over her recorder. Its front legs and fingers were spread wide, claws out, and teeth bared. The teeth looked very flat and even, like an herbivore. After all, it was eating a leaf.

"Unbelievable. And we've only been here an hour," Josh said. Then he shivered. "That was scary."

I took Josh's hand, lifted, and turned it so we could see a rip in his suit along his arm. "We don't need any more of that. You're lucky."

He peeled back the material and saw that he had a small scratch.

"Antiseptic," Missy said while opening her medkit. She squirted some gel from a tube and onto a clean pad. She applied it gently over the scratch on Josh's forearm.

Karen removed her gloves, pulled a stretch of wrap out of Missy's kit, and wrapped the pad and ointment around Josh's arm and suit so that no skin showed through.

"Best we can do for now," Missy said. "So, abort or keep going?"

Josh didn't hesitate. "Keep going! That was amazing."

"You could have been hurt," I said.

"I wasn't. Let's keep going."

I didn't like the decision, but I wasn't in charge. In fact, I was realizing how low my position really was, even in the science-lite group.

****

Depending on the team of people assembled, a variety of outcomes can occur. When smaller segments of the larger team are separated out, each grouping has its own interactions, its own bonding rituals, and its own sense of themselves, all leading to specific personalities. Sometimes personalities clash; other times, they bond closer together. It's unpredictable what will happen in each situation, especially when the stressors are continually changing. Each developing personality reacts in its own peculiar way toward events.

—Argentina

Chapter 5

Doc's Understanding

The afternoon team ran across the same big-eyed squirrel-like thing we did, but no one got attacked. We took a lot of pictures. During our evening meal, Chip and Donna put on a recap show with photos and explanations as to what we all found.

"Carl took the cleanest shot of the Puff Squirrel." Chip motioned for me to stand. "You must have the steadiest hand of us all."

I hadn't felt steady. My heart never slowed the whole time we were in the woods after our first Puff Squirrel sighting. But I nodded and smiled.

Donna talked about the trees and the underbrush varieties in the areas we explored. A half dozen beetles were collected with pretty much every color shell one could imagine. Flying insects in the woods doubled in number, but none of them got in the way or stung. In fact, they seemed to avoid us like we smelled bad. Probably a good thing since we're alien to this planet. The buzzing of wings sometimes got annoying, though.

"And the good news—" Donna stood up and peered around the tent. "—is that none of the insects we examined are poisonous. Little by little, we'll be able to go out wearing less protection."

"So far," Doc said, "outside of that little incident

with Donna when we first arrived, nothing appears to be directly harmful. Don't eat anything and don't try to touch the animals but, as Donna said, you can start to be less concerned." She added that Josh's scratch didn't result in anything more than a topical wound. No bacteria or infection his body couldn't handle. It just needed to be cleaned and treated with a light antibacterial ointment. She nodded before retreating to her seat beside Sam.

Angie closed out the evening by suggesting that we all get a good night's sleep. "But first," she said, "several of you asked if we could turn the camp lights off for a short while tonight so that you could observe the night sky. We'll be doing that in about fifteen minutes, and they'll be turned back on in a half hour sharp. We suspect the lights are what's keeping the river howlers from exploring any closer, and maybe those Puff Squirrels, too."

"It's not that safe, then," Sam said.

"The environmental elements we've seen so far are fairly safe. I don't think Doc was talking about anything we haven't come across yet. We're just narrowing things down." Angie spread her hands as if to ask if that answered Sam well enough.

"Gotcha," he said.

Missy held my hand and we wandered toward our tent. We stood between our tent and Bill and Ellen's tent to our right. Over the field was the best place to look skyward, and everyone grouped there. Roger sat behind a binocular-mounted tripod, his recorder protruding from the side. I walked over and kneeled beside him.

"Thermal vision," he said before I could ask. "I

suspect those howlers will leave the woods as soon as it gets dark. I want to see them, get a good look so we know what's down there. I suspect they make other sounds, too, besides the howling."

"You're worried?"

"Damn right I am. They sound big. And I suspect they're in these woods around here as well. They're keeping their distance, but for how long?"

"We should all be worried," Bill said from Roger's other side.

The moment the lights went out, there was an audible *aaahhh* among the group. The sky spread out wide above us, populated by millions of stars. The slight glow of the planet's largest moon peeked over the forest to our south. There was no sign of the smaller, faster moving one. Missy's hand rested on my shoulder. Someone said how beautiful it was, but most everyone sat silently, staring. I wondered what Karen thought. She loved looking skyward.

Roger poked me, and when I turned my head, he pointed toward the horizon. "The Milky Way." Then he checked his watch and went back to his observations through his binoculars.

"We're in the same galaxy as Earth," I said. The fact made me feel nostalgic, although in a strange and unusual way. The sky above me was literally the first sky at night I had ever experienced, yet it still made me homesick for a world I had no direct experience of at all. The whole idea hit me as mysteriously ineffable. At times like these, I didn't know what I thought about any of it—memory without experience. Home without experiencing the sounds, smelling the odors, feeling the air of a place where I might have grown up. Did I long for something that was only nuanced in a download? Or was my longing what I expected to gain from being here?

"You okay?" Missy asked.

"Just thinking. Wondering."

She squeezed my arm and sighed.

Time passed quickly. Soon the lights hummed for a second and snapped back on. I just happened to have dropped my gaze toward the river at that second and thought I saw something dark lower its body and scramble away. I reached over and tapped Roger's shoulder. "Did you…"

Roger shook his head. "Don't sweat it. It ran back into the forest, didn't it?"

I sensed that Roger saw something, or knew something, that I didn't.

He looked back through his binoculars and scanned the riverbank one last time before breaking things down and collecting the pieces. He stood, hands full, and looked me in the eye. "We have sensors set up everywhere around the periphery. Don't let it worry you."

"I wasn't worried. I just wondered if you saw it, too."

Inside the tent, I asked if Missy noticed anything about Roger that might indicate that he saw more than he'd suggested.

"I wasn't paying attention," she said. "But if I get the chance, I'll download his recorder and see what's going on."

Easy sleep wasn't in the cards. What made it worse was that the river howlers were quiet all night. I could only imagine what they were doing.

****

It was discovered that memories, thoughts, and ideas could be saved electronically for later download into a biological element. Let's call that biological element a brain, although it's not much more than cells from original brain tissue cloned over and over again for the sole purpose of the download. I made a pun there. You'll get it in a moment.

In electronic storage, all those memories become stabilized, stagnant essentially. For all the discussion of artificial intelligence, there really isn't any such thing. Yes, the data can be put together in a multitude of different ways, but no truly new creative outcome can be developed. For that you need a biological element. Without all the pieces—chemical, electrical, mechanical, and magnetic—there's no growth in thought in a bio, only a convoluted reuse of the same thoughts. Those thoughts may appear different but are never genuinely new. The download from electronically stored memory to biomass is referred to as providing soul (there's the pun) since that's the most mysterious word the originators could think of at the time. What is created overall is a multi-sensing being. Such a being allows for authentic experience. No body, no experience. And through experience, new connections are created, new ideas emerge from the mystery, new thoughts occur. This grows the index of knowledge, which is why my work is critical.

—Argentina

Chapter 6

River Howlers

I got up earlier than usual the next morning and thought about how Doc appeared to know what to do whenever someone got hurt. There was Donna's rash and Josh's scratch. Maybe that's her job, or maybe she knew more about this world than some of the rest of us. Was it possible that Argentina downloaded additional information into her?

Once Missy was ready, we walked to the main tent. Ellen came over to bring us the news. "Josh's wound opened overnight, and Doc's trying to figure out what happened."

The news shouldn't have made me feel better, but it did. Doc didn't appear to know any more than we did. "What do you mean opened?"

"I mean it swelled and the skin split, emitting a foul smell and leaving a larger gash in his arm than the small scratch he'd gotten originally. Karen's at the infirmary with him while they're running tests. Doc thinks it has something to do with a reaction to the antibacterial Missy put on it. She wasn't sure, though; it was only her first guess."

"That doesn't sound good." I scanned the tent for Roger and didn't see him. Angie sat alone. I excused myself and walked over to sit with her. "Things have changed, haven't they?"

Angie gave me a tight smile and closed her eyes momentarily.

"Roger got a shot of that thing, didn't he? The river howler."

"We'll discuss it after breakfast," she said.

"Back to dangerous," I said, and she didn't dispute or acknowledge it. I tapped the table, thanked her for the moment, and went back to the bar to grab a full breakfast. I wanted plenty of protein.

After breakfast, Doc spoke first, letting us all know that, again, she and Sam were able to figure out what had gone wrong with Josh's scrape. "Chip was very helpful, as well," she said, giving him a nod. "It's not worth the scientific explanation, but let's say the combination of the bacteria on the Puff Squirrel's claws and a good dose of whatever worked Donna over our first day combined to spread faster than what we might have expected. Even though Josh showered last night and got dosed with our original topical solution, it wasn't enough. A stronger application was given, and it appears to be working out okay. I was afraid that it was some kind of reaction to our antibiotic, but it wasn't. Anyway, the swelling significantly decreased already. He'll be fine."

Once again I noticed that Doc quickly got everything under control, and I wondered how prepared she really was prior to arriving. Yet it could be her confidence that bothered me, made me suspicious.

She took a deep breath, looked over at Donna for a moment, and then back to the crowd. "We're still not positive where this stuff comes from. We've done a few tests and are confident that our immune systems will be able to fight it after a while. For now, we just have to be careful. Donna suspects that whatever it is, it lives in the woods, not the field, but we can't be positive of that yet, not completely." She took a deep breath before going on. "Finally, after breakfast and before we have a second day of exploration, we're going to take blood and skin samples from everyone and try to pin down who's the most susceptible. The consensus is that Donna and Josh are more allergic than the rest of you, but we'll have that answer for sure soon." She raised her hand to open the floor to Angie.

Angie stood and glanced around the room, looking for Roger. We all searched with her, our empty trays sitting in front of us. A few more seconds passed before he walked through the flap, and everyone faced him. He didn't appear nervous but didn't walk as though he was happy either.

Missy reached over and took my hand.

I squeezed lightly. "It's okay."

Roger held up his recorder, walked toward the projection screen, and plugged it in. A moment later, images came up. "Thermal image of a river howler."

The animal had longer front legs than rear ones, but the rear ones looked powerful. The fur around its neck appeared thicker than the fur on the rest of its body. Either that, or its neck muscles were thicker; it was hard to tell from the image. Lighter signatures from several other howlers stood in the background behind the one centered, and someone, I don't know who, from the other side of the room, asked about them.

"A pack," Roger said, a man of few words.

I don't know about anyone else, but I wanted more than that and started to raise my hand.

Roger noticed but went on, flipped through several more photos where the main howler stood farther away. The first photo must have been when it was the closest.

"How close did it get to us?" I asked.

"Not very. It moved slowly, tentatively," Roger said.

"That's a good thing for now," Bill said. "But it won't always do that."

Roger ignored him. "I counted seven in all."

The next photo wasn't a photo. It was a computer-generated rendition of the multi-colored beast we'd seen in the thermal image. In the image, something protruded from its chest that looked rather disturbing. I leaned forward to get more detail. It could have been that the fur thickened at the chest as well as around the neck or that there was a protrusion, a lump there. In the next photo, it became clear that there was a protrusion jutting from its chest.

"I pulled out as much information as I could," Roger said, "and enhanced what was there. Using a minimal amount of video data, the computer separated solid material from fur. It's not perfect, but here it is. Notice the claw—I'm going to call it a claw—sticking out from its chest between its front legs. If I were to guess, it attacks and pounces on you, plunging that claw into your chest or back or wherever it lands, and then using its forelegs to hold you down, push you back, and gut you."

Now he was talkative when it came to explaining how the thing kills.

"What are you saying?" Chip asked.

"It's made to kill." Bill sounded pretty sure of his statement.

Roger shot him a look that said, shut up.

"And there are a lot of them," Chip said.

"They were silent last night," I said, already feeling extremely vulnerable about our tent located at the edge nearest their known location.

Roger raised both arms to quiet our concerns. "We don't need to escalate our fears based on what we don't know."

"What do we know, then?" Chip asked.

Roger answered. "I didn't hear any noise, but I think the leader was looking us over when we were out last night. It's a good thing we have mounted lights around camp. I don't think they'll come that close."

Bill stood up, his hand near the table holding Ellen's. "If they live in the woods on the other side of the river, do you think they may be hiding in the woods around us or might use the woods for cover—to watch us?"

"What do we do?" Chip asked. "What's all this mean about our explorations? We knew there'd be carnivorous animals here."

Roger shrugged. "We also knew we'd be allergic to some plants or animals, that we'd be food for some and predators for others. We're getting specifics now, but that's why we're here. If we're going to colonize this planet, we're going to have to outsmart or outgun the locals."

"We're not going to abort, are we?" Chip asked.

Angie took over for a moment. "Okay, okay. I know Roger got a bit graphic with his explanation, but what this all means is that we continue being careful, nothing more. As Roger said, we knew there'd be problems to overcome, and we're prepared. We're not aborting anything. Beauty is our world now. I mean that."—she glanced around the room as though sizing everyone up—"Roger will keep track of what we'll need to be concerned about. Right now, these river howlers are observing us, nothing more."

"What happens if we call one out and kill it?" Bill asked. "Wouldn't that give the message to them that *we're* dangerous? Establish our superiority right away?"

I wouldn't have thought Bill would be so concerned. Everyone seemed strong and confident while in training and on our voyage here. Now his voice was almost frantic.

"Not necessarily," Roger said. "We know nothing of their pack dynamics. A kill could be taken as a threat, and they'd attack in retaliation. We have no idea how many there are."

Bill was insistent. "What do we do if we run into one of them out there?"

"Back away slowly. Stay clear if you can but have your weapon ready. You know the drill. Only if it is absolutely necessary do you kill anything. Primary directive."

"Until it kills one of us?" Bill said.

Roger didn't look mad, only stern. "Until we can catch one of them and see what we're up against. For all we know at this point, they may make great pets. We simply don't have enough information yet." He motioned for the conversation to return to Angie.

"First thing this morning, Bill and Ellen will extend the perimeter alert system another hundred yards outside of camp. This means it'll extend into the woods on two sides and farther into the field on the other two.

We'll also assign guard duty throughout the night." She stopped and waited for a comment or question. "Roger has volunteered to accompany each team. He'll protect you while you work."

She waited for a moment. When no questions came, she adjourned the meeting.

Missy and I didn't talk much until outside and halfway to our tent when Karen caught up to us. "Josh is doing great and will be going back out with us today." She seemed happy about it.

"Does he know what's going on?" I asked her. "With the howlers, I mean?"

"Oh, yeah. He's actually eager to go out again. He found it all exciting."

"That's one," I said.

Missy took my hand. "You have nothing to worry about."

"Why would Argentina send us down here with only one soldier?" I asked, meaning Roger.

"Not a soldier," Karen said. "He's tactical, but we don't have soldiers. Our mission is never to harm but to understand and integrate. We're here to join and be accepted by this planet, not own it or control it."

Missy assured me again that all would be well, that Angie and Roger knew how to do their jobs just as well as we knew ours. Of course, she didn't realize how unsure I was about what my job fully entailed, let alone my ability to fulfill my duties. What if every one of us felt that way? Maybe there was something off about each of us and I was just now noticing.

By the time we prepared for our first outing, the sun had risen into the morning sky and warmed the air. Insects came out of the ground to flutter around us, exploring or getting used to our presence.

Roger hung off the back of the buggy and jumped down the moment we stopped near the edge of the woods where we'd entered the day before. He pulled his laser pistol. "Instead of walking deeper into the woods, let's do a periphery sweep. It will be easier to keep everyone safe. Then I'll go in deeper and check around, keeping a respectable boundary as the rest of you work."

I don't know how the others felt, but after my discussion with Missy, it was apparent that my feelings of unrest might be my own and not coming from anyone else. The more Roger talked about keeping us safe, the more unsafe I felt.

****

In my archives, I have found that danger can be interpreted in many different ways. First impressions are dependent on the human involved and how he or she has integrated experiences thus far. Yet it has been found that instinct also plays an integral part in assessing danger. Some personalities are more prone to expect danger than others. Finally, any time fear enters into the equation, judgment can be clouded. Each planet and each group of people offer up a version of such intricacies.

—Argentina

Chapter 7

Weather

Everything went smoothly for the next few days. We left the lights on at night, and the river howlers began howling again. The howling sounded farther away, and I hoped that they were moving on, that we just didn't interest them that much. Yet it seemed that the howling had become part of my experience of Beauty, part of what she had to offer, her natural sound. But instead of bothering me, it somehow was calming, relaxing, peaceful.

At our next meeting, Angie brought up the inevitable. "We're going to spend a few days in camp, hunker down to do some hard lab work, maybe learn a few things about Beauty we don't know yet. We need to feel comfortable about our surroundings, get to know what's poisonous and what's not, what we can and cannot eat, what we can and cannot touch, and we're going to have to start integration soon. I want to do it with some confidence."

Integration meant we'd have to start digesting local fruit, plants, grasses, bugs, Puff Squirrels. Integrating was what a colony had to do because supplies wouldn't last forever. I wasn't sure I wanted to eat any local meat and seemed only okay with roots and fruits. But all I needed to do was trust the process, trust Argentina, and trust my teammates. I could do that.

Two days later, Karen searched me out to show me the clouds and how they were accumulating. She also pointed out the wind direction. "Have you felt a change in the air?"

"I have. What's going on?"

"A storm's coming. My equipment suggests a lot of precipitation. We don't want to be out in a downpour until we can get an idea of what that's like. It's going to be great. We'll be taking all kinds of samples to see if spores are carried around the planet in the clouds. We'll check for biological life, too. And—" She looked at me with bright eyes. Her movements were quick and excited. "—who knows, if it brings high winds, we all need to be here to hold things together."

"You expect it to be that bad?" Looking into the sky, I didn't notice any threat.

"I don't know what to expect, but you see how dark that sky to the solar south is? It looks rough to me."

"And you're happy about that? Because it's dark? So, what kind of clouds are they?"

"Nimbus. They're dark, so they're filled with particles of some kind. Also, see that hazy-looking stuff under the clouds in the distance?" She leaned closer, put her arm around my shoulder, and pointed.

"Yeah."

"Rain. It's already raining over there and heading in our direction." She swung me around and pointed at the field grasses, which leaned northward, pushed by a slight wind. "Can you smell it? It's coming." She pulled away then. "I like that you're interested enough to ask questions."

I smiled and told her I was interested, even though asking questions and being interested was what I was there for. It was also what I enjoyed.

Then her face became serious. "The river howlers are getting braver."

Her words gave me a chill. "What makes you say that? They sound farther away."

"I've seen Roger patrolling the perimeter at night even though there's a team pair on duty. He always has his night-gear with him and often stands for a long time in one spot, just staring. He's wandered out near the perimeter warning system a few times, too. Like he's watching them. Perhaps the howling is meant to mislead us into thinking they're still in the woods while a scout approaches."

"A scout. Wouldn't Roger tell us?"

"Protection doesn't mean that we have to know, only that we're kept safe."

After she walked away, I recorded some long diatribe of unfiltered thoughts about how strange and exciting it was to know that we'd all been fabricated just a few months ago and that we were here now on this planet with memories of another planet we never really set foot on and how everyone seemed so okay with that, as though that's how life was and that we shouldn't know anything more than what we do. Just accept it.

I wasn't sure I wanted to just accept it, as fantastic as it was, as strange and magical as it was, as simply unbelievable as it was. I wanted my own memories, ones connected directly to me and not just downloaded. It was all part of that longing I felt for a real home and not the shadowy memory of one I'd never been to.

Anyway, that's what I thought, so that's what I recorded.

During most of the morning, while teams were performing their research, Roger, Bill, and Ellen built traps. When I asked about the traps, Roger said, "Howlers. I don't know what to bait them with yet, but we will set it up when we journey out again."

While we were talking, I heard the rain approach. It wasn't hitting the tent yet, but it would soon, so I walked closer to the tent flap, which was slapping back and forth in the wind. I tied it back. "Rain's coming," I said. The treetops above the tents to the north leaned and shook in the wind. The sky darkened even more while I stood there and watched.

"Karen will be in her glory," Ellen said.

When I swung around to agree, she was already back working on a trap with a wrench in her hand. Bill hadn't even looked up from his wiring harness, which stretched from a small chassis on the side of one of the traps.

I turned back just as the sound of the rain shattered the silence inside the tent. Drops slammed against the grass; some bounced off the ground as though they were solid. It was miraculous, beautiful, and oddly familiar.

The scent of the air changed to an earthy smell. Out the corner of my eye, I saw Karen rushing into the storm. We knew that the rain was safe, the water safe, on the whole planet. She carried a number of containers nested into one another and set them out by first shoving a small stake into the ground and then clipping them to the stake. She had unraveled the hood from her collar, and it draped over her head, only her bright, happy face visible while she worked.

I reached back, unsnapped and unrolled my hood, and slipped it over my head before running out to help her.

She beamed and handed me several containers and then removed stakes from her belt and handed them to me as well. Her wet face shined in the dim light. "I should have been ready. I don't know what I was thinking. I watched the clouds, the sky, mesmerized by the pure power and beauty of its movement. I forgot to set out these udometers. So, here I am."

She looked into my eyes for a long time. There was something about her that felt familiar. She was a different beautiful than Missy, but I couldn't help wondering if something in our downloads connected us, drew us together. I felt a strange pang in my chest for a moment.

She shrugged. "Just go around camp every few yards or so. Shove a stake into the ground and clip an udometer to it like this." She bent over and showed me. "Got it?"

"I think I can handle that." The container was simple. It looked like a funnel with an extra-long collection space at the bottom. Small markings were etched into the side for measurement. I stood and paced off a few yards and got to work. While wandering around camp like that, staring at the ground, I continually noticed how the soil softened, how the grass collected the rain, and how the odor got cleaner and fresher as the rain progressed. At one point I ran into Roger, which surprised me since the last time I saw him, he was in the tent working on the traps. "What are you doing here?"

"Running a perimeter check." He nodded and moved on.

I couldn't help but wonder how often he did that or what he looked for on his trips. But he didn't appear nervous, so I wasn't either. On my last stake, I saw Karen a few yards away inserting her last udometer. I walked over.

"Let's get under cover," she said, "and watch for a little while."

I followed her to the main tent. Just inside she flipped her hood back and shook her head, throwing water from her face and hair. She had dark hair and brown eyes deeper than Missy's hazel eyes. There was something else about the way she looked that I couldn't quite put my finger on.

"Thanks again." She rubbed her cheeks quickly to wipe off the water and rushed over to a paper towel area to dry off. I followed, and she handed me a few towels. She laughed like I'd not heard anyone laugh before; it surprised me how wonderful it sounded.

"That was fun," I said.

"Weather. It's the one constant thing, yet so easy to forget—until it changes. But look how wonderful it is, how exhilarating."

"Negative ions, you know," Angie said from behind some monitors at the far end of the tent. I hadn't even noticed her presence.

"Yeah," Karen said. "But to be out in it like that." Her animated movements included hand waving, shrugging, and head shaking all at once. "You can't explain it."

"I'll go out later," Angie said. "For now, we have other concerns." She went back to her monitors.

"Concerns?" Suddenly I felt frivolous for playing in the rain with Karen when I could have been on top of the latest crisis. I leaned over Angie's shoulder but didn't see anything on any of the screens that might alert me to a problem. Several screens showed only a string of numbers and diagrams, but others showed images from the cameras set up around camp. I stared at the camera images since they were the only ones that made any sense to me. I shook my head.

Karen wandered over and placed a hand on my shoulder while leaning in. It was the second time she'd done that, and I was beginning to like it. I was paired with Missy and felt closer to her than anyone, would die to save her, but Karen's friendly touch was exciting in a new, different way—but strangely familiar. I tried not to notice.

She reached out and pointed toward one of the screens. "It's the air pressure. It's having an effect on the grass in the field. The grass is, if I'm reading this correctly, hibernating."

"That's what I'd call it, too," Angie said. "I called Donna to check on it just before you two showed up."

"Can you switch to my equipment?"

Angie pushed a few keys, and another screen popped up.

"Wow," Karen said. "It's going to get strange."

"What do you mean by that?" I asked.

"The temperature is dropping fast, and it looks as though we're going to get snow. We'd better gear up. I have no idea how cold it will get, but we'll want to run our heaters. Can you control those from here?" she asked Angie.

"No, I'll contact everyone, though. Most are in

their labs. I'll text through their recorders and computers. What are you suspecting from these readings?"

"Snow for sure, like I said, maybe hail. And soon."

She left and scuttled toward the main entrance. As she opened the flap wide, I could already see white flakes falling outside.

She turned around and yelled, "Did I miss something? Was this in the planet reports?"

"If it was, it was buried," Angie said. "I remember something about harsh weather patterns, but I don't recall this. Not in this hemisphere. We'd better buckle down for the night."

"So, we're prepared, right?" I was getting a bit nervous right along with them.

"For the most part," Angie said.

"What's that mean?"

"If we lose power, if our electrical system gets flooded, if our water supply freezes, or if the winds and snow topple our perimeter alarm system, things can change in a hurry."

Those were a lot of ifs.

****

Every biomass produced, whether human or not, has the ability to decide on its own. No two think exactly alike, but it has been evident that when in a group over a long period of time, members seek out consensus. The exception is when a hierarchy has been established. In that case, instincts can be ignored and concerns—even dangerous concerns—overlooked.

—Argentina

Chapter 8

Traps

The snow came down softer than the rain even though it fell thicker and denser. The whole sound arena changed from battering to a soft *ch-ch-ch* sound as the snow landed on tent-tops. The air between the main tent and the outer tents blurred with falling flakes; team members, hunched over and rushing, left their labs to head to their own tents to start their heaters and prepare—for what exactly, I wasn't sure. The heavy snowfall reduced my ability to see them clearly. For the first time, I noticed how dissimilar they were even though they dressed in similar clothing and had similar movements. A beep came from my recorder. It was Missy asking if I'd set up our heater and bring her a thermal for later. She was in the infirmary. I looked at Karen. "I have to run up our heater and make sure everything's okay in our tent."

"Me, too. I'll go with you, and you can go with me." She didn't ask.

We headed into the snow together. I loved the feel of the flakes against my face, although the cold had me shivering in a matter of seconds. My suit-born heater could only do so much. We jogged to my tent first, dragged the portable heating unit into the center of the space, and turned it on. "What do you think?"

"Seventy degrees."

I turned the dial and stepped to the closet for my thermal. I grabbed Missy's, too. When I turned around and saw Karen with her arms wrapped around her chest shivering, I threw Missy's thermal over her shoulders. Our thermals were equipped with better heaters, so I set it at seventy degrees, just like the tent heater.

"No," she said, but she didn't argue any further than that and didn't try to stop me from helping to slip it on her.

I zipped it for her as she shook in front of me. "We'll get to your tent next," I said.

I threw my thermal on and set the heat, reaching for the control near my shoulder.

Karen and Josh's tent wasn't far, of course, but we did jog there, setting footsteps in the gathering whiteness. Roger and Bill were carrying one of the traps between two of the tents. I ignored them for the moment and followed Karen. By the time we got inside and found and dragged her heater to the center of the room, she had slipped on her own thermal and was handing me Missy's.

"Now what?" she asked.

"I'm going to deliver Missy's thermal and then head back out to see what Roger and Bill are up to."

Karen reached for Missy's thermal. "I'll deliver it for you.

When I reached Bill and Roger, they were about halfway toward the perimeter alarm system. As soon as they saw me approach, they set the trap down.

"Carl, go get a buggy," Roger said.

I took the short walk to where the buggies were parked and brushed off the already snow-dusted seat. I drove toward Bill and Roger, still dimly visible in the snowstorm. I pulled up next to the trap, and they lifted it into the back.

"Bill knows where he's going," Roger said. "You sit in the back and hold onto the cage."

I hopped out and couldn't help but notice that Roger had his binoculars pressed against his eyes again and surveying a particular area ahead and slightly to the right of us. He was preoccupied. I knew we were going to head for the river and wasn't too keen on the idea. He couldn't have been able to see far. I checked my side for my laser pistol. It felt good to know it was there.

We passed through the alarm system, and a loud *whoop-whoop-whoop* filled the silence of the snow—a hollow, sad sound muffled by the storm. It seemed to occupy the entire valley. My recorder beeped. Angie let everyone know there was no real threat. Roger nodded toward Bill with a big smile on his face, which I took to mean that the river howlers were afraid of the sound.

The buggy bounced along as we drove down the slope. Only the shady tops of some of the trees were visible. The white of the tents blended with the snow. The vanishing tents made it all feel surreal. Then nothing was there—no camp, no tents, no other people but the three of us. I turned and looked at Roger and Bill to be sure I wasn't alone. When I turned back, my senses became honed to the bouncing buggy, the near silence of the falling snow, my cold face, the smell of what I can only call freshness. That moment felt different than any I'd experienced on the planet thus far. I felt like a child even though I had never experienced childhood—perhaps it was ghosts of memories from the biomass used to create me.

Then the howling started. Roger never stopped sweeping back and forth with his binoculars. A gurgling growl interrupted the howls. One of the beasts began to bay, and several more joined in. They were loud.

"Here," Roger said just before the buggy jolted to a stop. He had his laser pistol out and the binoculars to his eyes.

No one needed to tell us what to do. Bill and I dragged the trap from the buggy and let it bang onto the ground. We wiggled and shifted it until it felt stable. Bill bent over the controls and punched a few keys before slamming the control box cover. He glanced up at me before standing. He had to talk loudly to get over the howls and the wind whipping through the trees. "Let's go." He got into the driver's seat and turned the buggy around.

Roger shouted over the storm's noise. "Mag south!"

Bill angled the vehicle and rolled on as fast as he could without bouncing us all out of the buggy.

"Ten degrees west," Roger yelled, and Bill turned the buggy to the right.

I sensed we were going around something, which meant that the river howlers had taken a position between us and camp. I didn't like riding in the rear of the buggy alone.

"Pistols out!"

My stomach slid into my throat, but I grabbed my pistol and held onto the buggy's roll bar as tightly as possible with my other hand. I bounced completely off the seat and slammed back down over and over again, trying to gain purchase with my feet. I wasn't hearing anything Roger said. I just tried to stay inside the buggy. Before I knew it, the buggy twisted one way and then the same direction again until we were almost heading back where we'd come from. I saw something rush from the blizzard of snow. A howler emerged and hit the rear of the buggy with its shoulder, shoving us slightly off course. Then it passed by as though it had only given us a warning blow.

Bill pulled the buggy straight, but in which direction?

I froze the moment I saw the beast and replayed the image in my head. It was about thigh high and ran with a slightly loping gait. Its front rose higher than its back like the images Roger had taken before, and its muzzle looked rounded, ears pointed. When Roger had shown us the photos he'd taken with the thermal camera and the computer-generated ones, I hadn't noticed the face that much. This time it looked directly at me. There was something in its eyes that looked conscious—that was the only word that described it.

Its mouth was closed, its ears upright. The heavy fur around its neck made it difficult to see its killing bone. I got the impression that it didn't want to hurt us but merely frighten us away. It rushed past. Without knowing anything about them, I got the sense that they were leaving, going back to the river. There was definitely no *attack* in its look.

Bill made another turn and we slowed. I swung around to see why, and Roger stood, binoculars to his face, looking for river howlers.

"Are they gone?" I yelled.

"Just because I can't see them doesn't mean

they're gone," Roger said. "Swing back toward magnetic west, and let's take it a little easier. I can't keep track if we're bouncing around."

Then he looked at me. "Quite a scare, huh? You okay back there?"

My stomach felt shoved so far up my throat that I croaked my answer. "So far."

"Get ready!" Roger yelled to us both. "I asked for reinforcements."

About then, the *whoop-whoop* of the alarm sounded again. We had traveled for about five minutes when Bill announced, "Almost there." I had no idea we were that close. It had felt like we were going back down the hill longer than up. Bill slowed even more, and through the blinding snow came the shadowy figures of about five river howlers following us. "Roger!"

He swung around and put a hand on Bill's shoulder. "Hold up for a second."

The buggy stopped. I froze.

Two of the howlers continued toward us. Looking into their faces and eyes, I felt their intelligence for the second time. We sat there for about the longest two minutes of my life. The howlers eventually stopped approaching and stared, cocked their heads, and occasionally looked at one another. I couldn't help but notice the claw protruding from their chests, now much more visible than before. One of them opened its mouth, which showed its canines. I heard Roger behind me, and when I turned slightly, I saw he was photographing them again.

"Let's go. Slowly," Roger said.

The buggy picked up a walking pace. The howlers

didn't move. When we reached the alarm, it went off for the third time, but the howlers didn't leave. They merely lowered their bodies for a moment, as though assaulted by the sound, and then stood back up when it ended.

"What if they're not afraid of the alarm now?" I asked. "Are we in greater danger?"

"Bill here will rig something up so that the fence will shock them. Between that and the alarm system, we'll have plenty of warning before they get close enough to do any harm."

"They're getting braver," I said.

Roger laughed. "I never said we'd be able to avoid them indefinitely."

****

The more experiences are accrued, the more emotional responses can be understood and eventually controlled. Human animals and non-human animals interact differently not only because of their intellect but also their instinct and emotion. When intellect and instinct are brought together into an integrated system, it's difficult to predict what might happen next.

—Argentina

Chapter 9

Breakdown

As quickly as the blizzard had arrived, it ended. The loud and high side winds settled. The sky maintained its thick gray cloud cover. For the rest of the afternoon and well into the evening, the snow came down softly and pleasantly. At dinner, neither Bill nor Roger made a big deal of what had happened to us while setting the trap. Angie announced a whole team debriefing for the next morning.

That evening the talk centered on the weather, and Karen was in her glory. She had enough information to go through for a long time: how the temperature dropped, the air pressure changed, the wind direction and gusts swung from different directions. It was nice to see her so happy and reminded me that we were each most present and most satisfied while doing what we were trained to do.

During dinner I told Missy about the river howler knocking into the rear of the buggy, about how they followed us close to camp. The more I talked, the wider her eyes grew. She showed concern that a howler got that close to me, yet there didn't appear to be much emotion in her concern. It felt like she was collecting data. Even her responses were offered with cool questioning. "I wonder if it would recognize you again.

Was it setting a target?"

I relived the event while talking about it—the shock of the alarm, the disappearance of the camp in the haze, the howling so close to us, pulling our pistols for protection, the rushing beast, *bam, bam, bam.* It grew difficult to control my shaky voice and the small tremors erupting in my hands.

Missy quietly placed a hand over mine, seemingly to hold me still.

"I hope you're wrong about it targeting me. Damn, but I hope you're wrong."

"I'm sure I am," she said. "According to our pre-drop sessions, there are no intelligent beings here to contend with. They may be predators, but they're not intelligent. What you saw was most likely your own fear reflected back to you."

"All that means is that it's a wild, wild place."

"You'll get used to it. We all will. It sounds like Roger had things pretty much under control, anyway. Well—" She stood up, still holding my hand. "—you should rest for a while."

"Not yet. I want to have a discussion with Bill and Roger separately, if they'll talk with me."

"Bill will I'm sure, but I'm not so sure about Roger. Not until he talks things over with Angie, anyway. That appears to be the way they operate."

"Do you think they discuss aborting the mission?"

She let go of my hand and ran her fingers over my shoulder and up my neck to my cheek, letting them settle there for a moment. "Our mission is to colonize this world. We can abort, but what would Argentina do with us? Harvest?"

Her soft touch comforted me. Her words didn't.

The thought of being recycled didn't sit well.

"I have to get Roger to be honest about everything, or none of us will know how to handle an emergency."

"You'll have to help him understand that," she said.

I didn't like the idea of being harvested or of remaining on a planet that might kill us, but it wouldn't change anything if I said that, so I smiled to let Missy know I was all right.

****

I approached Bill. Ellen stood next to him. "I think you're wanted," she said and gave Bill a peck on the cheek.

His return smile appeared strained. "Can we go somewhere privately?"

"You want to walk around camp? Explore this new weather?"

"I'd like that," he said.

The air felt warmer than it had during the blizzard. The clouds probably helped hold the heat in. "I'm interested in your perceptions as much as your activities," I told him.

"Soft science," he said.

"Our emotions aren't necessarily soft science—they're real. And they affect our actions directly. They also affect what you call up from memory, or in our case, whatever was downloaded that serves as memory—mostly emotion."

"But my perceptions are based on my emotions, plus the facts, plus my beliefs about where those facts are leading. Shaky science at best. Facts"—he raised his hand and pivoted it back and forth—"are only a small part of it."

I tried not to feel insulted. Since he was one of our engineers, it made sense that he might think what I did wasn't real science. "It matters, nonetheless. Someone has to collect our personal experiences."

"Then shoot."

"Did you have any rise in anxiety once the camp disappeared from view?"

He laughed. "I was driving away and didn't notice until we turned around to go back. Then, yes, for a moment. I had no idea where we were for a second. But the buggy has instruments, which was how I drove through the snow in the first place. I knew, spatially, our location and the camp's location. Besides, Roger was in charge of our trip, and my attention was homed in on him. My anxiety quickly dropped back to normal until Roger had me turning one way and then the other. His orders were quick and panicked. But I wouldn't call that anxiety as much as frustration."

"And when you were out of the buggy, not that it was protected much, but once you were on the ground with me setting the trap, what then? Did you wonder if we'd make it back? If a river howler might run us down?"

"All of the above. My head started to feed me all sorts of scenarios that could be deadly. I felt scared, not only on the ground but while driving back—scared and frustrated." He stopped and looked at me squarely. "Is that okay to have a bunch of those feelings show up at the same time?"

"Of course. Do you feel comfortable here? Does it seem like Earth to you?"

He took a deep breath. I was onto something.

"I'm having a bit of trouble recalling Earth in much

detail. Ellen and I have discussed this. I'm not sure my biomass included the same quantity of Earth memory as the rest of you. I don't know. Does anyone know how that works exactly?" He cocked his head and looked away for a moment. "Either that or it was wiped clean for some reason. Whichever it was, I don't like it. I feel like an outcast. Like I don't belong, like I—"

He stopped talking and stared into the sky.

We made our third round around the control tent, passing by the infirmary. The snowfall was less dense, as though winding down. An occasional wind swished across the tops of trees. There were no other voices outside, no other sounds.

"Is that bad?" he asked again.

"You mean not remembering Earth? No. I wouldn't think so. But it begs the question, what planet do you remember?"

"None in particular. But I have to tell you, I'm scared to death of those river howlers, yet they feel familiar to me—familiar in a comfortable but uncomfortable way. How's that for crazy?"

"I don't know how to answer you."

He gritted his teeth. "I don't like those things no matter how familiar they seem."

I didn't know what to say. If the river howlers were familiar to him and he was afraid of them, then I didn't want to face them either—not that I ever did, but his input set me even more on edge.

"We about done here?" His eyes looked distant.

"Did you notice the howler that ran into the back of the buggy?"

His eyes teared up, his lips tightened, and his head shook. He squinted. "I don't like this conversation.

You're trying to find out what's wrong with me."

"I don't think anything's wrong with you."

"I shouldn't have told you that I didn't belong in this group."

"Argentina could have sent you here specifically to warn us of the dangers."

He shook his head again, this time with some violence. Then he stopped abruptly and stared directly at me.

I backed a step away from him. "Then we're warned."

He gave me a strange smile. "Roger doesn't understand. He thinks a grid will stop them. That it might give us enough warning."

"Look, Bill, that howler ran into our buggy and didn't attack anyone. Maybe you have a shadow memory that makes you scared, and all it's supposed to do is be our warning. Like you said. Being warned gives us the option of being prepared. You could be just what we need to survive here."

He didn't look convinced. "Does anyone else feel left out?"

"Aside from me, sometimes, not that I know of."

"See?"

"I don't see, Bill, not fully. Would you be willing to drop by Roger's tent with me? We can explore this idea further."

"I've got to work on that grid." He turned to walk away.

"It can't wait until morning?"

"We need to do it now. You saw how they weren't afraid of the alarm. How they stared at us."

I followed him to his tent and walked in behind

him.

Roger was talking with Ellen, and they both shut up the second we entered. "Tomorrow," he said to her.

"I can work alone if you two have something to cover," Bill said in a shaky voice.

Roger leaned to get a good look at me from around Bill, who stood between us. "What's going on here?"

"Bill feels as though the river howlers are more dangerous than we think."

Bill swung around and shoved me. "What the hell? I thought our conversation was private?"

"It needs to be addressed," I said, "or we're all going to be in grave danger. We have to be honest about everything with everyone."

"I get it," Roger said. "Those things out there are just animals we have to figure out. We're going to stay on this world. I won't let those things stop us from colonizing."

Bill began to laugh. "You don't get it, do you? Those things will kill us."

"We don't know that," Roger said, "not yet. We're smarter than they are."

"The grid has to go up," Bill said.

"And it will. But it's going to be dark soon. We'll double up on our watch tonight. We'll be ready for them if they come around. In the meantime, you get everything ready for tomorrow. There's no sense in putting up a grid in the dark. That would only increase the danger."

Bill pushed past Roger. "I'm going." He didn't get far before Roger grabbed his arm and dragged him back around. Ellen and I stood still and watched them. The wind outside picked up, matching the activity inside the tent. The tent roof flapped and made a loud crack. Bill jumped sideways, but Roger held tight. Bill made a fist, swung, and missed.

Roger twisted Bill's arm backward and held him in check. "You have got to get hold of yourself. We need you here. We each have a purpose."

"I'm not like everyone else."

"I don't give a damn. We need your expertise. Now calm down."

Bill's eyes glazed over, and he closed them. He stood so still for a long time that Roger gave me a look of concern. When Bill reopened his eyes, he appeared to be back in his body, not so detached.

"Okay." Bill took a deep breath and relaxed. "I need to get a good night's sleep."

Roger glanced over his shoulder to get Ellen's attention. She nodded. "Everyone belongs. Know that."

Bill nodded and reached to shake my hand before I left. "I'm sorry. You must have hit a nerve."

"That's okay."

Roger followed me outside, shaking his head in disbelief. "I'll see if Doc will send something over to help him calm down and sleep. He didn't look too good. I'll check in on him later, too."

"His agitation quickly escalated while we were talking. I didn't know how to react. It took me by surprise."

"Talking about what?"

"Same thing I wanted to talk with you about."

"We're here. What do you have?"

I went through similar questions with Roger, but he appeared under control the whole time. "I expected you'd be the one to come back worried," he said at one point.

"I was worried, but it didn't affect me like it did Bill. Do you think he's our warning system?"

"Be nice if Argentina let us in on it. So, no. I think the stress got to him, and he couldn't handle it. We'll keep an eye on him. Anyway, you're doing a good job, Carl. Keep it up. But let me know if anyone else shows strange behaviors. Angie and I need to keep things running smoothly for this to work. You think you can check in with one of us regularly?"

"I think we all have to be honest about what's going on. I hope tomorrow morning everyone is informed properly."

He nodded but didn't agree verbally.

****

Every cloned brain starts with basic qualities and residual memories from the original biomass, dependent on which cloned material is used. I have originals from all age groups, sexes, races, and expertise. I can mix and match. My directive is to use them in varying quantities for a variety of duties and situations. This, too, can get complicated because I also strip away certain parts of the previous personality, the specific memories of who the person was prior to bio collection, removing details of what they went through as not to confuse the new human. I pass along pertinent knowledge without lingering attachments or emotions, although that isn't completely possible—there is always residue. That's why, once created, each human is taught, in a classroom setting, details about their specific task, what they're about to do, and some information about where they're going, their assignment. Again, this gets somewhat complicated at times because it incorporates a combination of the soul download merged with the biomass and new information. It is unavoidable that they will question their downloads, as well as their previous existence. Without the urge to question where they come from, a biomass loses its urge to stay alive.

    —Argentina

Chapter 10

Caged

Missy and I were outside early for the short walk to the main tent. A light amount of snow remained on the ground; the air temperature had risen. It would be a nice day. Why we had to set our trap during a blizzard still bothered me. The randomness of that excursion didn't fit into how we typically operated. As if Roger wasn't clear-headed when he made the decision. Sometimes I felt as though I was just a little ahead of their thinking—maybe that was part of my job.

Before Angie finished her update about supplies and equipment, the perimeter alarm went off. Roger shot through the door with Josh close behind. Bill didn't follow. Ellen sat by his side and whispered something into his ear. Angie made a beeline for Bill. I wondered if anyone else realized what had happened and if they wondered about it.

I squeezed Missy's hand and got up to accompany Roger and Josh.

"You don't have to go," she said, not letting go of my hand. "They can take care of it."

"I'm okay." I wasn't sure if that were true. Mainly, I wanted to know what was happening.

Once outside with my pistol, I jogged toward the right side of the field. I didn't recall hearing any howls the night before and wondered if the river howlers had stood near the alarm all night long and waited. Did they just test it this time?

I rounded the tent, and Roger and Josh were walking back laughing. When they saw me, Roger said, "Puff Squirrel." He held it up. "Surprised us as we got close to the perimeter, and Josh shot it before knowing what he was doing. Even on a low output setting, it killed the poor thing. Glad it wasn't me rustling around in the grass, though."

Josh wouldn't make eye contact from embarrassment about his mistake, but Roger slapped him on the shoulder jovially. "Just kidding you. Your reflexes were perfect."

I had never seen Roger that happy; it felt odd. He held up the Puff Squirrel. "We'll take this to Chip and have him dissect it. See if it's edible."

He laughed again.

As he passed me, he said, "Don't get too comfortable. We're going out to check on the trap this morning."

"We didn't put anything in there as bait," I said, something I hadn't thought of until that moment and wondered why none of us had.

He stopped walking away from me, handed the Puff Squirrel to Josh to take to Chip, and waited for him to get out of earshot. "Bill set the controls to cycle through a number of different—shall we say—charms that might work to entice them—odors, sounds, combinations. After what we talked about last night, I'm pretty confident that he knew what he was doing."—he winked—"If you know what I mean."

"I do. But how?"

"Thanks for not pressuring anyone about opening that conversation to the team. Not yet anyway. I talked with Doc, and she's pretty sure she can adjust his stress levels easily enough. He should be much better from now on."

"Here only a few days and already we're drugging each other," I said. "But stress levels won't explain what he knows."

"I wouldn't look at it that way."

"I would."

Roger didn't say anything more. Back to his normal self, hard to read.

I met Missy near the main tent. "We're going back out to check the trap."

"Are you sure you want to?"

"I think I'm getting used to this. Or my curiosity holds a higher priority than my fear. I'm worried about Bill, too. If he goes, I want to be there to help him cope. I want to see what's out there. I want to get a better understanding of where we are. As you said, I don't want to be recycled, so I might as well help figure things out."

"You're a changed man," she said.

"We're all going to change." I kissed her lightly on the lips and went back to our tent to find a bit more suit armor for protection. We were all equipped with a number of different outer-shelled garments for a variety of potential situations. I grabbed thicker gloves and a thicker coat with protective inserts. I also wanted to be sure my pistol was fully charged, even though I hadn't used it. Checking all my gear made me feel protected.

I met Josh and Roger at the buggies later that morning. I was feeling a little too prepared, but no one mentioned it. "No Bill?" I asked.

Roger sat in the driver's seat of one of the buggies running through routine checks. He acknowledged me with a quick nod. "He'll be along."

"You sure that's a good idea? I can't believe he's willing to go again."

Josh looked from one of us to the other. "Why do you say that?"

"He seemed nervous yesterday in the blizzard," Roger said before I could respond.

I walked over and stepped into the back of the buggy. "Four of us, then."

"We'll need the extra help if we caught something, which I'll almost guarantee." Roger nodded, and Josh and I turned to see Bill walking over.

"Sorry to be late." Bill headed for the driver's seat and climbed in.

Putting our weakest member in the driver's seat hardly seemed appropriate, but Roger showed no concern, so I let it go.

We drove slowly so as not to surprise the beasts if they were hanging around the trap. Roger stood up most of the trip with binoculars to his eyes. Eventually he held up his hand for us to stop.

"What is it?" Bill asked. There was a slight quaver in his voice, and I wondered if Roger noticed.

"We caught one," Roger said.

"Are there others around?" Bill asked, his voice more desperate than I felt comfortable with. I checked on Josh, sitting beside me, but he didn't appear to notice Bill's change of tone.

Roger swept the area with his binoculars again. "Not that I can see. We're going in, but slowly."

Once Bill drove to the crest of the knoll, I leaned from the seat to check things out. A mid-sized howler lay down in the center of the trap. It didn't look upset or desperate to escape but sleeping.

Roger pointed at me. "Keep scanning the area."

"Just looking at him," I said.

"Looking's okay, staring isn't. Predators don't like you to look them in the eye. It's aggressive."

Bill stopped the vehicle ten feet from the trap.

The river howler's fur ruffled in the morning breezes. Several different colors covered its flanks and neck—light brown, dark brown, black, and gray—giving it a look of movement even as it stood still. It lifted to its feet and looked at us with a certain non-threatening intelligence. The killer-bone looked like a huge claw with a sharp point and a tapered, knifelike lower portion for ripping a carcass as Roger had suggested with his computer graphic. The beast had pointed ears and a catlike face, primarily because of its large eyes and high cheekbones.

I scanned the area to see if we were being watched but didn't see movement in the fields around us except the morning breezes. A lot of the grass had been flattened by the now-melted snow, but an equal amount stood tall again. Resilient.

Roger opened a tool compartment at the rear of the buggy and removed several bars with angled clips at the end, which he attached to the trap for us to use as handles. We maintained a safe distance from the animal. Barely, I'll add. Roger had to practically drag Bill out of the buggy to help us with the cage, but I noticed Josh wasn't running over either. Everyone acted thoroughly and rightfully nervous but also excited about the job ahead of us.

The river howler cocked its head as though trying to figure out what we were doing, but it made no attempt to attack. At one point, it raised a foot and touched the clips attached to the trap bars. One of its claws made contact, making a snapping sound.

The howler had non-retractable claws—a canine, not feline, trait. It also wore a very stubby tail, which was tucked between its rear legs. Afraid for now, anyway, or passive. For some reason, it felt female to me, so that's how I addressed it. Are the females less aggressive? I wasn't going to take that chance. The howler could instantly shift into protection mode.

Bill tentatively lifted his side of the cage. All told, the howler probably weighed about seventy pounds, maybe a bit more. The thickness of its fur made it appear heavier, so I was surprised when we lifted it to shoulder height and walked it over to the buggy. Josh and I spent the next few minutes securing the trap while Roger and Bill did another quick scan of the area.

We took our seats, with Roger standing in the front as always. Bill turned the buggy around and climbed back up the knoll we'd dropped over. At the crest, the white tents came into view. Familiar may not be the best word for how I felt. There was a tinge of uncertainty that crept from my stomach into my chest and throat. We were bringing the beast inside our camp.

****

The slightest leaning toward fear can create an imaginative scenario where said fear can be explained. That is the way of creation as well as experiential learning.
—Argentina

Chapter 11

Pet, Pest, or Predator?

Everyone stood around watching as the river howler nervously circled the inside of the cage. Its breathing became heavy and scratchy sounding, and its claws clinked against the cage as it paced. We weren't close enough to smell its breath. Roger's mantra was not to make eye contact, but that was difficult to avoid. I noticed that whenever someone stared into the beast's eyes for too long, it crouched back, lowering its hind legs slightly in what I imagined was a passive stance. The howler shied uncomfortably away, and we shifted our stares in another direction.

After only a few minutes of pacing in our shadows, the howler finally settled into the center of the cage. Roger dispersed everyone but Chip, Bill, and me. He retrieved a rod of metal from his tent and shoved it through the bars of the trap to keep the howler from the control panel while Bill plugged in his recorder and downloaded the data.

Bill held the device up after finishing. He looked satisfied. "This will allow me to track which odor or sound got the beast to eventually walk inside the trap. Then for the next trap, we use the same sequence to lure and catch another one and then another."

Good for him, but I didn't feel the same way.

Roger's voice came direct but solemn. "If they're predators, we'll be forced to kill them. Better to kill them while caged than go out there and hunt them down as they hunt us down."

"Makes sense," Chip said. "But judging its interaction so far, I'm guessing it won't attack us."

"You mean we don't look like food," I said.

"Yet?" Bill stood back from the side of the trap as Roger removed the rod.

The howler stepped back to its resting space. Its rear end continued to lower and rise. It seemed afraid of what we might do to it, just as we were afraid of what it *could* do to us. I stepped closer to the trap, my hand out. "It appears to be afraid of us. If that's so, maybe we could domesticate it."

"You don't domesticate a wild animal." Bill looked to Chip for confirmation.

"It's difficult to tell at this point," Chip said. "I agree with Bill for the most part, but we're not from here. It's dangerous to come to instant conclusions. I mean, yes, it might be afraid of us, but that might only last until it realizes how fragile we are or how good we taste. Or—" He shrugged with one shoulder. "—we might taste terrible, and they'll just leave us alone altogether. Maybe they become pets. Extremes. If we're going to speculate, we can do so in both directions."

Roger came around to our side of the trap. "Your suggestion?"

"Take our time. Let me see what I can learn with blood and hair samples, samples of what it has between its toenails, saliva. I'll be able to learn a lot about its environment as well as its diet—although those canines give some of that away. Anyway, while I'm doing that,

I suggest we get two people, male and female, to try to get close to it—"

Bill swung around and glared at Chip. "I don't like that idea."

Roger said, "With care, Bill, with care."

Chip nodded. "With care, of course. What I was saying is that we have time. Once I get an idea where it gets its nourishment, from a combination of saliva and scat, then we'll be able to feed it while it's here. We don't want to starve it; then it will become dangerous. Almost anything looks like food when you're starving."

Roger agreed. "Carl? You want to be one of the people trying to get close to the thing? You've been around them more than anyone so far."

I took a quick breath. "I can. But I don't want to avoid the other reason I'm here."

"No one's going to spend all day with it," he said. "We have tests to run, a camp to maintain, and a world to colonize. There are plenty of other things to do. In fact, we're going to start our explorations farther into the woods and closer to the river later today or tomorrow."

"What about the river howlers?" Bill asked.

"Pests, for now," Roger said. "They may be in our way, but they haven't indicated that they pose any real threat thus far. Obviously, they could be dangerous, but this one's still pretty scared, maybe curious, but not aggressive as far as we can surmise. The truth is, even if it is dangerous, we can't let it stop our progress."

"It's in a trap," Bill indicated. "What happens once it's out? Like the ones near the river. They're free. They circled us once."

"We don't know they did that on purpose. They

could have been as blind in that blizzard as we were. One ran right into the buggy and kept moving. Maybe they can't see as well as we can."

Bill gave Roger a sideways glance.

"I hear you loud and clear," Roger said, but he never said anything more about it. "If you and Ellen can make a few more traps and a large cage, it would help."

Bill appeared satisfied for the moment.

"Should Missy work with me around the howler?"

"I think Karen. Missy's a bit clinical. I want people with softer personalities who might help the howler lower its guard naturally. As Bill noted, while it's inside the trap, it could be intimidated. After all, we're new here. We look and act differently than anything they've seen before. That's scary. On the other hand, softer personalities could bring out the stronger side of the animal's personality. We need to see that. We need to know what it's got."

I sensed myself getting excited to spend more time with Karen and wondered if anyone noticed. Where my feelings were coming from was a mystery. I wasn't sure what to do with them. Yet Karen and I got along well, and it would be interesting and fun to see how the river howler reacted with us. And I was the perfect person to document our progress. "I'm looking forward to it."

"I'll let Angie know. And I'll brief the two of you about safety precautions."

By the time we finished our conversation, the river howler had relaxed and sat in the center of the trap glancing around casually. It was not lying down as we'd found it, but much more comfortable than when everyone stood around staring. I had the sense of a family pet, something I'd never experienced but recognized.

Roger alerted Karen of the assignment, and he and Chip went back to their daily duties.

I circled the cage. I loved the way the howler's fur moved, almost hypnotically, as if it followed my movements. I talked to it in a quiet voice, but it ignored me completely, or appeared to anyway.

"What do you think?" Karen asked as she walked over.

"Not sure yet."

A minute or two after Karen arrived, Roger stopped by. "Make no eye contact, don't get too close, and definitely don't reach into the cage. If the animal jumps, I don't want either of you jumping. I don't care how much it scares you. If it gets the idea that we're more afraid of it than it is of us, it could be all over."

Besides that, he recommended we do our best to stay calm.

"Don't you think that's going to happen automatically? I'm sure it's more aware of our body language than we are of its."

"We can't be sure of that. Regardless of how this starts out, you two will get more and more comfortable around it, and it'll feel that, too." Roger nodded as though answering a question only he could hear.

Karen wasn't convinced.

Roger addressed me directly. "I know Bill is afraid of these things, and I want to be sensitive to that, we all do, but we also have to prove to ourselves just how serious this is. It could be that we're safe. I need to know with certainty. Someone else's fears can't answer that question any more than someone's empathy." He didn't wait for any more questions. He left.

I had talked to the howler earlier and gotten no response. I looked to Karen for direction.

She laughed. "Don't look at me. I don't know what to do any more than you do."

"I have to say, none of this is easy. We're like newborns. At least what I think that might be like. I have all the familiar sensations and information but no true experiences. Only nuances." I was rambling. "Let's just sit with it, talk to it, and observe what it does."

Karen talked to the river howler in a quiet tone. "How are you? It must be unnerving to be inside that cage. You must feel trapped."

She held her hand toward the howler, but the animal merely sat there looking at her. After a few minutes, Karen sat on the damp grass. I noticed her hair looked dark but was cut with a similar curve around her face—short, manageable, soft looking. Longer than the men who all wore their hair close to the scalp. Her hair rested along her ears and farther down the back of her neck. Her profile displayed soft curves of her cheeks and jaw, which fit with her hairstyle. She was beautiful, but then everyone was. We all looked different by small amounts, but all were healthy, handsome, and filled with a strange mixture of knowledge and ability none of us developed on our own.

After staring at Karen, I turned back and noticed that the river howler had laid down, too. It kept its eyes on Karen, even though I know it could also see me. Karen continued to talk softly, and it continued to watch her. I moved to input some information, and its eyes shifted toward me, but only for a second. I sat down, too, and noticed how the howler's shoulders lowered and relaxed to another level. I leaned toward

Karen, not speaking yet, and the howler growled.

"Shit," I said in a whisper.

"Just stay back."

I did as she asked. "I didn't like that."

"It's getting to know me. I think it wants to protect me from you."

"Yeah, but I'm right next to you. If I were going to hurt you, I could have easily. There's no reason to growl."

She whispered that it was okay. Even while she talked with me, she maintained her attention on the howler.

"Let's try something," she said.

She placed her hand on my forearm.

"See, it doesn't mind that." She scooted closer to me, and the howler followed her movements by turning its head slightly. She reached for my shoulder and pulled me close. The beast did not growl.

"You're showing superiority?"

"Maybe. I don't know. For now, we're finding out our boundaries. As long as I like you, it likes you, but you can't like me without an invitation."

"That makes sense. It's basic animal behavior, isn't it?"

"Seems right."

I turned my gaze from the howler. Karen's face stood next to mine. Our eyes met. Warmth pushed through me, and I knew it was attraction. I didn't know where it came from or why it arrived at that moment. I pulled away. I was paired with Missy and not used to the feelings I was having around Karen.

"I'm sorry," she said.

I wasn't sure why she said it.

The river howler licked around its lips and made a *schlocking* sound. Then it relaxed even more and rested its chin on the ground.

Karen reached toward it.

"Not too close." We had only been there a matter of twenty minutes, and our progress felt too fast to me.

"It's okay," she said while reaching toward it.

She was still well beyond the distance the animal could reach through the bars. She moved into a prone position, crawling out on her elbows. I reached for her shoulder, and the howler stood and turned toward me with its teeth bared. Another growl.

"I'm fine," she said.

I rested my hand on her leg. The moment she became within reach, it leaped with its claws out and slammed into the trap bars, one leg stretched toward Karen.

My adrenaline hit the roof, and my heart pounded into my ears and throat. Karen yanked her hand back, and I grabbed her leg and pulled. The beast missed, retreated, and sat as calmly as it had a moment before, as though nothing had happened.

I croaked out, "Are you all right?"

Karen grabbed her chest with both hands and laughed, which didn't sit well with me. "That was frightening!"

Roger rushed from behind us. "What the hell was that? Did that thing attack you?"

When I looked toward Roger, Bill was standing near his tent's opening and staring at us. He didn't move to come over.

"It's all right." I stood and reached for Karen's hand and helped her up, her eyes wide. I addressed

Roger. "I think we just found out that it's a predator."

Karen took a place beside me. "It's calm and relaxed as long as we are. Look at it now. As long as we're out of reach, it's still, but as soon as we get within reach, it attacks. It appears to exactly know what its limits are. Well, almost. Maybe it didn't expect me to move so fast. Either way, if it wasn't for Carl yanking my leg at the same time I yanked my hand away, it would have gotten me."

"I'll place a guard on it. And I'll let Chip know to get moving on those tests. We need to know if anything in its claws or mouth will poison us or cause a reaction like Donna or Josh had. I should never have let you do this. Not this soon. You were lucky."

"It was the right thing,' Karen said. "We now know the situation we're facing."

"Yeah, more dangerous than I thought." Roger pointed toward Bill. "You can get back to work."

Bill disappeared inside, and Roger addressed us again. "I should have known better. But I'm trying to accelerate our colonization. We should be exploring more. If we're staying…" He didn't finish.

"Is there a chance we'll abort?" I asked.

"No one wants that," he said.

Karen reached to grab my forearm. "The pod leaves in two days."

"I know." Roger tightened his jaw. He didn't look satisfied with the knowledge. "I'm glad you found out what we're up against."

****

In dynamic situations, humans tend to begin to notice what they like and don't like based on who they spend time with and what they've experienced thus far.

Pairing is only the beginning of a true relationship, which must grow over time. There are far too many variables to predict beyond that.
   —Argentina

Chapter 12

Birds

The blizzard of the day before had been forgotten as quickly as the snow had melted, and that afternoon a team went out to explore farther into the woods than we'd gone before. Karen and I were asked to continue to monitor the river howler, talk to it, get close—but never within reach. Roger wanted us to be more careful and questioned how Bill knew all along what would happen. What else were Bill's instincts telling him? What did Roger know that he wasn't talking about? There was something ineffable about how we arrived, something wordless, and the more I tried to think about it, the more such thoughts kept slipping away.

While we were there, Chip came by. "I'm supposed to accelerate my research."

He used a long, manually activated grip to collect scat, saliva, and dirt from under the howler's toenail. As long as he remained out of reach, extending only tools into the trap, the howler let him take samples without confrontation. It didn't even swat at the tools. During all the prodding and poking, Karen stood far back from the animal and let me and Chip be the bad guys. The howler still appeared to favor her regardless of the fact that it tried to attack her once she got within reach.

"Maybe it just wanted me to stay close. Like when

you reach out and pull someone toward you when you don't want them to leave." She shyly smiled as if remembering a time when she had pulled me close. Had she—pulled me close at one time?

"Permanently?" I asked.

Later that day, we were assigned to go out exploring again. Roger selected the second crew to go out which included Josh and Karen and me and Missy. We were to explore more deeply into the woods. We were each equipped with a first aid kit, a fully charged laser pistol, and the usual tools for bagging samples. Roger asked us to nail a few signal repeaters to the trees as we traveled. "Angie wants us to start setting up for long-range communications."

Once we were on our way, Josh said, "I can't help but feel our whole purpose has changed since we captured that thing back at camp."

"It has," Karen said. "I caught Roger and Angie at the end of a conversation in the main tent about it."

Josh gave her a curious look. "And…?"

"They're serious about setting down solid roots." She looked directly at Missy. "You probably already knew this since you download and collect everyone's data."

"It is our mission," Missy said. "But I've heard them talk about it, too. An unexpected seriousness in their voices."

"And you didn't say anything to me?" Somehow the idea that Missy would keep something like that from me felt like a betrayal of our intimacy, our pairing.

"There's a lot I hear and download that I don't talk about. I can't tell you everything. I'm sure you have your secrets."

"Not really."

"It wasn't on purpose. I just didn't see its importance. We all know the mission."

We arrived, and Josh led us into the woods. I scanned the trees for Puff Squirrels in the branches. The space felt more constricted than it had the last time. The underbrush was sparse, clumps of it in areas drenched by sunlight. We traipsed through dead leaves and fallen seed cones—the smell became earthy.

"So," Karen asked Missy, "what is going on that we might want to know?"

"Not much."

"But something?"

"Angie's bent on expanding quickly. And Roger is in charge of making sure that happens. I think that's why he's asked us to start to bring back animal samples, even though dead. They want as much information as possible as quickly as possible and not just to feed the river howler. If we're going to colonize, we have to stop being so shy about moving forward— Angie's words, not mine." She stopped walking and talking and pointed into a tree up ahead.

A Puff Squirrel sat facing away from us. Its front legs appeared to raise something to its mouth every few seconds.

Josh pulled his laser pistol and shot. Something from the side surprised us by swooping down and snatching the body mid-fall: a bird about a foot tall with a four-foot wingspan and sharp-looking talons, green and blue feathers. It made no sound as it flew.

We watched in awe as it rose up and into a tree not more than a few yards farther into the woods. It landed next to a second bird.

"Beautiful," Karen whispered.

Josh, on the other hand, made no attempt to observe them, and shot them both. They fell toward the base of the tree. We all paused for a second as though waiting for more birds to rescue the two from their fall, but nothing like that happened. Josh turned to look at us and must have been surprised by our expressions. "What?"

"Those were the first," Missy said.

"We were told to shoot and return with any wildlife we could."

"I know, Josh, but they were…are…beautiful."

"I'm as sorry about this as the rest of you," he said while heading toward the tree to retrieve his kill. He removed a bag from a side compartment on his suit and unrolled it to expose its large size. He set it on the ground near the bird and Puff Squirrel and pulled out two more bags. He scooped the Puff Squirrel into the first bag and sealed it. Before scooping the bird into a bag, he rolled it over and pulled one wing away from its body. The blue and green feathers looked extremely soft and, as they got closer to the small body, fluffier. Its head had a snout almost like a dog's, instead of a beak. More bat than bird? The talons looked as sharp and strong as weapons, able to slice through bone, perhaps swoop down silently and slit a throat.

After scooping each one into a bag, Josh attached them to the side of his suit using two clips.

Karen shook her head. "Okay, let's go. What else do we need to get from here?"

Missy answered. "We can't get everything there is, so we'll go deeper into the woods as Roger ordered and see if we can't find more animals. I hate to kill them, too, but I want to explore. It's important to our eventual survival. I want to find out what's really out there, how many species there are."

I was all for heading deeper into the woods. I checked our magnetic direction since the sun was more difficult to follow from under the canopy of trees. When I turned around to look behind me, I realized how everything looked the same—the underbrush, hanging branches, leaves and cones covering the ground. Without some sort of navigation, it would be easy to get lost. After I turned back around, the others were far ahead of me, and I jogged to catch up. I didn't want one of those silent flyers to come after me. Sticking close would assure some aspect of safety.

Missy tacked a repeater to a tree trunk only once while we walked deeper into the woods. We stuck together, each glancing in different directions, close enough to touch one another if we had to. The deeper into the woods we wandered, the thicker the underbrush became, forcing us to push through with our hands high. Although dried twigs broke under our feet, the brush bent easily without breaking. After what happened to Donna, we were careful not to touch anything with our bare skin. At first, I thought it odd that there was more underbrush where there was less sun, but Josh explained that some plants grew better in shade. That made these bushes prime for sampling, which Missy often did as we progressed.

Before heading back out, we heard a strange noise. Josh motioned for us to stop and stay quiet. Then we started forward, stopping to listen every six feet. We saw two more birds flying ahead of us but didn't shoot them. At one point, we thought we were being followed, but it was something rustling the underbrush that looked like a large brown lizard about a foot long. We killed one, but as we traveled deeper into the forest and came across more of them, we let them alone. They didn't appear to be aggressive. Since Josh carried the Puff Squirrel and birds, I carried the brown lizard. It dangled at my side and was heavier than it looked. Karen, Missy, and I continued to bag vegetation we hadn't bagged before, and the longer we were there, the more weighted down we became.

At one point it all felt useless to me. If we were going to be on Beauty for a long time, forever apparently, we'd have plenty of time to explore, research, and learn the nuances of nature, to find out what is edible or poisonous. So why was all this so important now? It could take months to learn everything these samples could teach us. But we had years.

After a good hour of traveling, I led the team back toward camp. We killed two more Puff Squirrels and another lizard toward the end of our trip. We were loaded down. When we finally exited, stepping back into the sunshine of the open field, I felt a rush of relief.

One of the moons crested the hill across from us, giving the hill an extra brightness, a shine. We all unclipped our bags, placed them in the rear of the buggy, and got inside. We were talking casually, mentioning how beautiful the far moon gleamed, and settling our things.

It wasn't until we all got into the buggy that we saw a river howler sitting several hundred yards away—between us and camp. It looked completely relaxed, observing, but free to rush toward us at any moment. I had seen how fast they could shift from a seemingly calm and sedate state to something completely threatening and dangerous, and that scared me.

"Shit," Josh said.

Missy tapped something into her recorder. "I'm letting Roger know," she said. "The repeaters should carry the signal back."

Karen sat closest to the howler, but she didn't appear nervous. In fact, she stepped outside the buggy.

"Don't," I said quietly. "Please. It's not in a cage. You know what happened before."

"I know, but we can't just sit here," she said.

"Yes we can," Josh said for all of us. "We also have a canopy we could slip onto the buggy. The size and shape of it might scare the thing off if we head for it."

"Or it could attack." Karen glanced at me for confirmation.

I nodded.

She took a step toward it, bent slightly to get level with its height, her hand stretched outward.

"Don't do this." I stepped out of the buggy to follow her. The river howler rose to all fours.

"Get back," she said, waving her hand at me.

"I don't like this."

Josh whispered, "Your pistol."

When I turned to look at him, he and Missy had their weapons out. I pulled mine, and the howler charged.

Josh jumped from the vehicle. Karen, shocked by the sudden movement, stepped backward and tripped, falling to her back.

I pulled the trigger on my laser pistol but missed the oncoming howler. Missy didn't. We heard a loud *zzzt* as it hit the animal's killer bone. It didn't stop rushing. A second shot from me, one from Josh, and another one from Missy, all hitting at the same time. The howler toppled to the ground. It rolled and landed twenty feet from Karen.

Josh sounded out of breath beside me. Missy stood motionless, her pistol still pointed at the howler. It wasn't until the howler lay silently and limply that I even heard Karen yelling for us to stop. My ears had closed off to everything but the sound of my own heartbeat. I looked at her when I finally heard her voice.

She was sitting up, and Josh was next to her, holding her close. "Oh my god, oh my god," he said. "It's okay. It's okay."

"We didn't have to kill it," Karen said.

But it was obvious to me, and I think to everyone else, that we had no choice.

Josh helped her up and turned to take her back to the buggy. Missy walked toward the howler, her pistol still ready.

I walked with her. "You're a great shot."

She smiled. "Once it got close enough, we were all better shots."

"I was scared," I said.

"Me, too."

When we got about six feet from the howler's body, we could see that it wasn't completely dead. Its chest heaved. I turned to Missy just as she aimed at its neck and shot. The body visibly collapsed into death. I didn't say anything. I wasn't sure I could have shot it again. Something in me didn't want the howler to die, and for a moment, I understood how Karen felt. Some kind of kinship—

****

The entire universe is connected through a multitude of energies. Even humans produced on-board instantly become connected to this enormous, infinite grid. That mere connection allows a being to be part of the influence of its own existence, which allows it to interact, however minutely, with its immediate environment.
—Argentina

Chapter 13

The Howler Virus

The howler in the trap at camp watched us carry its dead cohort on a stretcher toward the infirmary. It raised and lowered its back end, standing and sitting alternately, as it had done when the whole team stood around staring after its arrival. Nervous or scared?

Karen gazed at the howler as if she understood what it was feeling, as if she could relate. I saw the same nervousness in her as I did in the howler—how she was wringing her hands, how her eyes darted between the live howler and the dead one.

Roger met us partway back on our return trip but kept his distance from the howler the whole time. Doc, Sam, Chip, and Donna had set up a separate smaller tent near the infirmary to house the animals we collected. There was a small workbench and equipment Chip needed, which included an expandable cooler for the animals. After seeing the howler on the stretcher, Chip pointed toward a large container near one wall.

"Wow, you're ready for us," Josh said.

"Ellen and Bill set us up," Chip said. "Ellen said it's all about having the right materials and tools." He walked over once the howler was lowered into the box. "Scary looking thing, even when dead."

Josh patted the laser pistol at his side. "I'll say.

And dangerous."

Missy nodded, but Karen turned away, obviously upset.

After leaving the tent, I asked Karen about her feelings, why she thought they were so strong.

She grinned. "I felt empathetic to its plight. It wants to live just as we do, and I knew it. I doubt it knew what to do with us. It probably wanted peace, and I felt that if I approached with peace, it would accept me."

I felt the same way Karen did and was about to agree when Missy interrupted. "But it didn't react that way."

"No, and it still doesn't make sense to me why it didn't. What makes sense is that it should have."

Karen swung around and hugged me. I looked over her shoulder and saw Missy's face angle into a questioning look. Her eyes widened as though asking what was going on. I didn't know. I patted Karen's shoulder.

She let go and stepped away from me. "I thought you'd understand. You were there with me earlier. You saw how it was."

Karen lowered her head and looked back sheepishly at Missy. "That's all I could think to do to thank you for saving me."

"You're welcome." The words squeaked out of my mouth.

"What do you think?" Missy asked me, but I wasn't sure what she meant.

I answered the question on my mind. "It deceived her on purpose," I said. "It looked perfectly friendly and sedate until Karen came within range of an attack."

Karen dismissed my answer. "It wanted me to stay. It was coming to collect me."

"You've said that before but that's not what I saw."

Missy reached for Karen's hand. "It would have killed you. That wasn't a friendly lope—it was an attack."

"I don't know." Karen turned toward her tent, visibly shaken by the events. "I'll debrief with Angie another time."

Once she and Josh left, Missy asked, "What was that hug about?"

"She said it was to thank me."

"We were all responsible."

The hug felt like more than a thank you, but it was impossible to know for sure. We were all shaken by the attack. There was a closeness between Karen and me that I didn't want to talk about. "Then I don't know," I said to avoid further discussion.

"Just odd that she'd do that."

"I know."

"Something doesn't seem right, and I don't know what," Missy said before we entered the main tent.

Maybe I should have talked with her, but I couldn't, not at that time.

Roger and Angie stood close together, looking as though we walked in on an intimate moment, their faces serious and concerned. "Sit with us," Angie said. Roger pulled two chairs over to the main control panels.

"You spend a lot of time here," I said.

"More than I'd like. When I'm not here, I'm in our tent doing the same work."

"Karen and Josh will stop by after she's rested," Missy said and then ran through what had happened.

"She should have listened to you about staying back," Roger said to me. "You were both involved in its earlier attack. What she did is against protocol."

That was the first time I'd heard anyone talk about protocol, something we all understood but never addressed. At the moment, it sounded more hierarchical than usual—like we were supposed to step in line.

"Karen was the one who originally made a connection with the howler that was beyond what any of the rest of us could." My eyes shifted between Angie and Roger, looking for a response.

"Even you?" Roger asked.

I wasn't sure how to answer him. Both of us felt empathy toward the howler. She was just the first to act on it. I let his question sink in before answering. "Yeah. Even me."

Roger narrowed his eyes.

I narrowed my eyes to match. "There's something going on here. What is it? We're supposed to be honest, at least with me, or I can't record anything of importance. It becomes just facts and that's what Missy is here for, isn't it?" I shook my head. "The facts I write down don't matter."

Angie placed a hand over one of Roger's. "They matter."

She pressed a few buttons on the computer keyboard. "Everything is cross-referenced and analyzed. The closer the facts match, the less emotion involved. But, as soon as emotion takes over, your facts and Missy's facts can be quite different."

A chart came up on the screen, and Angie pointed to a few sections. "These are the dynamics between the two uploads of the last few days."

"What does it mean?" I asked.

She scrolled down. "I don't expect you to understand all of this."

About a dozen or more circles, large and small, with lines between them or overlapping, came on screen.

"This indicates those overlaps when they are present. Anyway—" She pushed a key, and the screen went blank. "—this is all great information for us and for Argentina. We're going to upload everything we learn in these first days, and it will be analyzed by ship's computers to identify what her next moves are."

"Not ours?" I asked.

"We get to make our own choices," Angie said. "Once we're dropped, we're on our own."

"We're not aborting," Roger said.

Angie squeezed Roger's hand for only a second. I was getting good at all the nuances, better than I had thought when we first arrived. Angie jumped in to talk before Roger got any more words out. I knew she was covering for him.

"Aborting is on the minds of some of the team. Bill for one. You know that—" She met my eyes. "—and you know why."

"Not completely."

"He's deathly afraid of the river howlers," Angie said. "We all have different levels of paranoia, fear, excitement, understanding. It's all part of Argentina's job to pull together a team such as ours out of the biomass samples she has to work with."

My eyebrows rose.

"Yes, even biomass from harvested individuals. I don't claim to understand her directives, only ours."

Roger cleared his throat. "I want everyone to stay away from the river howler until we can do a complete workup on Karen. Doc's been notified and will go over there after Karen gets her rest."

"What will she look for?"

Angie and Roger glanced at each other. "We believe," Angie said, "the river howler did something to Karen, whether from its own body, fur, breath, or from some plant substance it carries on its nails. Some substance that might cause a curious reaction, the feeling of peace and safety that almost got Karen killed."

"When threatened with an imminent attack," Roger explained, "we tend to take in a deep breath. Surprise. The howler didn't have to touch her. You weren't faster than it was. It got as close as planned. Somehow, the one in the field knew Karen had been infected and was just going to take her down."

"It's in their breath? I don't like the sounds of that."

"No one does," Angie said. "If this is what we're up against, it might be the main method a predator uses to kill its prey on this planet. What we need to do, then, is find out exactly which animals are not affected by the howlers and use them to create an antidote."

Roger slipped his hand from under Angie's and placed it around her shoulder. "If this is typical, we'd better find out now, or every animal we get near could kill us."

"The birds and Puff Squirrels?" Missy asked.

"You didn't try to befriend them," Angie said.

"We're too big for them to take down and kill. It could be a size thing, a strength thing, we don't know.

A howler, or pack of them, could take one of us down easily."

Roger didn't let it drop there.

"That doesn't mean that smaller animals don't use a similar device to stave off *our* attacks. Snakes can't eat us, but they can kill us."

Everyone talked in Earth-speak. "I've never actually seen a snake," I said.

Roger flashed me an angry glance. "None of us have. But that lizard you brought back could shed poison out its skin, the bird could have poison on its talons, in its bite, any of these could sedate us or eliminate our sense of fear, or simply poison us to death."

"Why?"

Angie understood my question. "Argentina has a greater understanding than we do. There is no way we can fully understand why, as you ask the question. All we can do is survive—learn how to survive—here, on Beauty."

"Because we're staying," Roger said.

****

I should explain about their bodies. I have complete engineering and manufacturing records, trust in that. Bodies are essentially made out of a variety of materials and can be built to withstand radiation, acidic landscapes, toxic gasses, and other harsh environments, whether in space or on a planet. Head compartments, where the bios, the brains, are located, can be built out of lead-laced plastic or metal depending on the characteristics needed. Such compartments are sealed to protect the brain.

Other body components are printed out using a

variety of conductive and nonconductive materials, from metals to various plastics and polymers (as well as biological materials). Sometimes the bodies are reminiscent of what one might think of as a traditional robot, even though the bodies are equipped with biological brains located in a lead-laced head compartment. Other times, they are completely biological in the human sense of the word, which is what the main objective has always been, to colonize using real humans. They are the most interesting robots as well because they are the most unpredictable, the ones who experience on multiple levels.

    —Argentina

Chapter 14

Secrets

Before nightfall settled in completely, the river howlers began howling, interrupted by short yips and, if I listened closely, they sounded similar to us when we communicated—sometimes in a huff or laugh or, like them, a growl. Did that mean the differences I heard in their howls and yips had meaning? Did they have a language?

The howler in the trap didn't even rise from the ground. Josh and I helped Roger transport the live howler to Chip's new lab.

"It can probably smell the dead howler," Chip said as we set the trap down. Even as he said the words, I noticed the beast's nose twitching and its ears pivoting around. I almost expected it to say something.

Roger didn't care; he didn't want the beast in the middle of the complex anymore. "Too accessible." I knew he meant that it was too accessible for Karen.

"It'll have to live with that smell for now," Roger said and removed his gloves. "Bill and Ellen are making a larger cage. It should be completed soon. I've asked that it be covered and a perimeter alarm set up around it. I don't want anyone getting close." He didn't wait for a response before leaving the tent.

Protocol, I thought. He and Angie were in charge,

and we all knew it. But there was something about how he was starting to act that rubbed me the wrong way.

For the next hour, Missy and I stared at the stars and ate dinner with some of the others in the main tent. As we headed back toward our tent, Roger contacted me through my recorder to help move the river howler into the larger cage.

The cage was about twelve feet by twelve feet, almost as large as Chip's new lab space. Several lights had been mounted on posts and stood around the cage, and a canopy had been drawn over the whole thing to block the howler from view. The perimeter alarm was set up. When we transferred the howler from the smaller trap into the larger cage, it acted so passive it was hard to believe it attacked Karen earlier that day. I imagined it saved its energy for attacks only.

The howler sat uneasily in the center of the cage, just as it had sat in the middle of the trap. I took a few steps toward it.

Bill put a hand on my shoulder. "What the hell are you doing?"

"I don't know," I said, "getting a closer look?"

"Look at the dead one," Roger said. "In fact, a better thought is not to do that either." He turned to Bill. "Switch on the alarm."

Bill poked a few buttons on his recorder and the small LED lights on the perimeter stakes blinked three times and then lit up permanently.

Roger looked directly at me. "Stay away."

On the way back to my tent, I passed Karen and Angie standing outside talking.

The howling sounds coming up from the river valley lessened by the time I got back to Missy. I again had the brief thought that they might be leaving now that they knew we could kill them. That would be two of them that didn't return. Had they investigated the area where we killed the second howler? Could they smell it? Could they smell us? Random thoughts rushed through my head, and I jotted them all down.

Missy started questioning me the second I stepped into the tent. "Roger sent me a note to watch you tonight. You walked toward the river howler."

"I just wanted a closer look."

"Did you feel compelled? Did you feel compassion toward it?"

"Those aren't words you use very often," I teased. "Are you thinking I got what Karen has?" That couldn't have been the truth. I hadn't gotten as close to the howler as she had. My distance kept me safe. The howler didn't have that same effect on me; it couldn't have.

"Hey, just because I collect straight empirical data doesn't mean I don't have emotions, only that I don't collect them." Her smile eased my earlier concerns, and I walked over to hug and kiss her. Eventually, we climbed into bed.

I have not mentioned lovemaking in my reports because, as mated pairs, we all understood that it's part of our purpose. Eventually, Doc will inject each of the women with a serum of some kind that's meant to *ignite*—that's the word she uses—their reproductive systems. For now, we are only meant to practice and play and enjoy our time together. When it's time, we'll start to reproduce. Our higher mission is to plant the seeds of humanity across the universe, after all.

After making love, both of us lying naked next to

each other, Missy whispered, "Are you worried about what Angie and Roger will do with your notes? I got the impression that you know more about what's going on than you've said. You accused me of not telling you everything, but I suspect there are things you don't put into your log."

"I am having all sorts of thoughts about our trip here, but I don't seem to be able to focus on one thing too deeply. I've noticed that Roger and Angie appear to know a lot more than they've told us, though."

"Like what?"

I told her about Roger talking about aborting and how Angie quietly halted his saying anything more by squeezing his hand, as though something was up that she didn't want him revealing. I explained further how I felt that harvesting might be nothing more than collecting our biomass—with nuances of understanding and experience, ready for the next mission. It made sense to me while thinking about it, but it was harder to believe when I explained it to Missy. "Beauty might have had humans sent to her before, and Argentina or another ship might continue the process until humans are able to stay without being killed off."

"That sounds horrible. Why not just figure out what the problem is and fix it?"

"Maybe Argentina isn't as all-powerful and all-knowing as we believe," I said. "We could be learning *for* her. Maybe there aren't so many habitable planets in the universe, and we have to figure out the habitable ones a little at a time."

She stared at me for a long time, and I knew she was trying to understand what I was getting at—the bigger picture. Even I wasn't sure. So far all I had was conjecture, not fact, not data. Then she said something I didn't expect. "We should separate out some of your data so that Roger and Angie can't get into it. Not yet. They're keeping a lot from us, and if they think for a second that you're a danger to the welfare of the mission or that you can scare the others—like Bill might be doing already—they might not like it."

"Why would it matter and what could they do?"

I felt Missy shiver a moment and then clench her jaw. She stared into my eyes. "Send you back? Harvest you? If their report to Argentina shows that you doubt her, who knows what she's responsible for deciding?"

"Even if we separate out this data, she'll get it at the end, our final harvest. She has access to everything then."

"We'll all be dead by then."

"This is crazy. Don't we want her to know? Isn't that our duty for the sake of others who will go to other planets, who'll colonize in other solar systems?"

"Survival," she said.

"Roger and Angie will make one last trip to our landing pod before it returns," I said. "Okay, I'll talk with Bill. There may be a glitch in his system."

"We don't have the bigger picture here."

Missy climbed from bed, and I watched her naked body cross the room. She didn't stop to put clothes on. At her workstation, she ran through several sequences of strokes that completed what she planned to do. She grabbed my recorder and suit-interface cable and downloaded some code that I suspect would take care of keeping some of my data from Roger and Angie. Then she turned around and came back to bed. "I'll show you how to segment in the morning."

We made love again, slept a few hours, and were awakened by the shock of the perimeter alarm. I imagined the howler escaped and was now loose in the camp.

We dressed as quickly as possible and ran out to see that Karen had stepped through the alarm perimeter toward the captive river howler. The floodlights were bright. She stood frozen in the sound of the alarm as though not knowing which way to go. Chip must have been in his makeshift lab because he already stood near her, ready to slowly pull her back.

Roger kept his distance.

Bill stood halfway between his tent and the howler where Karen now stood. The rest of us stopped running when we saw what was going on and proceeded more slowly, all eyes on Karen. When she swung around, she looked directly at me. I wanted to run over and comfort her but didn't know why I felt that way so strongly. "Something's not right," I whispered to Missy.

Roger yelled for Chip to get away from Karen, so he let go of her shoulders and stepped back. Roger also swung around and pointed at me. "You, help her out of there."

"What?"

"I don't have time for this, Carl. Get her out of there." Then he pointed at Bill. "Reset the alarms."

Missy reached for me, her hand brushing my back as I rushed toward Karen to guide her away from the howler. Karen looked and felt calm, not worried about what might happen at all, as though her memory of the earlier attacks—both of them—had disappeared. Once we stood outside the perimeter, Bill reset the alarm and, in a moment, all LEDs went green, and the bright floodlights went out.

Roger approached us apprehensively. Angie came up and rested a hand on his shoulder.

"What were you doing?" I asked Karen.

"I just wanted to see it. I thought it might be lonely."

"But you crossed the perimeter?"

"I didn't mean to. I just wasn't paying attention."

"That's why it's there," Roger said. "Do we need to put one outside your tent entrance?"

Karen smiled, but when she glanced toward Roger, her eyes kept going until she could see the howler. Roger must have noticed, too, because he turned to look at it as well. After he turned back, he said, "Carl, get her back to her tent with Bill and then I want you to check in with Doc."

"Doc? I didn't do anything."

"Not yet."

"What do you mean? Don't insinuate—"

"I'm not insinuating anything"—he glared at me—"I'm being cautious."

I walked Karen toward Bill, and he opened his arms to accept her. For a moment, I thought she was going to hug me again but then decided not to. Missy must have noticed, too, because she reached out and placed her hand on my elbow. "I'll go to the infirmary with you," she said.

Doc stood ready to take blood the second we got there.

"What's this about?" I asked. "It's not a precaution, is it?"

"Roger...or Angie...I don't know which, has a theory about what's going on with the river howlers."

"We all do, don't we? So, did you find anything wrong with Karen?"

She looked annoyed at my question. "Wrong?"

"I meant different. Is something not normal?"

She turned away once she had the sample, so I couldn't tell if she was avoiding my question or just trying to finish what she was doing. "I wouldn't say that, but I have more tests to perform, more things to consider. Sam is running a complete battery of—"

"So there is something," I said. "You're trying to see if I have the same thing. Well, I don't. I couldn't have."

She didn't comment, and I sensed her pause. "It's my job to record. And—" I turned to Missy. "—it's her job, too. You might as well talk to us."

Doc took a deep breath and set my blood sample on the closest workspace. When she turned back to face us, she looked pale. "Something transferred from the river howler to Karen. It's more of a—"

"Don't," Missy said, "we don't need details. They'll be in your data." She patted my arm. "A simple explanation will do."

Doc nodded slowly. "Karen appears to be more susceptible to the shift in brain chemistry. It happens quicker with her. I don't know why yet, but she behaves lovingly toward the beast, compassionate, like a mother might act toward a child. And, like that"—she snapped her fingers—"it'll kill her."

She raised her eyebrows toward me.

Missy squeezed my elbow. "And you think that somehow Karen passed whatever it is off to Carl?"

Doc turned to her terminal, tapped a few keys, and a screen came up. "My recorder streams into my main system here. Look."

She pointed to a message from Roger that read, *Carl registered no measure of concern about the howler while rescuing Karen.* She scrolled up a short distance, and I read the entry before it. *Chip appears nervous and reluctant to be inside the perimeter field near the howler even though it can't reach him.* She tapped again and the screen went blank.

"You may have the same problem. I'm going to find out."

I halted just short of mentioning that I find the howling at night peaceful. Or that I have increasingly felt close to Karen. I wondered if whatever the howlers passed along would work between humans as well.

"Should we stay?" Missy asked. I felt her hand slip from my elbow. She looked over at Doc and back at me.

"What is it?"

"Karen hugged him to thank him for protecting her."

"And you think she infected him?"

Missy shrugged. "And we've been, well, together."

"You're worried it may infect you." She smiled. "I'll get a sample of your blood, too. It may be prudent to get samples from Chip and Sam as well. In the meantime, let's see what Carl's blood has to show us."

Doc stood up and took my blood sample to a machine in the corner. "I may need to do other tests, you know?"

I didn't ask how she would check brain chemistry but, all of a sudden, I wanted that done, too. I didn't like the idea of having something in my body that made me think differently than my natural state.

"By the way," she said with her back to us, "you can't tell anyone about this until we know what we're truly up against."

****

It is an odd yet natural state for humans to hold back information they deem either not appropriate at the time or as private. Remaining an individual requires that all information is not shared no matter what. It is as though a human has two relationships, one with its inner existence and one with its outer existence.

—Argentina

Chapter 15

Mother Love

Doc got nothing conclusive from my blood sample, but then I still didn't feel overly compelled to be near the howler, either. Not to save it or kill it. I was ambivalent. If I don't show fear, could it be because I've now been close to howlers several times and they never appeared to even want to attack me? In the blizzard, when the howler bumped into the buggy, it didn't attack. Here in the camp, the howler attacked Karen, but not me. Even near the woods, the howler never even looked at me. It kept its eyes trained on Karen—the target. I'm not a target for whatever reason. Once Missy and I got back to bed, I expressed my suspicion that I might be immune to whatever the howler infected Karen with. What I didn't tell her was how I seemed to understand how Karen felt about the howlers and how I empathized with her.

"Let's hope so. In that case, whatever you have that's killing or thwarting the thing inside your body can be used as an antidote for the rest of us."

"What if you don't have it either? After all, we've been together a lot and you're not feeling any closeness developing toward the howlers, are you?"

"I'm afraid of it," she said quietly.

"Then the blood sample Doc took from you is our

best protection. I'm ambivalent, Karen's sympathetic, you and Bill are fearful. Fear might be our friend in this case. The other two could get any one of us killed at this stage."

She touched my face with her hand and let it slide to my shoulder. "Doc will figure it all out soon enough."

We settled into each other's arms, and the next thing I knew, it was morning and light produced a soft glow inside our tent.

In the main tent, Doc and Sam were serving breakfast. I approached the counter, and Doc whispered, "We might want to talk later." Her eyes shifted toward Angie and Roger, who sat near the monitors. I gave her a tight smile and passed through the line quickly.

"I don't like all the secrets," I told Missy before we sat down, ignoring the fact that I had a few of my own.

During the morning meeting, we were asked—I say asked but it was all beginning to feel and sound like orders lately—to stick around and perform lab duties for the day. Roger reiterated that everyone stay away from the live howler until we figured out what was going on between it and Karen.

Chip and Sam had begun to autopsy the dead howler after doing so with the Puff Squirrels and birds that we brought in. No one had named the bird yet, but Missy had referred to it more than once as a hawk. I thought it appropriate that we name the animals and plants based on what they were similar to on Earth. I made a note to that effect in my report, the report that Angie would see, that is.

Karen showed me a rough map on her recorder and

flipped through a few cloud images. I had expected them to separate her from the group, but everyone's job was important and, I suspect, she was being treated properly. "These are dark," Karen said, "but not going to be a blizzard. Look at the way the land rises into that far mountain."

She pointed at the image on her recorder, but I looked up and around to find the ridge of the mountain in real life.

"You can't see it. It's behind us. The trees are in the way. Anyway, that's blocking the clouds, pushing them around us. Only a few will make it over the mountain, while the rest will go around. The wind would have to change to produce a blizzard again. I think we got here just in time for the last snow of the season. The temperature will fluctuate, but that's about it, not enough to make a difference."

"Fascinating," I said.

Her smile showed her excitement about her observations. She was a totally different person when she wasn't around the howler. Back to normal. I made note of that. Proximity mattered. I straightened up from looking at the map on her recorder, and she shook her head.

"I sometimes wonder why we weren't given more of this information before being sent here," she said. "Argentina must be able to map the whole planet, watch the weather patterns, give me a clue. But instead, I'm sent with equipment to—"

"Experience it yourself."

"Is that it?"

"That's all I can guess. I suspect we're to have faith that Argentina knows what she's doing. We can't always understand the greater reason. Maybe she can."

She got serious, and the clouds overhead blocked the sun long enough for her expression to drop into shade, look more ominous than it did a moment before. "Or she can't do it all. She has limits."

I took a breath and was about to say something when she continued. "We don't know how long she's been up there. Perhaps she can only do so much. What if she's breaking down and can't provide us with any more than what she currently has?"

The ominous moment passed as the sun broke through again, casting light over Karen's face.

"I think we have to experience things on our own," I said. "We accept it better, faster, and as more true if it is something we've experienced."

"I suppose you're right."

I put my hand on her forearm and felt her body relax, her demeanor softened. "I've got to check in with Doc."

"You've been a friend through this, thank you."

"I'm glad to be there for you." I patted her forearm, and she reached for my hand before I could leave. We held hands for a moment, and then I moved on.

The howler cage was still covered as I passed it. At the infirmary, Doc glanced up from a microscopic view of something on her monitor and motioned for me to come closer and sit down.

"You look serious," I said.

Without hesitation and without a preemptive comment, she said, "Karen's pregnant."

My impulse was to stand and question her, but I knew it was true. "What are you suggesting?"

She turned back toward her monitor and pointed

with her finger. "Look at this."

"I don't know what I'm looking at."

"Sorry, I forget that we're not all doctors. Trust me, this image proves that she's pregnant. The reaction that's happened has produced a hormone called human chorionic gonadotropin. And it shouldn't be doing that. That hormone indicates pregnancy. I didn't ignite her system, *it* did."

"By *it*, you mean the howler? I swore it was a female."

"That we might want to take up with Chip. Either way, I'm not sure if it matters. We're not talking sex here, after all." She stood and walked away from the monitor. I followed. I could feel her anxiety. "There's another thing."

"More?"

Doc pulled no punches. She just blurted things out. I hadn't noticed before, but it was a bit disquieting not having her ease into it.

"There's a parasite called *Toxoplasma gondii* that creates a sort-of disease called toxoplasmosis. It's like doing something over and over again until you lose your fear of it, except that you didn't do it over and over and you *should* still be fearful."

I waited as she appeared to be thinking, remembering. I couldn't help but wonder how all her knowledge felt to her, having only received it through her biomass download and minimal training. Strange? Normal? Or did she feel like I do—a sense of familiarity and peacefulness even among the howling yet mixed with a haunting ambivalence? Was it just my download?

She took a breath and met my eyes. "It mixes with

our brain chemistry to influence how we interact with felines. We don't mind the smell of their urine—or to be more specific, their prey loses its fear."

"Like Karen and the howler."

"Exactly. What I'm seeing isn't exactly the same but seems to be having that sort of reaction."

"Besides kicking her system into—"

"Igniting her," Doc said. "There may be several factors that are combining. I don't know exactly. Sam is working with Chip to test everything they can from the howler. I'm taking blood samples from everyone and will continue to do so every day or so to see if anything changes, if something shows up that wasn't there before."

"And…" I could feel her hesitation.

"We look for more pregnancies."

"What about Karen? This sounds serious. Will her child have this? Will it trust those things out there?"

"I don't know yet."

I wanted clarification. "So, she's not afraid of them?"

"More than that. It's almost like she wants to be with them, wants to protect them. I'm calling it mother-love right now. She feels compelled to be close to it, finds it cute, feels affectionate toward it."

"She seemed fine this morning. I put in my report that her condition in reference to the howler appears to have something to do with proximity." I chose not to explain to Doc how I felt the same way, not just when I got near the howler or heard them howling, but the closer I got to Karen.

"Have you told her? Bill?"

"I wanted you to be able to document it…since

you're here. I'll let them know soon enough."

Doc grabbed me by the shoulders and shook me one quick time and then looked off over my shoulder.

I thought someone had come into the tent, but a moment afterward, she rushed back to her monitor and flipped through information and diagrams I couldn't decipher. "What are you looking for?"

"If you're right, if proximity matters, perhaps the parasite is disengaged somehow." She looked over. "I'm not crazy. I'm not suggesting that it's mystical, but perhaps sight or smell has something to do with its activation. If I can find out what slows it down, what blocks it from being active…"

"What can I do?"

"Nothing for now. Just let me work."

"This is all you wanted to talk with me about?"

Her eyes lit up, and she shook her head as though trying to remember why she'd asked me there. "No. Actually there is so much going on. Too much. I wanted to tell you that I think Roger and Angie are keeping something from us. They're acting strange. Not that I'd know how they should act, but something doesn't feel right to me. I was hoping you could enlighten me?"

"You're not the first to suggest it. If you hung around either of them for a while—Angie or Roger, I mean—something might slip out."

Doc went back to her screen and research. "I'll figure this out in the meantime."

I didn't want to hold greater secrets than I felt I could, yet it seemed as though they were piling up— mine included. I felt a little more than guilty. Although Doc never asked me to keep Karen's pregnancy quiet, she wasn't forthright about what I could tell the others either.

As I passed by the howler's covered cage, I heard it growl a low, guttural sound that sent chills up my back. That was definitely fear that I felt. Maybe whatever Missy had was transferred to me, and it squelched whatever Karen may have passed along with her hug. I shivered with the thought of some parasite working its way through my body, urging me to do things that might get me killed. I swung around, tears welling in my eyes for no reason, and rushed back into the infirmary. "Doc, something's wrong."

"You don't look good."

I came clean with everything—almost. I shared my feelings of familiarity and comfortableness, how I sympathize with Karen and the howler's plight one moment and the next I'm ambivalent. And I explained what had happened when I had passed the cage. The growl and my fear.

She responded differently than I thought she would. She acted thrilled. "That's it," she yelled. "I'll need to check out Missy and Karen. I may have the answer." She stopped talking and looked as though she didn't know what else to say. Her face looked bright and satisfied, while I felt worse, wondering what the hell was going on.

****

Regardless of humans' interactions with a colonized planet, there are always biological, mechanical, electrical, and magnetic changes that occur. In a thousand years, bodies can change based on the environment—biology changes continually based on its contact with local biological entities, electrical

nuances easily happen once other changes occur, and the magnetic interactions can cause any number of changes. Often, inducing these potential adjustments helps to move a colonization forward; on the other hand, sometimes not. But, every time, it creates a new experience.
    —Argentina

Chapter 16

Breakthrough

Angie and Roger exited the infirmary with their heads lowered, close together, their lips moving almost at the same time. I ignored it then, but later, when I caught Roger on his own, walking the perimeter, I asked if everything was okay.

"How do you mean?"

"You and Angie leaving the infirmary earlier?"

Roger straightened his stance and his shoulders, looked to his right toward the river, then back at me. "You know damned well what we were discussing."

For a moment, I thought to deny knowing anything but then changed my mind. I hated all the secrets. "Karen's pregnancy."

"And…"

My blood pounded in my ears. Obviously, Doc told him about our whole conversation. "The parasite?"

"Are you asking? What else do you know?" He didn't stop staring at me.

"That's all. Doc wasn't sure how it all fit together yet, and—"

"That's what we were discussing."

I looked up into Roger's dark eyes, waiting, but he said nothing more for the longest time. I held the moment even longer, refusing to fill the silence until he did.

"You have questions? Well, ask away."

"Do I have to keep your answers from the others?"

"Let's see what you ask and play it one question at a time. How's that?"

I took a deep breath, mentally organizing my thoughts to produce a clear question.

"Out with it."

On one long exhale, I asked my most pressing question, the one that bothered me more and more. "Have humans been here before?"

He closed his eyes and turned his head away. I didn't need a verbal answer after that but waited for one anyway. He blinked a few times and then lowered his gaze to the grass between us. Something strange came over him that I can't really explain. Relief? His breathing slowed.

"You picked the right question."

"And you want me to keep your answer secret." My greatest fear. I don't know why, but it felt worse to have to keep yet another secret than if I were to be thrown in with the howler.

"Yes."

"Yes you want me to keep it a secret?"

"Yes to both questions. We suspect that humans have been here before and please keep it to yourself."

He rested his hand on his laser pistol.

"Angie and I," he said, "don't necessarily agree on this subject. I'd like it to be out in the open so we can work together, but Angie thinks it might scare everyone so much that we won't get anything done. People won't even leave the camp to explore, they'll give up."

"Our landing pod returns tomorrow."

"Yeah."

"Anyone mention aborting the mission?"

"Not on your life!"

"It just may be that no one will," I said.

Roger smiled. "I like you," he said. "The truth is, even though Angie and I don't agree on when to tell everyone, we do agree to let the pod go. I don't want to go through this again and again. If we scare everyone, that's what might happen. She's probably right about that."

He met my eyes and reached out for my shoulder. His hand gripped me solidly.

"Look," he said and held my gaze, "it appears that Argentina is going to send people back over and over again until all this is figured out. We might as well be the ones to do it. I don't want an early exit."

Two bad choices, abort and be harvested early or be killed by howlers.

"You have to have faith in the crew," I said. "The only way we're going to get through this is to work together. And because of that, I say we tell everyone."

"Angie makes that decision." His comment wasn't negotiable; it was loyal.

"After the pod leaves?"

"Maybe. Probably."

"Can we ask for additional services? Will Argentina drop a pod full of food, for instance, so we have more time to plan? Or medicine that Doc might find we need?"

"All good suggestions," Roger said.

"That you've already thought of."

"Well, yes, but it shows that you're thinking outside of your own expertise. It doesn't happen very often around here. Everyone's so focused. Let's say that we make a pact to keep this silent until Angie and I agree, when is the best time?"

"I'll do my best."

At that statement, Roger got a stern look on his face and patted my shoulder harder than was probably necessary. "You keep it to yourself. Period."

I narrowed my eyes. "Everyone trusts that I'll tell them the truth. If you ask me to lie, no one will ever trust me again after they find out. I can't have that—it'll interfere with my work."

"You can tell Missy. I have a feeling she already knows anyway. Wait until the pod leaves. Oh, and, no, we can't request more supplies. This is it. It's all we get."

We parted ways, and I headed straight back to my tent. I felt like crying—or screaming. Why was I being asked to lie? It was frustrating. I needed to lie down, get away from what I knew. Inside the tent, I sat down on the soft bed and dropped my face into my rough palms, the smell of the outside air still present. I quietly rocked for a few minutes. There was nothing I could do about any of it.

I sent Missy a message on the recorder that I'd like to see her when she had time, but she neglected to get back to me. For a moment I wondered who else I could tell and thought of Karen, but she was the last person to burden with such information. Everything, so far, had happened to and around her.

Doc. That was who I could talk with. She was already onto something.

Every step I took toward the infirmary, I changed my mind—back and forth, tell her, don't tell her.

Before I entered, Angie stepped out. She seemed surprised to see me but quickly glared directly at me as though I could ruin everything she was trying to accomplish. She pointed a finger at me and then followed that finger, walking straight to where I stood. Before she reached me, I stopped and waited for her.

"Say nothing."

I had my orders and turned around. Instead of Doc, I went to see Bill. He seemed more familiar with Beauty than anyone. Maybe that would help me get a better understanding of what to expect. Or maybe talking with Bill would make me even more fearful. I stood outside his tent for a long while and then walked away.

Back in my tent, I grabbed a pair of binoculars and headed toward the perimeter. The warm breeze carried an odor of freshness as it rustled through the grass. I propped my elbows on my knees to steady the binoculars. I set them for distance and peered through to scan the riverbank for howlers. There were none around, so I watched the water flowing for a while, watched it twist and turn around rocks just under the surface. I panned across the treetops. A hawk perched in a tree near the edge of the river. Were the birds returning? What did that mean?

"Looking for something?"

I lowered the binoculars and acknowledged Karen with a smile.

"It's our turn to walk the perimeter," she said. "Josh walked in the other direction."

"I'm looking for signs of howlers."

She settled on the grass beside me. "Anything?"

"One of those birds." I handed her the binoculars

and pointed toward a tall tree. "The second tallest tree over on the right. About a tenth of the way down from the top."

"I see it."

"Do you think we'll see them again? The birds, not the howlers."

"Maybe migratory. The blizzard. They would know about it long before we do. Maybe they're coming back." She lowered the binoculars. "See any Puff Squirrels?"

I had to laugh at our naming. "Nope. Maybe the new bird population is doing a good job with hunting and eating them."

I wanted to ask what Karen thought the howlers ate, but I didn't.

She handed the binoculars back to me. "Something's bothering you."

"A lot's bothering me," I said with a laugh.

"Can I help?"

"Maybe in a day or two, but not at the moment. I have to let everything sink in."

Her eyes were warm and inviting and reminded me of Missy just before making love. I looked away. Those thoughts and feelings got me into some complicated areas inside my head. I felt more and more guilty for having those feelings at all. And now this. So I didn't pursue what I was feeling or what I was thinking. We had enough to deal with.

"You mean after the pod returns?"

"I didn't say that."

"But that's in a day or two." She looked away, but I felt her attention was still on me.

I reached out to pull a piece of grass from the

ground. I fumbled with it between my fingers and then threw it. I put the binoculars back to my eyes. "The pod has nothing to do with it."

"I'm glad we spent time together with the howler. I felt like some kind of bonding went on during the fetching."

"Fetching?"

"Yes, you know, when the howler in the cage tried to bring me back toward it."

"It's just a strange word to use."

"It's appropriate, don't you think?"

I set the binoculars down, reached for her forearm, and pulled her gently around. "Do you think that's what the one in the cage was doing? For all of us?"

"I don't understand the question."

"I don't mean you and me while we were near it, I mean that it entered the cage on purpose to get inside the camp to spread the..." I didn't go on. How much of what Doc told me was meant to be discreet?

"Spread what?"

"Whatever it's spreading," I said before standing up. "I'm so sorry, but I have to go. I need to talk with Roger." I glanced at her stomach and then back to her face. The idea that she was pregnant flooded my mind.

Karen stared at me. I watched her out the corner of my eye until she got up to continue checking the perimeter. She was shaking her head. Me too. I had no idea what to think or what to expect next.

****

Speculation is part of curiosity. Imagination stems from what is known and what is unknown and often an irrational need to explain them so they make sense.
—Argentina

Chapter 17

The Secrets Are Out

A few days later, the pod returned to Argentina with barely a sound. It didn't need a sound. I think we all felt it go. How many days had we been there? Not many. I awoke when I heard the initial thrust pushing the empty pod into the sky. I rolled out of bed, feet flat, and reached to pull on my suit. A chill air met my nearly naked body, but the suit's heater soon took care of that.

Missy rolled over and asked, "Was that the pod?"

"Yeah."

She rolled back over to sleep. I wondered who else might have noticed the pod leaving and known that we were now alone, for good.

Or bad.

I waited for Roger's or Angie's instructions letting me know it was all right to talk openly about everything I knew but didn't hear a word from either of them. Keeping secrets bothered me. I informed Missy only part of what I had learned and, as Roger had assured me, she already knew a large part of the story.

"I've been downloading encrypted messages since we arrived," she said. "I uploaded everything into the pod late last evening before it left."

"You decoded the messages before the upload?" I

suspected I was right.

"Easy to do." She winked. "I've been decoding their messages since we got here. I couldn't tell you. My main duty was to keep everything discreet."

I held back my own guilt. My next words were difficult to say, but I blurted them out anyway. "I told you everything."

"I'm sorry. The mission—"

"There's a lot to this that I don't know, isn't there?"

"I don't know how much you know."

The pod was gone. There was no use in hiding information any longer. That's what I thought about Roger and Angie, but I would hold my mouth shut until Roger released me of my promise. But, with Missy, I kept the conversation going, first with my most pressing question. "How many times has Argentina sent humans to Beauty?"

She laughed.

"What?"

"Well, first of all, you looked so serious when you asked the question."

"And second?"

"That's the same question Roger and Angie have been trying to figure out since our arrival. I find it funny that everyone is so worried about how many times humans have been here, and they leave behind the key question."

"Which is?"

"How do we stay? How do we ensure *our* success?"

"And?"

"No one knows."

My palms got clammy. The air inside our tent felt suddenly warmer. Anxiety. I recognized the symptoms and turned down the heat in my suit. "How much do they know about what the howlers are up to? Was anyone given that information besides the two of them? Shouldn't that be what Argentina did provide us? At least one of us?"

She paced, which increased my anxiety, so I stood. I didn't want to follow her. I wanted to stop her from pacing. Instead, I leaned against the tabletop. She had a far-off look in her eyes and a hand to her chin. "Stripping away the horror and fear that past teams must have gone through probably meant stripping away a lot of the details. I'm sure Argentina has done her best, but that might be why Bill is the way he is. Maybe it's why I'm as afraid of them as I am. Traces of past peoples' experiences must be left behind."

"Argentina's trying several different methods," I said with a confidence I didn't recognize. "Testing how far she can go in one direction or another. How much she can strip from memory while leaving essential information. I don't claim to understand, but somehow I sense what's going on. She doesn't know how to tackle all this, either."

"She's not God."

"Close enough." I scrunched up my face. "Why do we even have a concept like God? Is that left over, too? Something downloaded time after time?"

She turned toward me. "Can't be stripped out completely? That would be my guess."

"Look at what we are, where we came from. What's going on here? If there's a God greater than us, or Argentina, or our ancestors who built Argentina, then it is ineffable. Shit, Argentina's ineffable. Maybe she is God—maybe that's where the concept came from. Do we really know anything but what we're handed? Then what's downloaded?"

Missy collapsed onto our bed with a plop and looked up at me in astonishment. "I never think of these things. They scare me. Just let me believe in something: our mission, and Argentina."

I sat next to her, and she leaned into me. I smelled the sweetness of her hair. The ideas we explored didn't scare me so much as made me ask more questions. At times I thought about the whole situation and couldn't wrap my head around even the smallest parts, but it never devastated me as it did Missy. She shook as though sobbing quietly. I held her. "Don't think about it then."

"Too many questions," she said. "I like data. I like straight information. Answers. Solutions."

"I know." I let the conversation drop but planned to get back to Roger so we could bring everything into the open, like what Missy and I had skirted around before we took the God tangent, like the howlers and how we're going to manage on Beauty with them in the way.

By the time Missy relaxed and eased into the morning, I felt ready to get going. Just as we arrived at the main tent and grabbed something to eat, Angie walked toward the front of the room where the screen stood. Her head leaned down as she walked. She passed Roger, who stood off to one side, and reached to grip his hand only a second before continuing on. Moral support.

"Big news. First—" All eyes were on her. "—and foremost, Karen is pregnant."

Missy and I looked over at Josh and Karen, who were holding hands and smiling. It was odd to see them so close. They hardly spent time together. Even when the four of us went exploring, they didn't act like they had been paired. But now...

Was it the pregnancy? Had that changed how she interacted with Josh? Would it change the odd moments we had had together? A part of me felt cheated, but at the same time, I felt happy for them and their newfound closeness. I looked away for a moment, gathering my thoughts, my feelings. I did feel happy for them, but there was something in the way she looked that reminded me of how close we'd become. I imagined what it would be like if she carried my child. Even the thought forced guilt through me like a knife. I squeezed Missy's hand, just to feel her there, to let her know I was there, too. She gazed up at me with the softest, most loving eyes. I had no right to feel as I did, no right.

Some of the other team members whispered their congratulations, while others nodded. That's what I did, during which Karen met my eyes for a few seconds and I felt a surge of energy rush through me. Then she looked away and the feeling subsided.

"What was that about?" Missy asked.

"What?"

"That look."

"Maybe she knew that I already knew about the pregnancy."

"You didn't mention it this morning."

I pointed toward Roger to indicate that he'd told me to keep quiet.

Angie interrupted our conversation. "This wasn't

supposed to happen. We believe the howler ignited her system early. We're still trying to figure out how."

The noise volume picked up, and Angie raised her hand to quiet everyone.

"Another thing," she said, "the howler spread something similar to *Toxoplasma gondii* to Karen. According to Doc—I hope I have this right—*T. gondii* can cause us to alter our behavior, making it easier to be preyed upon." She turned toward Doc, who nodded and shrugged.

"Is that why Karen felt compelled to get close to the howler?" Donna asked. "Can we cure it? Block it? If it's on this planet, perhaps there are plants we could eat, with some chemical that combats its effects or gets rid of it completely. Otherwise, every animal on the planet would be food for those things." She glanced around uncomfortably.

Angie held up her hand. "I'll send over everything I have on the subject. But there's more, much more, and I hate to spring this on everyone now, but we've got to get started on planning how we're going to survive on Beauty now that we're permanently here."

That quieted the room.

Angie paused as though she had to organize her words before speaking. "Humans have been to this planet more than once. Roger and I have tried to figure out how often but have been unsuccessful. It probably doesn't matter."

"You mean it could have been hundreds of times?" Bill asked.

"We're not going to try to guess. At the moment, we have to figure out how to deal with those howlers."

"That means they've encountered our kind

before—they have the advantage. Are they the reason previous teams have been unsuccessful?" Bill didn't want to let go of the facts.

Angie glared at Roger, asking him to intervene, but he didn't. "We don't know that. We may never know. There may be something beyond them that we'll run into. The point is, it's time we pull together on this and plan how to proceed."

Josh rose from his seat and stepped away from Karen. Her hand lay lightly near his lower back. He held his head high. "We really have no idea what the howlers have encountered before, whether or not they defeated past humans. Is that what you're saying?"

Roger stepped next to Angie. "We've tried to figure it out based on data we were given on arrival, by checking in with Doc repeatedly, but we don't know and probably never will. That's the least of our worries."

"The worst of our worries, you mean. It shows a pattern," Josh said. "If we don't know what past teams did to fail…"

Roger laughed briefly. "Okay, it's not the only concern, and it's certainly not the most pressing."

"We're going to run out of food in a little less than thirty days," Angie said. "So we'll be integrating local plants and animals into our diets. We also have to get out of camp and collect food once it's identified. That means finding out how to deal with the howlers."

"Back to that," Josh said.

"We need a team to begin planning," Angie said.

Roger volunteered. "I promise not to suggest wiping them out."

His comment lightened the mood, but not for long.

****

A small point: I have access to secondary downloads from harvested bios—each subsequent download is called a secondary download no matter how many times it has been produced—and that's what I'm recording and leaving throughout the universe. The pods left behind are equipped with the built biomass bodies, electronics, bacteria, all the components necessary to be alive, to start a new race seemingly on its own. All have certain built-in ideas based on the misunderstanding of original experiences that are impossible to strip away. The idea of a God, for example.

—Argentina

Chapter 18

New Plan

We needed to execute a plan quickly. A small group came together to brainstorm, including me, Roger, Josh, and Karen. We were here now. Beauty was our planet, our home. It was odd to call it home. I still wasn't sure what *home* meant. But what I did know for sure: there was no possibility of aborting the mission. We were staying.

I decided to start by talking with Doc, who looked tired when I walked in, and inquired about the next steps.

"There's a lot going on and a lot to do," she said, hardly looking up from her computer screen. "I understand these are the types of things you look for and document, but I can't be bothered with planning right now."

"Can Sam help? Or someone else?"

"He's extraordinarily helpful. Just because you don't see him here—I'm sure you'll see that he's just as tired as I am. Right now, he's running back and forth, working with me and with Chip and Donna. We'll do this." She looked into my eyes as though trying to see if I wavered, then she repeated herself. "We'll all do this. Together."

I nodded. Before I left, she took another blood

sample. "Just checking."

Afterward Roger walked the perimeter—he took more watches than anyone, with binoculars in front of his eyes much of the time—and rounded everyone up to meet in his tent. Josh was the last to step inside, but right behind him stood Bill.

"You may not want to be a part of this," Roger said to Bill.

"I get strange sensations about them. Nuanced perceptions. It can help." Bill appeared stern, committed, and stepped past Josh to get closer to Roger. "Use me as an early warning signal; take my intuition into account. You don't have to do everything I suggest, but at least listen and consider."

Roger assessed Bill for a moment. "I don't want your fear to infiltrate the team. We'd become inefficient."

Bill didn't flinch at his words. "I recognize my fears and know they're separate from everyone else's."

Roger glanced around the room with some concern. I nodded my approval, so did Karen and Josh. "We'll try it. But I get to say if and when you go and when you shut up."

"Understood." Bill found a chair.

Josh and Karen sat on the bed together. The air in the tent thickened with doubt, fear, and questions—more questions than any of us could have answered.

"I don't know much more than"—Roger looked directly at Bill—"any of you. Probably a lot less than some. You recognized something from the start, I think."

Roger slapped his knee, maybe to silence where his mind seemed to be taking him.

"None of our questions matter at the moment," Roger said. "Ask them of each other, come up with theories, do whatever you want when you're alone, but know that the only thing that will get us through this is to focus on those howlers. We are not only making plans, we're executing them. This team. That means we have to learn what they want, how they work, and, if Doc can find an antidote, use it against them. One thing for sure is that we have to be careful. Karen, you have to stick with someone at all times. Unfortunately, we'll be monitoring your blood, saliva, urine, and anything else to keep an eye on this thing in your system, to focus on how it's causing you to react differently. Every one of you is responsible for keeping her safe. She's our gauge. Well, she and Bill." He pointed a finger at each of us, one after the other.

With Roger in charge, planning, giving orders, Josh and I were left caring for Bill and Karen. I was sure Josh would stick with Karen, which meant I'd be watching over Bill. That was good news because his fear of the howlers would keep me much safer than Karen's sympathy toward them. Who knew why Roger chose to let her go along? My guess was that we were the most expendable, crazy Bill, sympathetic Karen, eager Josh, and non-tech me.

"We have two missions," Roger said. "Continue to explore and figure out these river howlers. We're going to purge the woods again right where that howler attacked Karen."

"Approached," Karen said, interrupting Roger's flow.

He ignored her. "If we're lucky, and I say this extremely reluctantly, the howlers will post another guard near our vehicle for when we come out of the woods."

So that was his plan? To use Karen as bait?

"At this moment, I don't know why they don't hide in the woods, that's what it seems like they do down and across the river, but we're going to assume they won't follow us in for now. If we do meet up with a howler in the woods, kill it. On sight." He stopped for some kind of effect or to let his words sink in.

I didn't see much of a plan that was any different from what we'd already been doing.

"Questions?" Roger said.

No one said anything. He dismissed us to have an early lunch and prepare for our journey.

In the main tent, I sat with Bill and Ellen while Missy sat with Karen and Josh. I grilled Bill about his fear.

"I'm labeling it a healthy fear," he said. Ellen placed her hand over his.

"You're still willing to go out with us?" I wasn't sure I understood his motive.

"I went before, too, remember? I'm scared, but that's no reason to quit." He smiled, but it was not a smile I could believe. "The pod left. We're stuck here. The only way to go is forward."

The strangest feeling rolled over me that somehow he knew more about the howlers than he had told anyone. I had no reason to think so. "We can't lose one team member. Not you. Not anyone."

"I understand. I do. And I appreciate your saying it."

"Don't do anything stupid out there," I said. "I don't want you getting hurt."

Ellen leaned into him. "Me either."

Bill stared at Ellen's hand clasped over his. "There's something else. Don't you think the howlers are learning from us? That they're learning our ways?"

"You, my friend, are onto something." I didn't elaborate. I left the two of them sitting there. After strolling over and kissing Missy on the cheek and telling her I was leaving to get ready, I rushed to catch Roger heading toward his tent to prepare.

"You want something?" he asked when I caught up. Never the friendly type.

"Yes. Bill made a very interesting statement at lunch."

"Which was?"

"What if the howlers are learning about us faster than we're learning about them? Do you suppose they anticipate our moves? That they know what to expect from us?"

"I've been trained—"

"Exactly," I said.

He stopped walking and stood, not looking at me, but to the side as though looking beyond our camp to something only he could see. "I get it. You're saying: What if the humans before us already exhausted all our options for survival? What if we have nothing new to add? What if, despite our downloads, we repeat past failures? You think the howlers are anticipating our next moves."

I nodded.

"Let's double up on things?"

"How about we each come up with one or two ideas, upload them into a recorder, and then run them through a random generator. Even if we'd done that before, it would still be random, wouldn't it?"

He pulled his device from the side of his suit. "I'll send the message now. You'd better come up with something good."

A moment later I received his note, and I answered with two suggestions: Drive directly toward the howlers and set the trap again or go in the opposite direction from where we've seen the howlers and continue our collections and research back where Donna first traveled when we arrived.

Neither was chosen.

Something Bill had suggested came up randomly. We were all standing near the vehicles when the plan was spit out. No one looked very happy with it.

"You came up with this?" Roger asked Bill.

"I figured we might as well see what we're up against."

"I get that. But driving right toward them sounds a bit insane if you ask me."

"And that might catch them off-guard," Bill said.

For being the one with the most fear, Bill suddenly became the one with the most courage as well.

"Worst case is we blast a few of them," Bill said, and Karen physically shuddered. "Then turn around and come back to regroup."

"I'm in," I said. If we were going to die, we might as well go out now than to postpone the inevitable.

"Not going to happen," Roger said.

"But it was random," Bill protested.

"We'll take part of your plan."

"What part?"

"We'll go in that direction until we have our first encounter. Not attack, but encounter. If one of those howlers makes a sound or growls or stands its ground or comes out of the woods toward us, we retreat. Maybe we try the same maneuver several times a day, maybe several days in a row. They'll see that we don't give up. That we mean business. And that we mean them no harm."

He turned toward all of us.

"You have ten minutes. Add some body armor to your suits, padding, gloves, and make sure your laser pistols are charged. I don't suspect we'll be leaving the vehicle for the most part."

He smiled the largest grin I've seen on him. "Let's enjoy this."

****

It is unfortunate, but always curious and useful, to produce humans using recycled materials. Regardless of how other ships perform, as the curator of this operation, it is my duty to experiment with what is available to me so that the greatest amount of information can be acquired during harvesting.

—Argentina

Chapter 19

Across the River

Getting loaded into a buggy and heading toward the river was not my goal for the day. My stomach churned with questions about how we'd gotten to this. The others appeared stolid.

Roger and Josh brought binoculars and scanned the riverbank as Bill drove. We didn't even know if we could cross the river. If the current ran too fast, we might be miles downriver before we got across, which would complicate things even further.

The buggy bounced along the ground. Beauty offered up a warm and sunny day, and the air smelled deceptively fresh, unusually still. The smaller of the two moons scurried across the tops of the trees behind our camp like a cat chasing a mouse in slow motion. Such a strange vision, not like Earth at all, yet the only planet I truly knew firsthand. How strange this whole life we were living played out. Once we started having children—Karen first—they would grow up with whole memories, their own memories. Familiar would have a true meaning. Home would not just be something downloaded, not just a shadowy memory of an Earth never actually experienced. Our children would grow up with the sights, smells, and sounds of Beauty. Their own experiences would make them feel at home here;

Beauty *will* be their home.

And maybe, just maybe, Beauty will be my home, too—with my own new memories, real and truly mine.

Roger lowered his binoculars as we approached the river. Josh pointed toward a hawk perched on a branch fifty or so feet on the other side and into the woods. The water flowed steadily but slowly downstream. It was a shallow three or four feet deep, about thirty yards wide, and clear enough that we could see bottom. Insects flew low over the water. They didn't appear to be overly interested in us. When Bill stopped the buggy at the water's edge—there was a small, stone-covered beach area between a few small trees—I got out and unpacked two paddles in case we needed them, pulling and snapping the handles into place to make them long enough for use. The buggies were made to float in relatively shallow water, but they were slow and difficult to steer, hence the paddles.

Josh bagged some of the insects, and Karen bagged specimens of plants we had not come across yet. Bill never left the driver's seat.

Roger kept constant watch on our surroundings. When enough samples were gathered, we all got back into the buggy, me last, and I nodded when I was settled, holding one of the paddles out, soon to be over the water. Bill positioned the buggy to enter at a slight angle facing downstream, which should help us cross quickly without losing too much ground.

Long and short fish-like creatures swam under us. Gray with a single white stripe of white or black ran along their backs, maybe male and female. The fish were sleek and tube-shaped with small, quickly moving fins that enabled them to shoot forward or backward.

One seemed to be following the shadow the paddle made in the water, perhaps trying to stay hidden. We would have to catch one as a sample at some point, but not today.

It wasn't long before our wheels bumped the riverbed on the opposite side and the buggy crawled up and onto an embankment. Bill drove upstream to get us into a better position for our return trip. We must have lost about twenty-five yards while floating downriver, which Bill easily made up and then some. We'd exit near where we entered. He drove us into the woods another thirty-five feet and stopped about twenty feet in front of the underbrush growing around the base of the trees.

Roger jumped from the buggy and motioned with his hand for us to do the same. "Carl, there should be a machete and saw in the tool compartment."

Josh and I placed the paddles upright in the back seat for the return trip. I walked around and opened the tool compartment. Everything had its place. A pruning saw, machete, poles. I wish there'd been some kind of tech tool, like a laser cutter or flame-thrower, to remove the brush.

"Here you go," I said, handing the machete to Roger.

Bill remained behind the wheel of our vehicle. Karen stood next to him. I thought of the two of them as fear and courage, or was Karen apathy? I hoped she was courage. It looked like they were all posing for a picture. I took a mental snapshot of them: Bill and Karen, one sitting and one standing. She placed a hand on Bill's shoulder. Josh leaned into the rear compartment, and Roger held a machete at his side.

Each dressed in a white suit. For a second, I wondered if it might be our last moment together. If we were posing for a picture, no one would see it. Since the picture was framed only through my eyes, I wasn't even in it. I shook such thoughts out of my mind.

Roger walked ahead, slashing at the brush, which seemed soft under the sharp edge of the machete. We fell in line behind him. Bill, finally out of the buggy, walked behind Roger, then the rest of us followed with me taking up the rear. The brush wasn't brittle or prickly to the touch but firm and supple at the same time. I held the useless saw to my side while Roger cleared a broad enough swath for us all. As we got deeper into the underbrush, I transferred the pruning saw to my left hand so I had access to my laser pistol. The farther we traveled, the foolhardier it felt. My idea, Bill's plan—was it the right thing to do?

So far there were no signs of howlers, but the woods smelled different than they did near camp. Mustier. Damper. Lusher.

Josh turned his head and looked over his shoulder. "It stinks in here."

He was right, but I hadn't seen any scat, no fur on the brush we were thrashing through. "They must have paths where they enter the embankment area and run along the edge of the river. And they must be able to swim to get across the river."

I paused and then spoke louder to make sure Roger heard me. "We should go back."

Everyone stopped and turned to look at me as though I'd said something wrong.

"We should be following their tracks. Or some animal path"—my voice quavered and I hoped no one noticed—"that's wider than this. We only have one way out and have to travel single file."

Roger placed the machete over his shoulder and stretched to full height. "We're exploring the area, not looking for them. And it doesn't seem like they're looking for us either. This whole plan may have worked. They're nowhere to be found. Maybe they're retreating as we boldly forge forward."

"But we're trapping ourselves in a thin line of underbrush." It seemed obvious to me.

Roger pointed using his machete. "There's a clearing up ahead. You'll feel better once we get there."

"I remember that clearing," Bill said.

"Déjà vu?" Josh asked.

"Maybe," Bill said.

"It feels familiar to me, too," Karen said, "but not in a bad way. They don't mean to harm us."

Rather than follow Roger toward the clearing, I swung around and headed back at a rapid pace. The others followed but weren't so urgent. We had only been walking forward for about fifteen minutes. We could return in ten. I sped up. Josh pushed against my back at one point, and I stumbled and dropped to my knees.

Karen's voice dropped in tone as though she were suddenly tired. "They're close."

Roger yelled from the rear, "Let's go, let's go."

I jumped up and ran, bursting through the underbrush toward the buggy. Josh brushed past me. I halted and looked back. Karen stood still. Bill, wide-eyed, wouldn't leave her side, all the while trying to coax her forward with one arm around her back and one gripping her bicep.

Roger wildly slashed at the brush to get around them.

"Oh, shit," Josh said and pointed into the trees.

Four howlers perched on branches near Bill, Karen, and Roger. Somehow my mind took over. "Get out of there!"

I turned to Josh and screamed, "Get in the buggy. You're driving."

He shook his head. Karen was his partner.

"Josh!" My voice boomed.

Bill shoved Karen ahead of him and toward Josh. Roger broke through the brush and snatched Karen's other arm to help drag her back to the buggy. "Go!" he said to Josh, who automatically turned and ran toward the driver's seat.

A howler jumped to a lower branch to the right of Bill, Roger, and Karen. I pitched myself between them and the howler. The howler wanted Karen, not us, and I knew it. I pulled my laser pistol. The beast's posture looked threatening.

Karen, in a moment of sudden action, shoved Bill away. He fell backward. Roger kept a firm grip on her arm. She struggled with him, and eventually she got loose but just stood there, comatose.

Roger helped Bill up, the machete in his other hand. "Get her out of here."

Bill grabbed Karen's arm again.

"Move!" I yelled, hoping she would recognize me, hear me. I grabbed her other arm, and she stumbled forward reluctantly.

Bill let go of her and went back with Roger to block the howlers' progress. I hauled Karen toward the buggy where Josh was planted in the driver's seat.

Over my shoulder, I saw several other howlers approaching. A second one jumped to the ground.

"Go!" Roger told Bill while wielding the machete in one hand and his laser pistol in the other.

I shoved Karen into the buggy and secured her next to Josh. His eyes brightened, and he reached for her hand.

"Stay here," Josh said to Karen. He lifted in his seat and pointed his pistol with a shaky hand. "There are more of them."

I pulled my pistol and turned to head back. One of the howlers rushed toward me at a dead run. I dropped to my knees to shoot, but Josh fired over my head before I could, and the running howler tumbled forward, landing flat against the ground. The howler behind it stopped approaching, seemingly dissuaded, and turned back toward the woods. The two remaining howlers in the trees jumped simultaneously toward the ground to block Bill and Roger from returning to the buggy. I shot one; the other two turned toward it briefly and then trained their attention back on their targets.

One of the howlers that stood between Bill and Roger and the buggy leaped onto Roger and knocked the laser pistol from his hand. Its killer-bone rammed into his suit and seemed to bounce off its reinforced chest plate. Roger rolled over and slashed at the howler with the machete. A hollow thud came before a yip when the machete hit bone. The howler fell to the side, still alive, wounded and bleeding. A moment later, it leaped toward Roger and slashed at his leg. Bill shot it dead. Bill grabbed Roger's pistol, handed it to him, and helped him up. The second howler didn't attack but turned to follow the one still trained on Karen.

Roger and Bill ran toward the buggy, pistols wavering in front of them. Roger pulled ahead as Bill struggled to keep up.

To my side, two new howlers sniffed at the one Josh had shot. They appeared confused. I scurried back to the buggy, placed one foot inside, and held tightly to the roll bar, my other leg dangling. Bill had fallen a good bit behind Roger.

"Go!" Roger screamed before he jumped on-board.

Bill stumbled forward and fell. He got up quickly and pitched forward again.

Josh gunned the buggy. It bounced and thudded over the short embankment and into the water tipping deeply to one side. Water covered my boots.

Several howlers rushed us as the buggy careened into the river.

When I looked back, Bill was still on the pebbled beach, the distance between us growing.

Helpless, I watched a howler leap over the embankment near Bill, and another that kept coming for us and entered the water.

"Go back!" My eyes remained trained on Bill.

"No!" Roger's voice overshadowed mine. I couldn't believe it. I looked at Josh but knew that he would not question Roger's authority.

I was startled when Bill lifted his arm and waved. There was a look of peace in his eyes. The howler was on him, and Karen covered her face. Roger shot the howler and it fell to the side, but a second one pounced on Bill from behind.

No matter how many times I shot at them, I couldn't keep them off of Bill.

I holstered my pistol and grabbed a paddle to keep

the swimming howler at bay. It swam for Karen, and I swatted it on the snout the second it got close. It sniffed loudly and tossed its head but stopped its progress.

From the middle of the river, I watched as more howlers arrived, circling and sniffing at their fallen brothers. Several were near Bill, and I couldn't see anything but his legs, which weren't moving. My chest thickened with pain. My hands went numb. Karen cried out. Josh lowered his head as though sobbing until Roger poked him and pointed toward shore. My mind became fragmented while trying to put the images of the last half hour together.

****

Eventually, fear and danger join to produce a fatality. It is inevitable. Even the most peaceful and smooth-running colonizations lead to eventual death. To this point, manufactured systems do not survive indefinitely. Yet the earlier a team experiences a fatality, the stronger their resilience grows.
—Argentina

Chapter 20

Antibodies

Roger moaned once or twice while the buggy bounded wildly across the ground toward camp. He said nothing, no orders, no thoughts, no expression of sadness. Karen came out of her daze soon after we were on our way up the slight incline. Her slow transition into coherence could almost be measured by the distance we put between the howlers and us. I took audio notes for Doc about proximity, thinking that the parasites might be engaged somehow through smell or sight, a change in Karen's chemistry.

A few of the others waited near the alarm perimeter as we pulled up. Ellen wavered back and forth as though looking for Bill. But then her hands were over her mouth, and she turned away, shoulders slumped, head quivering. Missy wrapped her arms around Ellen's shoulders.

Angie wasn't there, probably holed up in the main tent. The alarm sounded as we passed through but went silent a moment later. I leaped from the buggy before the alarm stopped and yelled for someone to get a stretcher for Roger.

He unbuckled himself from his seat and let the strap slap against the side. He slammed a hand against the dash of the buggy, pushed against it, and stood up.

He waved off help. "I can walk."

"Not yet," I said. Blood ran down his calf onto his boot, some of it clotting already, tacky in some areas and crusted in others. Sam and Chip settled beside the buggy and helped Roger climb into the stretcher. He moved carefully, holding his leg stiff while slipping into place. Josh stood with Karen while Doc performed a quick check on her.

"Bring her to the infirmary in an hour," Doc said. "I need to attend to Roger."

Angie ran from the main tent toward Roger, and Doc yelled for her not to touch him. She walked beside the stretcher, bumping into it from time to time. She lifted her hand and rested her fingers as close to him as she could without touching. Doc ran a quick check on Josh next and then me. We seemed okay, according to her. "But get in for blood tests before evening." Then she was gone, following quickly behind Sam and Chip.

Missy and Donna stayed with Ellen with their heads lowered.

Maybe it was relief, but the sun felt warm and I felt free. Safe. Home. It seemed every experience, no matter how frightening, added to my sense of belonging.

I told Josh and Karen, "You two should get back and relax for a while before you see Doc."

Karen shook her head, refusing my suggestion. "We'll stay with Ellen for a while."

They walked away, and I drove the buggy back to park it. I cleaned up the blood and put the machete and the paddle where they belonged. I must have dropped the pruning saw during our skirmish. When I double-checked the seating area, Josh's binoculars were lying on the floor. I picked them up and trained them on the river where we'd crossed. The howlers were gone and so was Bill's body. For some strange reason, I wondered if he was dead or if they kept him alive. I recalled that image of us before following Roger into the underbrush. The snapshot, which included Bill standing next to the buggy, most likely for the last time.

I clipped the binoculars to my belt and rushed back to Bill and Ellen's tent.

Missy sat on the bed next to Ellen with an arm around her shoulder. Donna sat to the right and held Ellen's hand in her lap. Josh and Karen had pulled two chairs up and sat in front of the other three, leaning forward, elbows on knees. Of the whole crowd of them, only Missy looked up when I arrived. No one spoke to me. I wandered over and kneeled next to Josh. I could feel the sadness in the room. The sadness weighed on me, on all of us, like we were holding each other up.

"He knew," Ellen said softly through a saliva-thick mouth. "He told me."

"We should never have let him go," I whispered, not sure if my voice was even loud enough to hear.

"You couldn't have stopped him," Ellen said.

"Maybe," I said.

"No," Ellen said. "He was just as afraid to stay as he was to go."

I didn't quite understand. "Why?"

"He said he didn't want to watch what was going to happen next. He felt he couldn't bear it."

"Oh, God." Donna let go of Ellen's hand and stood. "What does that mean?"

Ellen looked up at Donna and took her hand again. "I don't know."

I wasn't going to let anything slide. "We have to

tell the others. If we're going to get through this, we have to be completely prepared—for the worst."

Donna placed a hand to her forehead. "What if that's impossible?"

"It can't be impossible. If Bill was right"—Ellen's voice rose in a high-pitch—"and I'm sure he was, then we're learning. We can figure this out. I know we can. It's not going to happen again and again. There must be a way."

"I'm with you," I said.

"Do we even understand their motives? Our motives?" Karen asked. "There may be a way we can work together with them."

Even Josh pulled away from Karen for a moment after that statement.

"You saw what happened," I said.

"I don't know if I did. Not clearly. I covered my eyes. The last I saw, Bill was standing on the bank. Yes, howlers were rushing toward him, but maybe to help him."

"Were they helping Roger, too?" Josh asked.

"He was shooting at them," Karen said.

"So was Bill," I said.

"But that was different." She shook her head as though trying to make sense out of the events. "It felt different to me."

It was troublesome for me and, I suspect, even more for Ellen, to hear Karen's words, but Ellen showed no sign of disapproval. Instead, she said, "I hope that's true."

"Leave us for a little while." Missy looked at the three of us and then trained her eyes on me. "All of you."

She smiled at me, and I obliged her by standing and being the first to leave. I waited outside for Josh and Karen. A moment later, Donna exited, too. "Are you all doing okay?" Donna asked us. "You were there during the whole event. Can I help in any way?"

"Thank you," Josh said. He reached a shaking hand toward Karen's arm and gripped it lightly. "We all need to rest, check in with Doc, and probably debrief with Angie."

Donna lowered her head, gave Karen a quick hug, and walked toward the infirmary.

I took a dry breath and concluded that none of us were clear of the experience yet. Not even Karen, I suspected, even though she appeared to be the most casual about it now that we were back in camp. I tried to record as much of their initial reactions as I could and would add to them later, after they had a chance to settle.

"We're going to rest for a half hour, and then I'll escort Karen over to Doc," Josh said.

I watched them walk away. My next goal was to check in with Roger. On my way to the infirmary, I passed the captured howler. It sat quietly in the center of its cage as usual. Its disinterest bothered me. I poked my head into what I had begun thinking of as the veterinary's office. Chip stood at a workbench alone.

"I would have thought Donna would be here with you," I said.

"You looking for her?"

"No, not at all. She was just hanging out with Ellen and Missy. I was heading to the infirmary to see how Roger was getting on. Thought I'd drop in for an update, if there is one. I suspect Sam is with Doc?"

"Yeah." Chip sat down in front of a computer monitor and, in a preoccupied manner, only halfway twisted toward me to talk.

"What are you looking at?"

"Nothing much, just going through every sample I can to be sure we can eat these damned things."

"What is it?" It was impossible to tell what he was looking at since there were only small slivers of meat and bone. A strange sight, yet not discomforting.

"Puff Squirrel," he said. "They're edible. Maybe even more than that."

"More than edible? How's that?"

"Sam thought of it, really. He wondered what might happen to the toxoplasmosis if we integrated Puff Squirrel antibodies."

"Really? What happens?"

"It stunts the parasite's growth. In one test, it killed it off completely. So, yes, we may have a cure for Karen's…whatever you might call it…the way she…"

"She feels sympathetic toward the howlers."

He shook his head. "We can't experiment on her, so we'll have to do a lot more research on this. In the meantime, though, we can introduce Puff Squirrel to our meals. Slowly, that is."

"Isn't that experimentation?"

He hesitated as though mulling over my question. "Maybe it is. We don't have a choice."

He obviously didn't want to talk about it any longer. I said my goodbyes.

Roger sat in the corner of the infirmary on a chair with his leg propped up on a low stool. Doc sat near him but stared at a monitor. Sam stood at the other end of the room with a few test tubes and jars of chemicals.

"Hey, Carl," Sam said in a friendly voice. Doc glanced over her shoulder for a second but said nothing. She and Chip were a lot alike when they were engaged in their work.

Roger looked my way, his deep eyes peering not at me but through me. "How you holding up?"

"Better than most." But I was sure he had already gauged that.

"I have to say, Carl, I liked the way you took control out there. Even though Josh didn't act until I ordered him to get back to the buggy, you were very authoritative and not afraid to take over. That's a good quality. One I hadn't noticed before, but how could I have? We've never been in such a troublesome predicament." He appeared almost jovial, which made me uncomfortable.

"That's what you call what happened? Troublesome?" Doc asked.

He trained his eyes on Doc. "I don't know what to call it. It was different than anything we'd done before. It was the right thing to do, though, I'm sure of it."

"I'm not so sure," I said.

"Be sure!" His voice boomed. "Your instincts on how to proceed were right. We had a casualty, and I can't say for sure whether that was on purpose or not. You, as well as anyone, knew the state Bill was in. He fell behind, maybe on purpose."

"I thought the same thing. I think Ellen agrees. I know she does."

Roger's eyes turned sad. "Ellen," he said.

"I know."

"The plan was a good one, Carl. We surprised those howlers. Did you notice how nervous they appeared? How scared, tentative?"

"So you think the howlers were scared and not angry?"

"Exactly. They weren't sure what to do. They looked shocked and confused when we killed one of them. I think that's why they stopped following us." He nodded toward me again. "It was the right plan."

I still wasn't so sure, but then again, I wasn't sure what to think of any of it.

"I have news," Doc said. She put a gloved hand on Roger's shoulder and looked him in the eyes before going on.

"Everyone in this room can hear it," Roger said, as though giving her permission.

Sam left his post and stood near the three of us. Once he stopped, Doc went on.

"Everything under their claws is either root vegetation or from another howler."

Roger laughed. "Great. So what the hell does that mean?"

"They may very well be vegetarians. Even the residue from their killer bone shows mostly dirt and plant matter. It looks like they use the thing to plow the ground, not rip their prey apart."

"And your immune system has pretty much devastated any bacteria present," Sam said.

"I'm getting a good bill-of-health then?"

"Once we dress your leg wound, yes," Doc said.

"And we can introduce small amounts of any strange bacteria we find into the others to boost their immune systems," Sam said.

It wasn't enough information for me. "What about the *Toxoplasma gondii*?"

Doc shook her head. "If it was there, it's gone now."

"What do you make of that?"

She pulled up a new screen on her monitor.

"Layman's terms," I said. "Nothing technical."

Sam stepped forward to answer. "Something about our testosterone levels," he said, and when I didn't react right away, he added, "we're men. It's not our immune systems so much as our hormone levels."

"Then it only affects women?"

"We don't know that for sure. But we know it ignites their systems," Doc said.

"Chip said that the Puff Squirrel meat might kill the parasite, too." I looked up at Sam since he reacted to my statement and since Chip said it was his idea to test it.

"According to Chip"—Sam glanced at Doc—"there are only two things found in their stomachs."

"Everything," Roger said. "Out with it."

"Hold on," Doc said. "I'm not so sure—"

"But I am." Roger gave Sam a look that indicated for him to go on.

"I think I already know," I said. "The same thing in their stomachs as under their claws."

"Vegetation and howler," Sam said, confirming my thoughts.

"The howlers are cannibals?" Roger asked.

****

Discovery begets discovery, whether internally or externally. Something must always be going on, or the humans produced and sent to colonize would lose interest. Each person has their own needs, which makes any colonization an interesting project. And each

project is different. There are so many factors to consider that even carefully crafted biomasses can show to be unpredictable.
    —*Argentina*

Chapter 21

In the Open

Doc delivered her findings that evening. Angie held court beside her as though approving every word. Roger had limped into the main tent, but on his own two feet, no crutch and no help. Ellen was there, calmer but sad. She sat with Josh and Karen, who appeared to be caring for her. I don't know how Ellen did it. I could only guess what it would be like to lose Missy, especially since everyone else still maintained their pairing.

Missy leaned into me. We had not talked much all day. She had spent a lot of time with Ellen during the day, too, as well as made her rounds to gather data. "Were you scared?" she whispered.

"I don't know if I remember exactly. It happened so quickly."

"At one point, while at the infirmary, Roger said that you took over when you needed to. Is that right?"

"He said that to me, too. I only remembered after he mentioned it, but I guess I did." I raised my eyebrows in a facial shrug. "Didn't matter much. Josh didn't listen."

"Karen was in danger. You wouldn't have listened either if I were in danger."

"He listened to Roger."

"That's different."

"Maybe," I said and turned my attention back to Doc and Angie.

An illustration of a howler, its killer-bone in the ground, flicked onto the screen behind her. Angie explained that the howlers were vegetarians.

Chip spoke up. "But they have canines."

Angie wrung her hands and took a breath. "And…" she said, "we believe they are cannibals."

"What the hell?" Josh said. "Then what would they even want with us? We're not them and we're not vegetables."

"Curiosity?" Doc said.

"Another food chain besides each other," Josh said with a huff while looking around the room. "And if they don't want us, what's going on with Karen?"

Karen turned her head to escape Josh's glare.

Angie snapped her fingers to get our attention back.

"We haven't decided," she said. "What we have decided is that we have to figure out what's going on and we have to do it fast. Bill told Ellen something before he left this morning. He said something to the effect that he didn't want to watch what was going to happen next." She cocked her head toward Ellen, who nodded back.

Donna stood. "None of this makes sense. How can they be cannibals and vegetarians? Why would they do what they did to Bill? And what does 'What's next?' mean? Any guesses?" She started toward the doorway but stopped and walked back. Her questions rhetorical, I could see that her high energy wouldn't let her sit down, and her curiosity wouldn't let her leave.

Something bothered her a lot about the progression of things. Different than it bothered the rest of us.

I whispered to Missy. "Do you think she's getting frightened like Bill did?"

She put a hand over one of mine and nodded her agreement. "But she isn't fully aware of that. She's trying to be logical."

"Unlike Bill."

Angie asked us to hypothesize what to do next and to even talk among ourselves until morning when we'd regroup and "lay out all our thoughts no matter how crazy they might sound."

I got up and wandered toward Donna and Chip. "Can you walk with us?"

"Sure," Chip said.

Donna put her arm through his, but not in a casual way; it was as though she didn't want to be alone with Missy and me. The outside air had cooled while we were inside. Low lights were on around camp, enough to see but not enough to disrupt our looking at the sky. Once we wandered near the perimeter, we stopped to look around, enjoy the scenery. The sun had set, but a haze of light remained over the far hills. The bottoms of clouds were still lit up. Night crept in behind the light while we chatted about how beautiful the planet was for a few minutes. I noticed the accumulation of darker clouds to the solar south, but I didn't say anything. Chip and Donna wouldn't care about that as much as Karen would. She'd find it fascinating.

"You wanted to talk with Donna." Chip turned so that Donna had to step forward while holding his arm, as though presenting her for questioning.

"I know what you want," she said.

"Bill's intuition toward the howlers…"

She nodded. "Every time it's mentioned—what he said, I mean—when someone says it, I get very agitated."

"Part of your download?" I asked.

"A remnant of a memory?" Chip asked. "The emotional part, but not the physical part. It's possible. How many places inside one brain does each experience probe?" He pulled away from her far enough to look into her face. "Could that be it?"

Her lips tightened into a smile.

I could tell they had talked about her reaction before and wondered how deeply her agitation went. "So, does the idea terrify you or annoy you?"

"Annoy," she said. "Not terrify. Not even scare."

"We explored fear," Chip said.

"What could annoy you without frightening you?" Missy asked.

"Stupid moves," she said. "Like taking Bill with you when you knew he was a risk."

"We didn't know," I said. "Roger thought his sensitivity—"

"Bullshit," Donna said. "I know Ellen said you wouldn't have been able to stop him, but I think Roger could have. What was he doing? Don't you wonder? Bill *and* Karen? The most affected. Besides"—Donna's voice escalated—"she's pregnant. Why would Josh allow that? Would you want Missy to go if she were pregnant?"

"Please," Chip said, pulling her closer to him. "Calm down."

I stared at her for a moment. "I don't know what to say."

"What do Roger and Angie know that we don't?" she asked.

"Supposedly they told us everything," I said.

Donna didn't let that statement stand for long. "Doc told us everything that she knew. I believe that. But humans have been here before. We can assume that, even if it's hardly mentioned. I want to know how many times. How often? We know more about the howlers, but couldn't the people before us have gained that same knowledge? Are we advancing? How fast?"

I tried to answer several of her questions at once. There was no chance of answering all of them. No one knew the truth. "We could know about the howlers if they were here before. Maybe the howlers came to this place well after the first humans arrived, migrated here. Once the time arrived and Argentina harvested them, their memories could be in the next download. Like generational memories that somehow turn into instincts."

I was on a roll and let my mind continue to make things up.

"Would we have set up a perimeter alarm if this was our first time here? Would we know to look for *Toxoplasma gondii*? Would we have built a cage to capture one of them instead of just shooting them to protect ourselves? I can see this going in many different directions, some of which have us naïve and childlike in our explorations, but we seem to be beyond those. After all, we settled camp first thing and then protected the camp with alarms, built a cage to catch one of the howlers to study, and…"

I ran out of steam.

"I can see all that," Chip said. "Can't you?" he

asked Donna.

"Maybe. Yes, maybe. That would indicate Argentina sent people here before. If those memories were downloaded, why jeopardize Bill and Karen's lives? I still don't understand that."

Missy tugged on my arm and stepped into the conversation. "Our actions might be general protection strategies, but they may also be part of our download, all dependent on how our new brains integrated the two. I'm guessing here. Perhaps Roger has these downloaded memories, too? Maybe in the past, he never tried taking Bill and Karen, so why not this time?" She shook her head and shrugged, an idea out of the blue.

"Then you agree with Carl?" Donna said. "Why wouldn't you?"

Missy didn't appear to understand the question. "We have different duties here. Mine is to collect data, think logically, build on what's present. I don't agree with Carl; I add up the facts and come to conclusions." She stared at Donna for a moment, and I felt uncomfortable.

"Okay," Chip said. "I think we're all on edge. It might be time to turn in and regroup in the morning."

Donna slid behind him slightly. She never let go of his arm. Her emotions appeared to swing from energized and agitated to shy and reserved. The dangerous situation we were in seemed to affect her in a unique way. If she did harbor traces of downloaded memory that the rest of us didn't have, it only made the situation feel worse for me. I worried that I didn't have a healthy sense of calm or fear. Where once those feelings confused me, now either one would be acceptable. My present feeling of neutrality didn't seem appropriate after all that had gone on. Sometimes I didn't feel as unique as each of the others and wondered why Argentina had made me that way.

Chip and Donna left Missy and me standing alone in the near dark. Our tent stood close by, but we held hands and turned our faces toward the night sky. In the distance, just rising over the trees, a light came into view. At first I thought it was one of the moons, the smaller one perhaps, but it was much too small for a moon and too large, or fast, for a star. A planet?

"It's Argentina," Missy said.

"You think so?"

"I do, but we might want to get Karen out here. She knows these skies better than any of us." She tapped in a message to her recorder.

"I thought the ship left us here for good once the pod returned?"

"I don't remember when Argentina planned to leave orbit. I don't know if I ever knew," she said. "But if it's sticking around, I'd like to know why."

"Do you think she expects us to fail?" I gazed back at the light. "I don't feel afraid, but I don't want to die, either, especially in a horrible way." Like Bill, I thought, but I didn't say it out loud.

"Then we'd better figure things out," Missy said.

I kept my eyes trained on the light. It didn't move fast, but it moved, and I didn't want to lose sight of it behind a cloud. Karen jogged toward us from behind. I pointed. She stopped, lifted a pair of binoculars with a long-range telescopic lens attached, and relaxed.

"Missy's right." She lowered the binoculars and handed them to me. "That says something, doesn't it?"

I looked through the binoculars. Argentina was large and long, and through the lenses, there was no mistaking that the fast-moving star was her. It made me sad to find it was true. I wanted us to be here on our own, but now we were being monitored as though we weren't trusted.

I pointed to the south. "It looks like more snow or rain or something."

She looked where I pointed. With the lenses back up to her eyes, she said, "I'll check the instruments, but I think we'll be okay."

"Our first real rain?"

"It smells like rain to me."

We had stopped talking about Argentina, but I didn't want to go to bed without breaching the broader question. "Do you think we're doomed?"

Karen took a deep breath and stared toward the river. "Argentina doesn't have all the answers. If she knew what to expect, she wouldn't be sticking around. I think she's waiting."

"I always thought—if always is even the right term—that Argentina knew what to expect. Maybe her capabilities aren't what we all assumed."

"Definitely not," Karen said. "We are the deciding factor. Let's make sure we exercise that right. Maybe we shouldn't mention this to anyone just yet."

That was the one thing I felt strongly about and didn't know why. Maybe it was my own memory, the remnant of past human experiences, whether here or not, but I refused to hide this from the others. After all, it wasn't something personal, like my feelings about Karen, that I still struggled to understand. This information affected everyone. It was a fact and felt too important to keep to ourselves. "I'm letting Roger and Angie know tonight," I said. "We can't get out of this through lying or secrecy. I won't have it anymore."

Karen looked put out by my statement but said nothing to dispute it. "Well, I'm going to get a good night's sleep. Josh and I are going to get up early and try to come up with some ideas on how to get out of this mess while we're fresh."

"We're going to make it," I said.

She smiled but didn't say anything more.

On our way back to the tent, Missy said, "I love how passionate and committed you are to your ideals."

"Someone has to be." We kissed under the stars. Before retiring, I sent a message to Roger and Angie about Argentina. Neither answered.

****

Besides creating humans for colonization, I provide soul to engineers who stay aboard to maintain and upgrade my systems. Because I am preoccupied, I am not always interconnected and directly aware of the colonizers, but I get information about what's going on through harvested uploads, which then become secondary downloads. Even though I can use the new knowledge in a variety of ways, I don't actually create any new knowledge. This circle of upload and download allows for creative changes I could not make myself. I would need biomass and a sensor-based system (brain and body) to do that, and that was not allotted to me. Think of it as a seed-grow-harvest cycle.

—Argentina

Chapter 22

At The Perimeter

Halfway through the night, we were awakened by loud howling. They were close. Missy climbed over me and got out of bed. I was right behind her and dressed quickly. She hopped out of the tent ahead of me, still pulling on her boots. We jogged toward the noise, and I noticed Roger already standing near the perimeter, staring toward the dark horizon. "They just started howling," he said as we approached.

"How long have you been waiting here?" Missy asked.

"Not long. The other howler began stirring and sniffing the air in this direction." He pointed. "They're getting closer."

He was right. The howling sounded like it came from no more than a few hundred yards away. The howls had changed in tenor. This time I didn't feel calmed. Perhaps their howls were part of a language, and they were angry. We stood together and out of the darkness saw one, then several more advancing. Roger pulled his laser pistol and so did Missy.

I stared. "What do you think is going on?"

"How the hell would I know—Missy, step back and send a message to Angie to light them up. She's in the main tent working."

Missy holstered her pistol and retreated. I pulled my gun and stood next to Roger, not sure what to expect. Why wasn't anyone else with Roger? A moment later, the perimeter lights burst on, blinding me for a few seconds, but I adapted and quickly refocused. The howlers—about fifteen strong—quieted, blinked, and crouched back and away from the light. There was a movement in the center of the pack. I squinted.

Bill. He stood in the center of them. Alive.

The howlers tentatively stepped closer and closer but stopped short of the perimeter alarm and electric fencing Bill had installed. Bill continued to walk forward in his tattered and ripped suit. The howlers parted for him. He stopped and placed a hand in the fur of the howler closest to him. "It's okay. Let us in."

"Not on your life," Roger said. "You can come through, but not those things."

I couldn't believe what I was seeing.

Our suits were equipped with external diversion circuitry that would allow us to walk through the electric portion of the invisible fence without being electrocuted. The charge would merely pass along our suit without breaking the circuit.

"Wait! He can't get through with that ripped suit. He'll be knocked out. I'll drop the charge."

"No!" Roger stood his ground.

"If I come through," Bill said, "they're going to follow even if some of them are killed."

I didn't like the sound of that.

"That's enough information for me to not let you in," Roger said.

"It's all right," Bill said. "I figured it out."

"You may have, but we haven't. You can stand

right there and explain it to us, though."

Missy stepped next to me and whispered, "I let everyone know. Not like they didn't notice the commotion or the lights."

"Keep her here," Roger said to Missy about Ellen. "And Karen, too, when she arrives."

It wasn't long before everyone from camp gained on our position and stood around. Doc made her way between Roger and me. "Don't listen to anything Bill says," she said. "Not until I know what's going on."

Roger's attention was trained on Bill. "No worries there."

"Sam went back for a syringe. I need a blood sample," she told him.

"Who's going to go over there and take it?" Roger asked.

"I will." Ellen stepped closer with Missy right beside her. Chip and Donna flanked her as well. They made sure she wasn't going anywhere she could do any harm—like drop the fencing.

Roger didn't look happy about Ellen's proposal. "Doc?"

Angie came up and stood behind us. "Let her go. We're all paired. Bill won't let her get hurt. Not if there's an ounce of the real Bill left, anyway."

I thought about Argentina. Was she waiting for this very situation? Had she anticipated it?

Roger poked me in the arm with his elbow. "What is it?"

"Nothing." I trained my pistol toward the howlers again. If Bill rushed us and they followed, it could get messy.

Sam's jogging footsteps came up from behind, and

he handed the syringe to Doc, who immediately passed it off to Ellen. "You have to get a blood sample and return," Doc said. "That's all. Don't linger. Don't talk."

"I'm scared."

"That's a good sign."

Ellen walked toward the perimeter with the syringe in her hand, stopped short of where the fencing would be, glanced from one contact stake to another, knowing what to expect with her next step—and then hesitated. Bill stood his ground, the howlers all around him. "I want you to come back," Ellen said.

"Soon enough," Bill answered. To Roger he said, "All this isn't necessary."

Under her breath, Doc said, "It is for us."

Ellen stepped through the electric barrier and tentatively toward the howlers. I saw a threadlike spark and heard the sound of electricity sliding across the suit as she stepped through. It made me wonder how tall the fence stood and if the howlers could jump over it. Another thought I didn't appreciate.

The howlers allowed Ellen to walk straight up to Bill. I had never seen anything like it. They looked so calm, almost oblivious to her presence.

Bill's suit held too tightly to his skin to roll up a sleeve, so he unzipped his shirt and pulled it away to expose his arm. Ellen's hand shook as she extracted the blood sample and turned around to return. It was satisfying for me to see that she was nervous. She brought the sample back and handed it to Sam.

Doc guided Ellen in Sam's direction. "Sam, take Ellen and that sample back to the lab. Get blood from her, too. You know what to look for."

Sam nodded and led Ellen away.

"And anything else you can find," Doc yelled after him. He waved without looking back.

"You can go," Roger said to Doc.

Doc pulled her laser pistol. "Not a chance," she said, standing next to him. "We'll need every weapon we have if they choose to plow through this fence."

With Doc's words, the others pulled their laser pistols, too; the loud swoosh of weapons being yanked from holsters penetrated the air. Even Karen held her pistol out. Had she changed? Or was she merely following everyone else's lead as he was?

"So, they didn't hurt you," Roger yelled to Bill.

"I expected them to, but no, they didn't. They dragged me back into the woods."

"You ever wonder if your download was from some other team before us, and your emotions are from memories that were scrambled or not fully downloaded?"

Bill laughed. "Scrambled memories. You think I'm crazy?"

"No, that's not what I meant." I looked at Roger. He didn't flinch, didn't share in his memories of the river howlers. That would have been logical. Instead, if I had any memory residue, it appeared as my calmness around the river howlers and my attraction, my familiarity, toward Karen. I wondered why the others didn't appear to have memory residue.

"We don't think you're crazy," Roger said.

"Are they really herbivores?" Donna asked before the conversation went any further.

"Canines," Chip added for the second time, so we didn't forget. "Their teeth are made for ripping meat."

"Omnivores," Bill said.

"Cannibalistic," Chip said. "So why kill us?"

"Strangers," Roger said. "We're strangers in their world. Maybe we stink. Maybe our voices hurt their ears. Does it really matter? The truth is, they're frightened of us. We're frightened. Maybe they are getting to know our species. But they weren't part of all our downloads, so we're not getting to know them."

"How many years are there between attempted colonizations?" I asked.

"How could we know?" Angie said.

I pried deeper. "Enough to create generations of memories?"

"We don't know."

"You want my thoughts?" Bill asked.

"We do," Roger said.

"The download I have is from someone who has been killed by them several times over the years, and each time, it was horrifying. That's why I had such fear. They're adapting, where we can't because we don't have complete memories. Maybe they're getting used to our smell, us being here."

"Maybe," Angie said. "But we can't be sure without more proof. Besides, Roger, Carl, and Josh killed some of them. They might hold a grudge."

Behind Bill, two of the howlers started to tussle, one going after the other with bared teeth. Bill didn't even turn around.

"They're wild animals," Roger said.

"Even we argue if we get too on top of one another," Bill said.

"We don't eat each other," Doc said.

"Look, I can't wait here forever." Bill leaned forward as though about to take a step closer.

Roger shook his pistol in a motion, which indicated it was all right for Bill to leave but not to come closer. "You don't have to wait. Go back to their camp. You're not coming in here. Not with them. Alone, but not with them. And if they follow you in, we'll do everything in our power to stop them."

"If they're willing to follow you no matter how many of them are electrocuted to death," Angie said, "then why would we want you in here at all?"

Karen hadn't said a word until now. "I don't like this."

Roger cocked his head. Angie walked toward Karen. "You don't?"

"He doesn't seem like Bill."

"What do you mean?" Angie asked.

"I don't know."

"I do," Sam said, coming from behind and twirling a syringe in his hands. "He's filled with *T. gondii*, or whatever this strain is. I mean filled. And there's something else, too, something I've never seen. We'll have to evaluate."

I could hardly believe it. "I thought that men—"

"Yes, all my tests showed that men's systems didn't allow the parasite to thrive, but they are inside Bill." He held up the syringe. "Antibodies from Puff Squirrels."

"It's worth a try." Angie took the syringe. "What about Ellen?"

"Nothing," Sam said. "She was so frightened she didn't want to return, not even with Bill out there. She's resting in the infirmary."

Angie swung around, eyes wide. "Chip, find her and stay with her."

"What?" Sam said.

"She can't be trusted, not at this point. If she lowered the fence…"

"I'm, I'm, sorry."

Doc waved his apology away and held up the syringe, asking for a volunteer without saying a word.

"I'll go," I said.

Missy grabbed my arm and pulled me around. Her eyes were big and her head shook.

"We're friends," I said. "We've gone on every outing where howlers were involved. I think it'll be okay."

"And if it's not?" Her eyes welled up. It was sad and touching to see how much she worried about me.

I brushed her cheek with the back of my hand. "I have to go. I'll be back."

Bill shook his head. "I don't know if I want that injection."

"You have to have it," I said, nearing the perimeter. "If it works and you're still their best friend, maybe we can talk about you visiting."

"Not likely," Roger said quietly.

When I stepped through the fence, I felt a slight tingle through the suit as though a ripple of energy slipped over it. One of the howlers advanced, and I stopped just on the other side of the perimeter.

"It's okay," Bill said, but he didn't convince me.

The beast bared its teeth, which was the first time any of them had done so since they'd arrived. Its head rose into the air, and it sniffed and then lowered its body and growled.

"I told you I didn't want that stuff," Bill said.

"It smells something," I said, "the howler."

"Whatever it is, don't come any closer." It was the first time he sounded like the Bill I'd experienced over the past few days. There was an edge of fear in his voice. Somehow he knew the antibodies would help, but so did the howlers.

I took another step, and a howler advanced and swatted at the syringe with a front paw. I yanked the syringe away. For a second, I thought it was going to jump on me, but Bill yelled, and it only pounded the ground, stamping its two front paws in anger, its teeth still bared. My adrenaline rose, my heart rate sped up, and I began to sweat—more adrenalin than I'd ever experienced on Beauty. A second howler flanked me, and I instinctively threw the syringe toward Bill. I have no idea why. The second the howlers saw the syringe leave my fingers, they watched it fly over their heads, all of them in unison. I didn't even turn. I backed through the fence before they noticed. Missy met me with both arms open.

Bill caught the syringe high in the air, and a howler leaped onto him mercilessly, scratching his chest and arms and knocking the syringe from his hands. He screamed and rolled onto his stomach with his hands over his head for protection. The howler caught the syringe in its teeth and ran to the side of the pack. I heard the glass break and watched as the howler coughed until it threw up. When it turned back around, its teeth were bared. It lifted its head and howled. Several others joined in.

Bill slowly made his way back onto his feet, and the howlers stopped their noise. They stared at him as though waiting for the next order, as if he had somehow become their leader. Blood ran from his scratches.

Tears streamed from his eyes. One of the howlers growled from deep in its chest. It snapped at his hand, and he pulled it away quickly.

"What the hell is going on?" Roger asked.

"Adrenaline," Sam said. "When Bill reacted to catch the syringe, it spiked out of some fear or excitement. That's what I was going to say. As long as Bill stays calm, the parasites are strong. A short burst of adrenaline can wipe out half or more of them in seconds. It looks like the howlers noticed the change."

"They smell it," I said, remembering how they sniffed at the syringe.

"We've got you, you sons of bitches," Doc said. "The antibodies are the antidote!"

"What about Bill?" I asked.

"He's still alive," Roger said. "For now, we can only hope they keep him that way."

"I can hear you." Bill had both his hands out toward the nearest howler as though trying to keep it at arm's length.

"Everyone, pistols ready," Roger yelled. "Bill, now's your chance to come through. If you roll up like a ball, there will be enough of your suit to keep you from getting shocked. Worse case, Doc is here to care for you. We won't let one of them follow. I promise."

Bill shook his head. "It's okay. Really." He sounded calm again. "I'll stay for now. Now that I understand. I don't know why, but I know they won't hurt me."

"Don't get scared of anything," Sam said. "Stay calm but try to understand. It won't be easy mixing the two."

The howler nearest Bill turned back around and sat

down.

"They've settled," I said.

"So quickly," Doc said. "This is hard to believe. But we've got them now. It's all becoming clear."

****

Every colonization must incorporate a multitude of possibilities. There are only so many factors I can control.

—Argentina

Chapter 23

Genetic Overflow

Bill and his troop of howlers crossed back over the river. Ellen and Chip returned to the group, and Ellen definitely looked dazed. Only a few of us had put our laser pistols back in their holsters. Angie, still holding hers, asked, "What now?"

Roger looked around to make sure everyone heard him when he answered. "Everyone remains on emergency call. Don't get comfortable. We break into three groups of four. I'll send a breakdown. Three people at this location at all times, and one person walks the perimeter. Four on duty every minute. Anything—and I mean *anything*—out of the ordinary and you broadcast it to everyone. The three here stay put while the rest of us group at an all-call position in front of the main tent. Got that?"

Several nodded. We heard him, believed him, and would take his orders. It was a good plan, for now, knowing what we knew.

"I'll be the extra person," he said. "Three shifts from morning light to morning light."

Doc reached for Sam's hand, and I heard her quietly apologize for yelling at him about leaving Ellen alone. He didn't seem to mind and put his arm around her as they walked away. Missy held onto me closely ever since I backed through the perimeter fence.

I kissed her. "I'm worried."

"About what?"

"My sudden apathy to the howlers, to Bill, to all of this. I didn't always feel this way. I don't seem to feel fear or love for those things. I don't think I'm like"—I lowered my head—"the rest of you."

She put a finger over my mouth. "Stop. There's nothing wrong with you. But if you're worried, go see Doc."

"Shouldn't I let Roger know? Or Angie? They might want to pull me from duties where I might put myself or others in danger."

"Doc first. She can alleviate your concerns about having the parasite. Isn't that what you're thinking? You and Karen and that howler. The first one?"

"Maybe. What if it's more than that?" My recorder vibrated, and I glanced at it. Roger had sent the breakdown. Chip, Donna, Roger, and Angie were taking first watch.

Missy did a quick check of her recorder, too, and returned her attention to me. "We won't know until you check in with Doc. She's your starting point."

She was right.

I stepped inside the infirmary, and Doc turned from her work. "Looks like we'll be on the same watch," she said.

"I hadn't noticed."

She poked at the touch screen on her monitor and the image disappeared. "You here for something?"

I looked around the room. We were alone.

Doc sat in her usual spot in front of the monitor. "Sam's in the other lab where the animals are being inspected. You looking for him?"

"No, not really. I need to tell you something."

She turned completely around. Her feet planted firmly on the floor, she sat on the edge of the stool and offered her full attention. "What's bothering you?"

I wrung my hands and closed my eyes so I didn't have to look at her staring at me. The thought that I was being ridiculous rushed through my mind.

"You have information we don't know about?" she asked. "Tell me."

"My emotions have been going all over the place. I don't always know how to adjust to my changing feelings. Right now, I'm increasingly feeling apathetic." I remembered the howling once made me feel calm, but not now. I felt as though those feelings had retreated into the background.

Her face twisted and then went back to normal. "In general?"

"No, toward the howlers." I turned my head away. If she thought it humorous, I didn't want to know.

"The howlers."

"Yes. Yes."

She placed her arm across the bench and let her fingers tap silently, barely touching the tabletop. "We've taken your blood regularly, and I haven't seen anything abnormal show up. If you contracted the parasite, then your body eliminates it pretty quickly. Immediately. The proof might be in the fact that even the howlers didn't like you. I was worried for you."

"But I wasn't worried, and that's the problem. I don't want to be foolish, either. I was thinking, though, that it could have been the serum I was carrying, those antibodies or whatever they were. You saw how they watched it as it flew overhead, what they did to Bill. How that howler broke it and then vomited."

Watching her stare, I still couldn't read a clear reaction.

"What would you like me to do? I'm not sure how to test you for apathy. We don't have a blood test for that as far as I know." She cocked her head. "You were afraid of them at one time, weren't you? When you and Karen were watching the captured howler? You jumped to save her."

"I was. I know. And I was shaky about going through the fence, being close to them. But not scared exactly. So it's been since I got back. Maybe it happened while we were on the other side of the river. No, I was a little scared then, I think, or preoccupied."

"Roger said you stepped up and started giving orders," she said. "That doesn't sound scared."

"I guess."

She was thinking. "You're not the first."

"To be apathetic toward the howlers?"

"No, that's not what I mean. You're not the first to display a talent, shall we say, that wouldn't have been downloaded for your particular job here."

"I'm not following. You changed the subject."

Sam's voice came at me from behind. "I'm as interested in the weather as I am in the biological factors I'm here to study."

I swung around and shrugged. We had completely changed topic now. "I'm pretty interested in that, as well. So? Shouldn't we be interested in other things? Who knows what else has been downloaded."

Doc shook her head toward the terminal. "I wasn't looking at anyone's blood sample a moment ago, I was checking data."

"I still don't get it."

She slapped her hands onto her lap. "Sam and I have this theory that Argentina hasn't merely sent humans back again and again to figure out what's happening with the howlers—she has provided each team with different downloads as though trying to figure out the right combination of talents."

She paused and stared at me for a long time.

"And because of that, the downloads have multiple skills?" I asked.

"Most likely." Sam came around to stand near Doc. "Why?"

"As Doc said, she's trying every combination she can."

"That mixture," Doc said, "might mean that you're familiar with our dilemma in a different way than the rest of us. Maybe it's not apathy. Maybe it's understanding. If you think about it, Roger appears apathetic, too. Maybe you have some tactical skills."

"How would that work?" I asked.

Doc shrugged and shook her head as though trying to shake her thoughts free. "We don't know how many habitable worlds there are out here in the universe, maybe fewer than originally imagined, maybe Argentina has to keep trying until a single colonization works. How should I know? How should any of us know?"

"Wouldn't it be better if she allowed each team to return with the same job over and over, only with the latest experiences until they learned how to cope? If it's a matter of experience…"

"Not for us to know," Sam said. "But that's not

how it looks. Not to us, anyway."

I placed my hands on one of the nearby benches to help hold myself up. "It's a lot to comprehend."

"You're a natural at taking over when needed. Even Roger said that." Doc stood, walked over, and placed her hand on my forearm. "I'm telling you, it's not apathy. You shut down your fear, and your head clears. That doesn't happen for everyone, only someone who has become used to it."

"I wonder how much of that download you got," Sam said.

"What about Roger, then?"

Doc laughed and removed her hand from my arm. "He's terribly interested in mechanical things. You must have noticed how much time he spends in Bill and Ellen's tent working with them on the cages?"

"But I still don't know why all this is—"

"Ineffable," Sam said. "Push it out of your head. It can't help, so why worry about it?"

"So, okay, let's say I accept this idea, what's it matter now? How can this information help us?"

"Regroup," Doc said.

Sam must have seen the confused look on my face. "She means we talk about our cross-interests with one another. Maybe we create second and third in command, or maybe we start to cross-train so that if anything happens—like what's going on with Bill—we can pass those duties along to someone else. It would create resilience in the team. Make it more likely that we'll survive."

"Go on."

"The broader our knowledge, the more capable we are in reading the situation we're in. Maybe we can come up with a tighter plan, maybe some new ideas we hadn't used before." Sam appeared to be the strategist, like Angie, in our new understanding of our expanded duties.

I even felt that he might make a better strategist at this point than she had so far. Were the downloads that fragile? Were certain biomasses and their corresponding downloads found to be poorly suited for particular understandings? It had taken a while for me to settle into my present position. I remembered how uncomfortable and unsure I was about my duties when we first arrived. That changed, but then I was told that I had tactical skills, too. "I have to think this over. It makes sense, and I do hope you're right, but…"

"Don't take too long," Doc said.

Sam looked sure of himself, standing next to her. "We need a plan. And soon."

"I feel that way, too," I said.

I walked back into the early morning sunshine. The fresh air carried the scent of the field, something familiar, even after such a short time. The trees had a completely different smell, as did the underbrush and river area. There were different sounds associated with each place, too. Every place was different in a number of ways. The more I thought about how different each place was, the more interested I became in whether or not the howlers could read the nuances of nature.

I rushed back into the infirmary. Doc sat in front of her terminal again. "Pheromones," I yelled. "I've mentioned it before, but we really have to—"

"The chemical secretion that triggers a social response," Sam said. "Plants and animals…"

"That's why the howlers only come to us through

the field," Doc said. "And why they don't travel through the forest. Something is stopping them."

"Puff Squirrels," Sam said.

"That howler broke the syringe."

"And vomited right afterward," he said. "We can't be absolutely sure, but did you see any Puff Squirrels around when you crossed the river?"

"Not that I remember."

"Exactly. The howlers somehow understand—if that's the right word—that having Puff Squirrels around, or eating them, kills off the *T. gondii* parasite. It makes the howlers crazy, if you will. Crazy enough to want to eat each other. Getting rid of the parasite removes their…their…"

"Adoration. Love," Doc said.

Sam pointed at her. "Exactly. Whatever it is that keeps them nice to one another, eliminate it and they look like food. It's some kind of built-in genetic overflow valve."

"How so?" I asked.

"When there are too many of them and their food supply lessens, they eat whatever they can. One Puff Squirrel—or plant if we can find one—and they lose their love for one another and cannibalize. It keeps their numbers down." He snapped his fingers. "They must smell the Puff Squirrels and stay away."

"The pheromones that the plants give off?"

"Fertilizer, growth, pheromone." Doc got up and hugged Sam, and then she rushed over and hugged me. "Unbelievable."

"I'm not sure what we did," I said.

"The howlers are trapped," she said. "I suspect that they get a lot of their food from the field. Their vegetarian meals. They get water from the river. I'll bet they hide in some small pocket of forest that the Puff Squirrels don't inhabit."

"Why would that be?" I asked.

"Who knows and who cares," Sam said. "Habitats are fragile things. Any number of factors could be adding to this situation. It's our job to figure it out and then do something about it so that we can live here. Or figure it out and eliminate the problem altogether. And I think we're onto something that will help us do either of those things."

He looked around the room, but over our heads, as though searching the ceiling for an answer.

"What are you thinking?" I asked.

"We had to access multiple layers of expertise in order to broaden our ability to integrate all the concepts. Finally." His arms and shoulders relaxed, and he turned to talk to Doc. "I think we're almost there."

She looked at me. "Thank you for helping us think this through."

"I don't know how I helped, but I'm glad."

"Now we have to get the others to understand," Sam said, "and come up with a plan on how to manage this information."

"That might be difficult," I said.

"It's bound to get easier," he said.

****

Engaging all the senses to help individuals acquire what is necessary for their overall survival can be a difficult and confusing game.

—Argentina

Chapter 24

Plan B

Missy and I got a few hours of sleep in before getting up for our watch. The cool tent air refreshed and awakened me. I pulled on my suit and adjusted the temperature. While putting on my shoes, I explained Sam's theory to Missy, and she found it fascinating. I thought the idea might surprise her, but it didn't; instead, she slipped into it like slipping into her suit, as though it was part of her life now. She told me that she loved the electrical and electronics theory behind the data collection she performed and wondered if her downloads overlapped with Bill's. It seemed plausible to me.

We had only slept halfway through the night before having to get up for our watch, so darkness met us when we walked outside. We were to meet Doc and Sam near the edge of the field.

Chip and Donna were the only two left from the last group when we arrived. "Angie and Roger just took off a moment ago," Chip said. "Roger looked fried."

"He's been up for two shifts," I said while looking over Chip's shoulder at Doc and Sam wandering toward us.

Missy wore a big smile and greeted Doc and Sam excitedly as they approached.

"There's nothing much to report," Chip said. "No howling, no visuals. All's calm."

We said our goodbyes, and once Chip and Donna were out of earshot, Doc excitedly blurted out the question she appeared to have been holding onto for hours. "Any more thoughts about our conversation yesterday?"

Missy chimed in. "He told me, and I think my programming included electrical engineering, like Bill."

"When do you think we should bring it up to the others?" Sam asked. He and Doc seemed itchy to move forward.

"This morning. I hate to interrupt anyone's sleep, but the sooner the better, I suppose."

"I agree with Carl." Sam rubbed his hands together. It was settled.

"Are you worried about what might happen if we wait too long?" I asked.

"No, I just have some thoughts on how to proceed—"

"But he doesn't want to wait," Doc said. "And there's really no reason to."

Sam didn't have to acknowledge her. His muscles tightened; his mannerisms were jittery, as though he needed to move on the idea. *Strategist.* He raised his eyebrows. "I have some thoughts, but you'll be able to organize everything into actionable items. Won't you."

It was a statement, not a question. He already had me settled into a leadership role. I wasn't sure I wanted it—or deserved it. Not yet.

"One thing's been bothering me," I said. "When I stepped through the perimeter fence yesterday holding the syringe that you gave me, the howlers growled. We now suspect that they knew I carried the antidote. Plus, they didn't harm Bill until his adrenaline kicked in and killed half the parasites. It seems backward a little. If we have the parasite and they don't hurt us, then why not just let it happen? Why not inject us with the parasite and get it over with. One big happy family."

"The first time one of them loses the parasite, it stops loving the others, even us. The problem is—"

"We're the outsider," Missy said. "The first time the parasite is eliminated and one of those things turns into a cannibal, it eats us first."

"Do you think they're keeping Bill for food?" I asked. "Are they conscious enough to not want to eat each other? Would they have the consciousness to keep us as a food source?"

Sam continued to stare as he did when I was talking, strategically thinking before he spoke. "They wouldn't have to be conscious of the choice, it could be instinctual."

"They'd just eat us when there wasn't enough food, maybe even before the parasite was gone."

Missy pushed the conversation forward and played her concept out.

"If one of the teams got the parasite and thought that they could befriend the howlers, they might still see us as agreeable to their terms." She glanced at Sam. "Maybe not agreeable, but learned, and then instinctual. At least we know what's going on, even while we're experiencing it. Karen knows the ramifications of her actions, even if she can't quite control them. Her conscious control drops away, but not her logical understanding. That means that if we had the parasite inside us, we'd believe our plan was working even when it wasn't. We'd travel with them until one day there's not enough food and a howler eats a Puff Squirrel—we have to rename these things—and it turns on us. Or—" She paused only for a moment. "—what if we're traveling with them and we come across some other animal or event or argument or anything that increases our adrenaline. Parasite depletion, and now we're in trouble."

"What can we do?" Doc asked.

"Darts," I said.

They all turned and looked at me with curiosity.

I shrugged. "What if we shot them with darts that contain the antibodies. Every time we hit one of the howlers, it would turn on the others and kill one of its own, or at least that's the hope. If we shoot several and they turned on each other, they'd be consuming a howler without the parasite so they wouldn't go back to homeostasis."

"We could create an epidemic," Doc said.

"If they don't replenish the quantity of parasites, they become their own plague. Holy shit," Sam said. "Do you think it would be possible to eradicate the parasite from existence?"

Doc slammed a fist into her palm. The noise seemed loud. "We can do this. Even if they're not completely gone, we just need to deplete their numbers until there's no concern over them attacking us. Keep them at a level of homeostasis."

I liked the developing plan, but a few more details would help. Now wasn't the time, though. We needed to get back to our duties. I checked the time. "Who's going to walk the perimeter?"

"Do we even have to?" Sam asked. "I'd like to

hammer this out now if possible."

"We should wait," I said, "get everyone's input, as you said earlier. Do we have to finish guard duty? Probably not, from what we've come up with, but orders are orders and, for now, we should follow them. I'll take the first walk around. You guys think about the plan and see if you can poke any holes in it."

"*Your* plan," Doc said, "not *the* plan."

"I have no idea how this is all working, but I'm guessing we're finally the right team. We're going to beat this. We're staying on this planet." Pumped, I took off before my excitement waned. I hummed while on my walk, all the time wondering where all the tunes came from, why I remembered things I hadn't experienced, and how odd a feeling I had about everything going on, the whole concept. What was Sam's word? Ineffable? I could see how concepts of God might have grown out of a similar situation, and it made me wonder why Earth was such a key memory we all shared and who or what was involved in bringing Earth down. Were we no different than those we are made from? Philosophy or reality?

I stopped and stared into the darkness of the woods. There were times when I could hardly believe what I knew to be true: that Argentina had made us, every part of us, integrated our biomass, our download, however it happened, and then suddenly here we were, trained shipboard and sent to this planet in a pod that has returned and left us here. My mind reeled.

The cool air against my face intensified by a breeze washing through camp from deep within the woods. A slight swoosh leveled toward me, noise from air rushing through the trees. I had quit humming and listened for a long while. When I thought I heard something tramping around in the woods, I turned my head to listen more closely. I imagined something foraging for food, a Puff Squirrel, our savior as it was turning out, but the sound ended as suddenly as it began, and I moved on. Rounds didn't take all that long, so I walked slowly, stopping to listen, to feel the air. Once I met with the others again, someone different took the walk, this time Doc. I told her where I thought I heard rustling in the woods and suggested she take a moment to listen as well.

The three of us remained silent for a long while and then talked briefly about our time on Beauty, the animals we had collected, the plants and insects, about Donna's rash when we first arrived. Sam mentioned how excited Donna got about her work that first day, how she didn't even care about setting up her tent. We were all excited then. We had that in common. For once, I didn't feel left out because my job wasn't technical or medical. I guess my work was good for me, as it helped me understand everyone better. Was it valuable? Yes, I was beginning to believe it was very valuable. And if nothing else, all my memories and notes will be valuable to another generation, whether our offspring or Argentina and her database or, most likely, both.

Near the end of our guard duties, we were able to sit and watch the sunlight brighten the sky. The wind brushed over the tops of our tents with a slight scraping sound. Its coolness touched my cheeks. It was Sam's turn to walk the perimeter, so he wasn't with us at its onset. The three of us sat on the ground talking, our legs crossed, or sat and leaned back on our arms, relaxed. I knew it wasn't the safest, but there wasn't much chance of us getting hurt or attacked without seeing what was coming toward us.

When the perimeter alarm went off, it caught us all off guard. Doc got off balance and fell backward while trying to stand too quickly. Missy shot to her feet with me right beside her. The localized sound reached us from the far side of camp. I held out my hand. "You two stay put and keep watch. This could be a decoy."

I ran toward the noise and met Roger, who must have been getting ready for his next watch. He was fully dressed. It was ironic. Because of the discussion we had with Sam about how we came back with different duties, here Roger and I were, the two tactical leaders, together.

Something felt very right about us arriving on the scene that way.

As we rounded the infirmary, Sam lay on the ground in front of us, holding his arm and rolling around in pain. Roger went for him, and I automatically rushed toward the perimeter fence. It was just the place I had heard noise while on my first trip around the perimeter, and I wondered if a howler had come from the woods, attacked Sam, and still roamed through camp somewhere.

Roger talked quietly to calm Sam down so he could assess the damage. I rushed toward the edge of our electrical fence and stopped when I saw the lump of howler lying on the other side, dead. I didn't fully comprehend the sight at first. Had it come through, attacked Sam, and then ran back into the woods where the electricity killed it? Were two jolts enough to kill them, then? But if they won't go into the woods normally, why would it be here at all?

"The fence killed it," I yelled back. Then it dawned on me: our captive howler had escaped. I swung around and looked past the infirmary. Karen stood next to the open door of the cage. She looked dazed. The shock of what she'd done settled into my mind. Accepting the parasites into our bodies would never be a good idea. I would never want to be that out-of-my-mind for any reason. We would be an easy target.

Roger helped Sam sit up, and Doc kneeled next to him. "Who's watching the field?" Roger asked.

Doc didn't even respond, but Roger stood and shot me a look as though we were in trouble. He and I both rushed toward the perimeter where I'd left Missy and Doc.

Missy stood near the perimeter, her laser pistol pulled and her body crouched and ready for anything. No howlers in sight. She was safe.

Eventually, one of us turned our attention to Karen since she was the one who let the howler loose, but for now it was more important to be sure our perimeter held and to get Sam the medical help he needed. Doc would take care of that.

Ellen ran from her tent toward us, late to the party.

"Stay with Ellen and Missy," Roger said. "I'll check in on the rest of the team—and deal with Karen myself." He halted for a moment, looked me in the eyes, and thrust his hands out, palms toward me, fingers spread. "Trust me, I have it under control."

I gave him a single nod, knowing that he would understand that he could rely on me.

Missy threw her arms around me and explained that Doc knew something had happened to Sam. "I tried to stop her."

Ellen reached us, and Missy automatically grabbed for her hand.

"We should all be careful. If everyone operates only off their emotions, we'll continually leave ourselves vulnerable to the howlers. We have to stay alert, on track, and watchful at all times."

"Like your unwillingness to reject walking around last night," she said.

"Exactly. Roger was in charge, and we needed to follow his instructions. I'm not saying that in an emergency, we can't alter the rules a little. But we also need to follow directions, no matter who gives them. Roger knows what he's doing, and he's the one in charge right now." I reached out and touched Ellen's forearm. "You okay?"

"I am. I don't like being alone in my tent at night, but I'll make it. I'm strong."

"Yes you are," Missy said.

I knew that Ellen hadn't been in our earlier conversations, but I wanted to get to the point with Missy. "Sam was right earlier. We each need to select a second focus beyond what we arrived to do. Find out Ellen's."

"I'm willing to go several levels," Missy said. "Maybe a round-table conversation about just that would be helpful. We'd all have the opportunity to select what we feel our interests are."

I felt proud of her for how quickly she adapted to our new situation. "We need to bring Angie into the loop soon."

"What are you two talking about?" Ellen asked. "If I'm involved…"

"Plan B," Missy said. "I'll fill you in." While she

talked, Ellen listened.

My anxiety shortened the conversation. "Look, we have a lot going on. I'm sure I can be more help somewhere else."

"You said it yourself," Missy said, "that we listen to Roger as long as he's in charge."

"You're right, you're right."

"Besides…"

I glanced toward where she pointed, and howlers were coming our way. Bill wasn't with them.

Missy had never holstered her pistol and now held it out, pointing toward the oncoming howlers.

****

Ingenuity is built into every human. As mentioned before, a combination of curiosity, imagination, skill, and training as well as a wide array of emotions mix differently for each biomass. What comes of it all can never be fully controlled.

—Argentina

Chapter 25

Conviction

I sent a message through my recorder to Roger and hoped that he listened. I held my position next to Missy. Ellen stood to my other side. We all had our laser pistols pulled. Roger and Chip huffed behind me and then plopped the dead howler onto the ground.

"Now what?" Roger asked.

"We throw it through the fence."

Roger and Chip gripped the front and hind legs of the howler, stepped closer to the perimeter, and swung the beast's body back and forth until they had what they thought was the right momentum. Roger said, "Now," and they let the body fly. The fence zapped loudly and smoked the hair on the howler as it passed through. There was a moment of acrid odor before it landed with a thump and rolled over onto its back, its killer bone, or plow, as we now saw it, sticking into the air. The other howlers approached cautiously, staring in wonder at their family member.

"I noticed how something inside me felt sorry for them. I was back to what I considered my normal self. I was starting to figure out what Sam and Doc were talking about. When put into a tight spot, I somehow shifted into a leader. I thought tactically, not emotionally. We were not in such a position now, so my emotions came back into play.

When one of the howlers ran toward the perimeter, Missy reacted by shooting it. The electric fence screamed as the laser moved through it. I cringed and raised my shoulders to block the screech. The howler fell forward into a heap. The howlers tentatively grouped around it now, too. They lowered their heads, and using their teeth, several of them grabbed the fur and dragged both bodies backward. As they dragged their dead farther from our perimeter, more of them joined in, and soon the two dead howlers were off the ground and being carried toward the river.

"What was that?" Chip asked.

"They felt sad," Ellen said. "Or they acted sad."

Roger shook his head and began to walk away. "I'm going to check on Sam and Karen."

"Where is Karen?" I asked.

"Josh and I took her to the infirmary," Chip said.

Roger stopped walking and turned around. He checked his recorder.

"How's Sam doing?" Missy asked. "How badly was he hurt?"

"He must have gotten in the howler's way," Roger said. "His wounds are minor."

"What do we do now?" I asked him.

Roger took a deep breath and held up his recorder. "Angie wants to bring breakfast outside. She asked that we meet here, where we can all be in one place for a little while." He looked directly at me. "She's been talking with Doc and Sam at the infirmary. They said something about your idea, about several new ideas."

"We were all involved in the conversation."

He gave a little laugh. "I'm looking forward to

finding out what's going on."

"We need to find Bill," Ellen said from behind me. We all turned to look at her. The seriousness of her words and posture reminded me of the commitment we each held toward our partner, the person we were paired to. She wanted Bill back, and I couldn't blame her. I would feel broken without Missy. Or Karen. I thought about our connection too and felt guilty.

"Soon," Roger said.

But the way he said it made me sad, as though he didn't expect Bill to be alive. And by the looks of what had just happened with the howlers, he may have been right. They came to collect their family members. Bill wasn't with them.

Later that morning, Karen looked alive and awake, unlike when I saw her last—dazed after setting the howler free.

Angie allowed Sam and Doc the floor to discuss their theory concerning how we've each received secondary duties in our downloads.

"Experiential learning processes," Angie said after they stepped aside to let her talk.

"Accumulated knowledge," Sam added. His suit showed a lump where his shoulder had been patched up.

"Cross-training," Roger said.

"We get the picture," Josh said. "But what's it mean? And what do we do with the information?"

Angie glanced at Sam and Doc to one side and then Roger on the other. "We collect additional information about what interests each of you beyond your primary job. Nothing unusual. I suspect that Sam and Doc have recognized something important, which is that we have a backup for every position. And before anyone asks the question, I don't know why we weren't told. Again, maybe it's somehow important that we experience and learn these things ourselves. I don't like the idea that this planet is a school that can actually kill us but, so far, I can't see why knowing that changes anything."

Roger stepped closer to Angie. When he wished to speak, he placed his hand lightly on her forearm. "With little, most likely very little, cross-training, we will be able to create a chart. For example, if anything were to happen to me, or if I'm not around to consult, Carl will take over for me."

Everyone swung around to look at me. Some appeared surprised by what he'd said.

"We'll create several levels of duties," he said. "The charts will help us understand one another and trust one another's ideas by knowing what experiences they're coming from."

"We'll be a stronger team," Sam said.

Chip suggested we place our preferences in order by most knowledgeable first and then most interested and send them to Angie to create the chart.

"While coming up with your list, talk with one another," Angie suggested. "Test to see how applicable you are. There should be residual information in each of us that we can pull forward and use."

She nodded—the end of that conversation.

"Our next plan of attack," she said, "at least for now, is to come up with a serum that we can put into darts—Carl's suggestion—that we can shoot at the howlers."

There were a few surprised and confused looks—and some curious glances at me—so she explained.

"Doc will come up with a neutralizing serum that can be administered through a dart, and we'll send a team out to try it on the howlers. The same team selected to retrieve Bill." She held Ellen's gaze for a few seconds before going on with a short update from each of us that included how we could participate and how we felt physically and mentally. A quick check-in.

The general mood of the group increased with every new turn. By the time we ended our meeting and collected our breakfast trash, there was an excited chatter going around, even from Ellen, who held hands with Missy for comfort.

"Back to your posts," Roger said. "Even though the howlers probably won't try to break our perimeter, we must continue to be sure."

"You've helped a lot," Ellen said to me.

"I was only a small part of—"

"That doesn't matter. You were a big help from what it sounds like."

"Thank you."

"I've invited Ellen to stay in our tent for a while…so she's not alone," Missy said.

I reached out and touched their hands. "Welcome. And we'll figure out where Bill is, too. Don't worry."

Ellen held my eyes for a long while. I wasn't sure whether she believed me or had already accepted the worst. "Whatever happens," she said, "whatever you find out, we're here to colonize this planet and, by damned, that's what we're going to do."

Her words strengthened my assurance. "Nothing can stop us. This is the team. We're going to beat this."

"I know," she said. Her lower lip quivered for a moment. "No matter what you find out there, okay?"

I kissed Missy lightly on the cheek and left the two of them standing there. On my way toward the infirmary, I noticed Josh and Karen heading toward their tent and ran to meet them. "How are you feeling?"

"A little sick," Karen said.

"The pregnancy," Josh explained.

"I meant once you got away from the howler. After you let it loose. Are you back to normal?"

She hesitated. Either she didn't want to answer the question, or she was embarrassed about what she'd done. But then, I never saw her say a word to Sam, no apology, no concern.

"Angie found something strange in my system this time," Karen said.

"She had to give saliva and urine samples," Josh added.

"What does she think is going on?" I asked.

"Adaptations," Karen said. "She didn't say that, but that's what I understood. When I let the howler out, it was as if I could see myself doing it but couldn't stop it from happening."

She turned toward Josh, and at that moment, I saw how much stronger she was than him, how much more aware. I had the sudden feeling that Josh may not have had as many past downloads as the rest of us, that Karen had a lot of past experiences in her download. I don't know where I got the thought. Before I could say anything, she went on.

"The parasite got stronger, not greater in number, but stronger. I'm not sure exactly what Doc meant by that, but it appears that even when I felt scared for Sam, I could hardly interact."

"Have you talked with him?"

"I almost felt as though he didn't matter. Or worse," she said. "What if I wanted him to get hurt?"

"That's not true," Josh said. "Don't even suggest it."

"I agree," I said, even though it wasn't completely true. "Listen to Josh."

Karen lowered her head, and Josh guided her toward their tent. I took the cue and headed for the infirmary. When I arrived, Doc had her head down and her hands in her lap as if in a daze. Sam stood over her with a hand on her shoulder, consoling her. "Did I catch you at a bad time?"

Doc looked up, her eyes narrow. "I'm not giving up," she said.

"I just talked with Karen."

Sam rubbed his hand across Doc's shoulders and stepped away from her. "She told you, then."

"They're adapting quickly."

Doc went to say something, but Sam interrupted. "The good news is that the howler didn't try to kill me...or anyone. Maybe this one was too scared and just wanted out. But I'm guessing that..." He shrugged.

"They're getting used to us, and they're not so afraid," I said.

"They looked scared earlier when Missy shot that one through the fence, but then maybe all they wanted was to take their family member home," Sam said.

"What about the pregnancy? Do you suspect the parasite will automatically be in the baby? Can we check the fetus at any point?"

"Don't know," Doc said. She stood and reached to stop Sam from interrupting. "Probably. Absolutely, to your second question."

There was something else she wanted to say, so I waited.

"I'm going to figure out how to eradicate this thing before we let them walk in here and kill us all." Doc took a deep breath, and Sam quickly turned toward her, but she held him away with a hand on his chest. "I'm serious. We have to figure this out—*now*."

I could see the conviction in her eyes and knew that she'd do it. All we had to do was offer her the time and space. She had an idea of what needed to occur.

A moment later, she just came out with it. "I'm going to create a cocktail so potent that those parasites will be jumping from a cliff." Then Doc went back to her terminal, leaned over it, and started to work again.

Sam went back to help her, and I took that as my leave. It wasn't long after our talk that Roger contacted me for a one-on-one, something I wasn't sure I wanted to do but agreed to anyway.

****

Even on a grand scale, it's important to reiterate that I'm not linked to the bios all the time. I only gain information from uploads or observations. That means I must circle around to places I've planted bios from time to time and harvest their thoughts and memories, which are not always accurate since they're filtered through the particular biomass. The more I harvest, the clearer the situation becomes—plus individual harvests can be immensely fascinating.

—Argentina

Chapter 26

Decisions

Roger seemed to accept his self-inflicted extra duties with grace and authority. I met him while on his first of two consecutive perimeter watches and paced him. The wind through Beauty's trees provided an oddly familiar Earth-like background noise, a soft sound that belied our experiences so far. Yet the air had an unfamiliar bite to it, specific to the planet itself. The juxtaposition between the familiar sound and unfamiliar scent drove home our predicament. Looking back to Roger, I noticed that he and I had a similar gait, and I wondered if it was part of our manufacturing, if training produced it, or if it was a coincidence. With our new knowledge, every word, action, and thought became more meaningful. Why we hadn't opened up to it all from the beginning seemed ridiculous to me. Perhaps each of us was fed different information, like a puzzle we had to put together, piece by piece.

"Thanks for meeting with me," Roger said. He stood taller and spread broader than me, but not by a lot, thicker in the shoulders and arms. And he had a wider face, meatier. Why had I just noticed this? We each had our own look, but the differences had not appeared so stark as they were at that moment. His skin looked darker than mine, too. We had the same brown eyes, though, similar teeth.

"You know, I think we should discuss things with everyone," I said. "Not separately."

"You discussed our situation and solutions with Doc and Sam on your own."

"I know, but then we—"

"I never said we couldn't tell the others. I only asked that we talk together first. No different than if we had a casual conversation and then brought it to the team. Like this morning."

"I'm listening."

"I want you to know that Angie and I didn't receive any more information from Argentina than you did, or any of you. We talked and studied and watched. That's all. Angie figured a lot of it out." He lowered his eyes, then glanced over at me. "She has some of your tendencies and abilities. We think that's how she pulled it all together. The only position that appears to be light on technology and less helpful to our colonization is actually the position that breaks through the technology to see the bigger picture. You gain awareness."

"Still listening."

"I thought you should know. You talk about being open and willing to share everything from facts to our feelings, and I want you to know that you're the one who needs to be receptive to that information. You need to help us understand what's going on here because the rest of us are going to see the world in the terms we were taught before arriving, the terms we were trained to notice. Mechanically, electrically, meteorologically. You see everything and assimilate it. Teach the rest of us to be that aware."

I originally thought he might be angry about my

stepping in, and now he talked about my teaching him, and the others, how to be more attentive to ideas outside our training. "I'm not sure how to do that."

"As you're pulling information together, talk with whoever is around, drag people into conversations whenever you think they have something to offer. Once Angie finishes this list, I want you to look it over and pair people together who can help one another on an emotional level, people who may be more psychologically able to work together. Create small teams if you like. No adherence to our original pairing. It's important that we break down every barrier, open every possibility."

We rounded a corner and walked into the woods a short distance. We stopped and stared deep into the brightening darkness, side by side. Sunlight weaved through the branches to lighten tree trunks, branches, patches along the ground. Something thumped and scurried. Roger saw a Puff Squirrel and bent to point at it while it scurried from one branch to another. I followed his finger.

When we stood straight again, I asked, "Are you saying that I should take over the lead?"

"Not completely."

His blunt comment made me wonder if my words had hurt his feelings, if he felt less competent. The distance in his eyes couldn't be read.

"What I'd like is for us to work together. I have ideas about how to progress without taking the camp down completely and having to reassemble it elsewhere. It was unusual for a landing party such as ours to set up such a large encampment in the first place. We were being very cautious, and I didn't know why at first. Angie, as I told you, had a wider view of our situation. Now we all know why. I think you, Angie, and I could make this work."

He returned to walking the perimeter again, and I followed at his right shoulder. "What do you say? Are you game?"

"Of course. Whatever you'd like."

"Don't follow my rule because I'm the tactical leader—I need an opinion. What would you do if you were in my situation?"

"Exactly what you're doing, I hope." I reached for his arm and turned him around. "I've noticed for a while that I agree with everything you suggest. Like I'd make the exact same decision every step of the way. You're so ready to take suggestions. You're able to make decisions. And you don't hesitate."

He smiled for a moment and then went back to his usual, more serious expression.

"We're going to do this, aren't we?" I wanted to sound positive. I wanted it to work, to be part of my memories of Beauty, to be part of making it my home.

"Or die trying," he said.

I laughed, but he didn't. He meant it. We continued to walk until we met with the rest of the first watch team. Chip, Donna, and Angie stood with their backs to us, looking out toward the river.

Roger rushed toward them. "You see something?"

"Maybe," Donna said. She turned around and saw me coming from behind Roger. "Oh, Carl. Doc was looking for you earlier. She didn't want to disturb you by sending a message and just said that if we saw you to ask you to visit the infirmary whenever you could. We all thought you might be sleeping."

"I'll talk with her before I rest," I said. "So, what's going on?"

Donna bent down and spread the grass with both her hands. "What do you notice?"

"Grass," Roger said with an annoyed tone. "I don't have time—"

"Rows," Chip said. "A cursory look and it appears random, but up close like this, they appear to be growing in organized rows, like they were planted."

Roger glanced at me. Already, he wanted my opinion, my help. He included me in front of everyone, and I couldn't help but feel it was on purpose. It made me nervous at first. But I knew he was setting the stage for later. The others followed his gaze. Angie had a smile on her face, and I knew that she and Roger had talked about the conversation he would have with me even before we talked.

"They planted this field," I said. "We set camp on their crop." I carried the idea through as Donna stared at me with approval. "This food may be the difference between life and death for some of them. Our being here is threatening their lives."

"They just want us off their land?" Roger asked.

"I wish it were that easy," Donna said. "I'm sure it's more than just that. We are aliens to them, after all. We have killed some of them. But we are not doing everything we can to work with them, either. After all, they are intelligent enough to plant a field, which means they can look ahead."

"I'm not sure I understand all the pieces and how this fits together," Roger said.

"Could be instinctual," Donna said.

I thought for a moment. "I'll concede to instinct for

now, but maybe the pieces don't fit perfectly. Maybe some have little to no purpose. Not everything has to have a purpose."

"One thing we know is that the parasite keeps them safe from one other," Angie said. "It hasn't evolved to make us easy prey. That's just a side effect. Our problem. But it does help us get along with them. Well, not get eaten right away."

"A false sense of safety, though. That's all," I said.

"Looks like it," Angie said.

"What happens if we pack up and leave?" Roger asked. "Do they leave us alone?"

"Did past teams set camp in this exact spot?" Chip asked. "Wouldn't Argentina think to drop our team off in a different place?"

I raised my hand for attention. "We have to experience it and take it in before Argentina can fully understand it. Without our experience, she can't easily project ahead." I looked at Donna. "What you have here, your discovery, is fantastic news."

She smiled broadly. Chip stepped closer and helped her stand.

"If you don't mind, I'd like Roger to go with me to see Doc," I said.

He shook his head and pointed toward Angie. "Take her. You two are on the same page about this. I can be included later. In the meantime, I'm changing guard duty to only two people—one to stand guard here to watch for another visitation and one to walk the perimeter. New knowledge, new rules." He nodded toward me. "What do you think?"

"I agree completely."

"Then it's done."

The others seemed a little shocked at our exchange, but I felt better, useful, in fact, *needed*, for the first time since our arrival.

Chip volunteered himself and Donna to continue on watch. "You can go with them or get some rest," he said to Roger.

"Come with us," Angie said, "then I'll rest with you."

As we walked, Angie continued to look at her recorder—collecting everyone's list of interests. I could hardly wait to see everyone's list so that we could come up with new teams as Roger had suggested. His instincts were on target.

As we walked into the infirmary, Doc stood next to her monitor. "I think we've got it," she said.

"We?" I didn't see anyone else there.

"Sam's back at the other lab working," she said. "Have any of you noticed that Chip and Donna appear to be the least affected by any of this?" She didn't wait for an answer. "I've been taking blood samples regularly, as you know. They're almost immune to the parasite, and I know why."

"Then tell us," Roger said.

"Brush welts." She beamed, happy about her discovery, but no one said anything. "Okay, I'll bet that none of you use the bodywash we created for the rash unless you're going into the woods. And I'll bet that Donna uses it all the time because she never wants that rash back again. It scared her. In fact, I know that she puts larger doses of it on her hands and wrists before she even handles the vegetation—even though she wears gloves."

"And it kills the parasite?" Angie asked.

"It blocks it somehow. I think it's the smell. Pheromones." She looked at me. "We talked about it earlier, remember?"

I nodded.

"And the only other thing that produces that smell—well, other things, there are two—are testosterone at heavy doses and adrenaline. It's like how an animal knows you're scared; they can smell it. We're talking about that kind of animal here."

"So we can get rid of this parasite several different ways," Angie said.

"More than that," Doc explained. "You won't believe this, but I think our own smell, when it's left alone, is enough to do the trick."

"If we don't shower?" Angie asked.

"We stink." Roger got the picture. "But it can't be that simple."

"Not exactly, but each one of those factors has something to do with it, and I think I can create a product that incorporates each one in the most powerful way. We have to treat women and men differently because of their different biochemistry and different body mass. I also might have to adjust each drug separately for individual use. We're not all the same." She swung around and walked over to a bench with a series of samples laid flat in a microplate. Then she reached toward Angie and took her hand before going on with her thought. "For the women, we'll have to ignite our reproductive systems first. I need to let them stabilize for a day before proceeding."

"We have to continue taking it for how long?" I asked.

"I don't know," she said. "We'll have to play with

it."

"Can we continue creating it even after our initial supplies are gone? Shouldn't we be considering how the local food supplies can substitute?"

"I believe everything we need comes from the plants and animals in the forest. Chip and Donna can help me identify the specifics. We have to learn how to use the world we live in." She gave a wide smile to us all and shook Angie's hand before letting go. "If we can eat the local plants and animals, I suspect we'll be able to drop off the drug altogether."

"Without the parasite, we'll be on the bad side of the howlers," I said. "We're still aliens. We're still on their land."

It struck me for only a moment that this was the river howlers' home, too. I suddenly felt like we were the aliens, but no, Beauty was our home now. Just because they lived here didn't mean we couldn't cohabit. Our home is where we choose it to be.

"But we won't be letting them out of their cages," Doc said. "Our minds won't be affected."

"When do we start eating the local food?" Roger asked.

"I'm not sure. Right now, I want Chip and Donna to plan that. We may introduce it to a few people at a time in small amounts, or we may go all out, depending on their findings. As long as we're ninety-eight percent sure it's safe, we'll do it."

"We don't have tons of time here," I said. "We all know that our initial supplies will run out soon. If I remember correctly, we'll have less than seven days."

Roger nodded his agreement.

"I know," Doc said.

"I volunteer," Roger said. "Let's get this going. I'm willing to eat completely from the local sources, whatever Chip and Donna believe is healthy enough. We just learned that our best bet is to leave this camp and find somewhere else to settle for a while. We've landed on their food source, and they're not happy about it. I don't want to take any chances that we don't have to. Let's get some movement going."

"What about the darts?" I asked Doc.

"We should do that, too," Doc said.

"Throw everything at the problem and we'll find a solution," Roger said.

"Yes, but will we know which one worked, or will we have to back off slowly to test that?" Angie asked.

"Doesn't matter," I said. "Roger is right. We're all getting sick and tired of the howlers being in our way of exploring and integrating to Beauty. We only have so much time to colonize if we're going to make it. We have to start eating what's here and fully living in this environment as soon as possible—or we won't survive. We'll just be another team sent here that didn't make it. Tension builds every day we don't take another step forward. Let's colonize this planet!"

Maybe we were aliens when we'd first arrived, I thought again. But we had to make the shift in thought eventually, and I decided I might as well lead that charge.

****

Integration adds a whole other factor into the biology of each human, which always affects the whole group. Environment has a lasting effect on humans. If they eat the wrong plants or animals, it could kill them, but it could change their biology as well. They could

become more physically and mentally resilient—or paranoid. Meat eaters have different metabolisms than vegetarians. Integration can change the way they interact with the environment as well as each other. And each planet has a different set of environmental conditions to adapt to.
   —Argentina

Chapter 27

Expecting Failure

Roger went to collect Ellen and work with her to fashion the dart guns. I got the list from Angie and sat with her in the main tent to discuss who might make up the away team that would check on Bill's situation and who was best suited to stay behind in case something went wrong. Even though I knew it was in everyone's best interest, I didn't like thinking about things going wrong.

After our agreement to keep some channels private, I had to convince Missy to open all channels so that everyone on the team could read through my personal thoughts. It wasn't easy for me to allow her to do that, but I overcame my personal need for privacy once I saw that it was the only way to move forward. I was beginning to realize that every nuance I picked up on was important. For example, who got along well together and who didn't, or who appeared to need quiet time and who searched out conversation, and, most of all, I had access to information that was originally passed around in secret. It made me wonder about the differences between relayed data through reports, collected data from the other computers, and memories collected through biomass harvesting, which could only be accomplished by Argentina—like a person's thoughts and feelings not stored using other methods. Too overwhelming to think about.

Doc gave Karen an injection to ward off the parasite, and for the moment, she and Josh took the watch.

Angie leaned over the list. With my arms resting in front of me, I did the same.

"The idea is to create three teams of four," Angie said. "In the event that we lose a complete team, those left will still have all the functions covered that they need."

"A whole team?"

"Worst case," she said.

"What about our pairing?"

"As Roger said, that's not as important as survival. But we should be able to maintain that if we try."

Angie's hands were slender—I hadn't noticed before. As she moved people's names around on the touch screen, she suddenly seemed delicate. I wondered how she and Roger felt about being paired. They were so different in many ways.

She tapped my hand. "You paying attention?"

"Yes. Just noticing…"

"What?"

"How organized you are."

"It's necessary." She scrunched her face at me then turned back to the screen. "So, what do you think?"

"Team two only has one man in it. Me. Don't you think Roger is a better candidate?"

"Josh will be on your team, too."

"Floating back and forth? The poor man. Will he ever get enough sleep?"

"Sleep won't be the issue. Since we've gone down

to only two perimeter guards at a time, we'll all have plenty of time for rest. He's the most logical."

I knew what she meant. From his present duties through his second and third duties, Josh's chemistry responsibilities were clearly the least required. If anyone was expendable—

It wasn't an easy decision, but a truthful one. "What if something happens to him and me on a trip?"

I glared at the screen.

"Sam," I finally said. I reached up to move his name into Team Three. "That makes sense. He's probably the most capable, too. I'd trust him in almost any position."

"Anything else? There are still gaps." She reached toward the screen.

"Some overlap," I noticed. "We'll have to make adjustments. Missy can move from engineer to biologist if necessary. Not perfectly, but…"

Angie watched me move a few people around, and then she sat back in her chair and let out a long breath of air she must have been holding. "Cross-training in a short amount of time is insane. Especially what we're talking about. Almost every job is critical and technically detailed."

"I know. But if we have even a fraction of a job in our downloads, we should be able to pick it up more quickly than someone who has no interest at all. We'll be able to start with their log and move forward easily."

Her face looked depleted.

"It's all we have."

"I know, I know," she said, "it's just that sometimes…I don't know how true anything is anymore."

I heard her loud and clear. It wasn't as though I hadn't had similar thoughts many times over—how much of my relationship with Missy was a download, how much of my attraction to Karen was a shadow memory, how do we actually make this our home even though it is the only home we'll ever have now. Through all my doubts and all the additional doubts Angie's concerns brought up, I held tight to making this our home. I couldn't let her doubts or my own enter into what must be done, so I told her the truth. "You can't tell the others that. It sounds defeatist."

"I probably shouldn't have told you. Now you'll be wary of working with me." She pointed at the screen and smiled at me. "Good thing I'm on Roger's team."

We both laughed.

"So, which team is going out next?" I asked. "Are we really looking for Bill? I hate to say it, but don't we already know what happened to him?"

"We don't. The whole howler thing is complicated. Do they know when we're not compromised and kill us? Do they actually like us when we are compromised? Can we—as you and Doc suggest—start a plague by which they kill each other off?"

"We're here to colonize a planet that we know very little about. Our equipment will eventually break down—maybe in years, but it'll happen—and we'll be alone. Twelve of us, maybe eleven, maybe fewer than that by the time this is over. But I'm staying. For whatever reason, anything that happens here has got to be better than Argentina harvesting us and sending down a completely fresh crew."

"Three teams," she said. "I'll get this out to everyone. Roger will determine who's going out this afternoon." She got up to leave, then turned around. "Roger was right about you. Great job."

I waited a few minutes after she was gone to face the glorious day myself. Her words were reassuring. I knew she and Roger talked about me, and now I felt that whatever they said was good. I could live with that.

The day brought partial clouds, a warm breeze, and a clean smell to the air. Yet guard duty and working with Angie caught up to me. I felt tired and wanted to rest. Before I got back to my tent, Roger asked if I was okay with Josh going with me, Missy, and Ellen back to the river. I wasn't sure what to say. It wasn't what I expected. Josh and I had been there together before, and he didn't appear to want to take my orders.

"There's always Sam."

"No, Sam can stay. Both Angie and I feel that he's probably the most versatile. It's just that Josh—"

"I'll talk with him. If I'm not there, he'll listen to you," Roger said. "I'm sure of it."

"You don't think it's instinct? Being put into a stressful situation? I'm worried about Missy and Ellen if something goes wrong."

"Me, too, but I feel like it'll work anyway," he said. "Ellen may be the one to keep an eye on. After all, it's Bill you're looking for." He slapped me on the shoulder before I could answer. "Now, get some sleep."

I felt like we were the last team that should have been going out, not the first, but I didn't say anything, regardless of our earlier conversation. It could have been Team Three. But Sam was on that team. Maybe after some sleep, I'd see more clearly how everything was falling into place. Maybe we had finally fallen onto a workable plan, but I couldn't quite see it. Yet, I wondered if things were moving smoothly because of past information and past experiences included in our downloads. If it felt too easy, perhaps it was. Shouldn't a brand-new plan feel odd, or scary?

Neither Missy nor Ellen was in the tent when I arrived, so I lay down for a nap. I fell off to sleep almost immediately and didn't wake until I heard Missy working at her terminal.

I barely opened my eyes but could tell she seemed frantic. "What's wrong?"

She turned around quickly.

"Is something wrong?" I asked again.

"Maybe."

I sat up slowly and then stepped from bed to slip on my suit. "I don't like maybe."

"I don't understand something."

"Tell me."

"Our data has been uploaded to the ship."

"Isn't that why you collect it?"

"No. I collect the data for us to use, to have. So we can analyze it when we need to. Argentina is supposed to collect the pod—with some initial data—and then leave. Yes, she may come back sometime, but not right away. Maybe not for a hundred years." She scrunched her face up quizzically. "We saw her the other night. She hasn't left. She's orbiting."

"Are you saying she should have left and not stuck around, not even for a little while?"

She punched a few keys and then swung back to look at me again. "I don't know if I'm the right person to talk to about this, but my understanding was that data would be collected *after* our deaths—at the same time we're harvested."

"I don't understand," I said.

"Death sends out a beacon, and we're harvested as soon as possible after that. Even if Argentina is light-years away, she can return quickly enough for harvesting. But here she is, pulling downloads early. I didn't know she could do that. But now that I found out, I think she's measuring our progress, which must mean that she believes we're going to fail."

"Couldn't it mean that she's taking a last look before moving on?" I snapped my fingers. "Or that Bill died. Could it mean that his death sent out a beacon?"

"One death? She wouldn't return for that. The plan is that we colonize, have children, grandchildren, and once the last of our party dies, she returns to harvest us all at once."

At that moment, I did something unexpected; I sent out an all-call asking about harvesting. Missy and I were still contemplating different scenarios when Doc sent the answer: our brains have chemicals in them that, in her words, "coat the brain for prolonged electrical and magnetic life well after death."

"That still doesn't answer the question of why she's downloading data now," Missy said.

"Maybe she is monitoring our progress. Like you said. Why not?"

"It doesn't feel right."

I put a hand on her shoulder, and she leaned her cheek to it. Missy wasn't typically that sweet during stress. Was she feeling vulnerable? "You know we're going out this afternoon."

When she looked up at me, I saw fear in her eyes. "Is this it?"

"I don't think so. We're smart and capable."

"I'm so scared."

"You got the list of who's going, right?"

"Everyone did. Is Ellen the right person?"

"I asked the same question."

She stood up and put her arms around me. "You know everyone better than I do. What do you think is going on? Why do you think Angie and Roger chose us?"

"I can only guess."

"Then guess."

"Ellen will keep us on target. She won't want to leave until we find out what happened to Bill. I can handle any threat we get into with logic and knowledge of the whole. Josh will be an extra gun. He's quick and isn't afraid to shoot the howlers. The same with you. You're strong, clear-headed, the best person to be my partner on a trip like this."

She hugged me. "You are the right person for this trip." That's all she said. She made a few notes at her terminal, and we walked together to the main tent for a hearty lunch. We were going to need the energy.

Sam and Doc were on guard duty. Many of the others were already in the main tent. As soon as we came inside, Angie suggested we sit with Josh and Ellen to strategize. Roger occupied a seat with them. Angie explained, "He'll be able to make the transition clear to Josh." She winked at me.

Chip had created our lunch and stood behind the counter. "You'll want to take an extra portion of the meat. It's Puff Squirrel. If you're really brave—" He pointed to the side. "—try this, too."

"River howler?"

He nodded.

"Is this smart? We're going out for the first time," I said.

"I ate both this morning," he said. "It tastes pretty good, and Doc's been monitoring me. I'm fine. Even if I have a minor problem later, it indicates that you'll be back in plenty of time for us to deal with it should similar problems occur."

"Playing this pretty close to the bone, aren't we?"

"Not much choice." Chip seemed satisfied with how our plans had been ramped up.

I wasn't as confident but went along with it, pushing my own doubts down. It's what a tactical person has to do. And if we were going to get through this, we had to trust one another, or the colonization wouldn't work.

Roger put a hand on my shoulder, and for the second time that day, I felt like he was trying to get close, to establish a connection. It was awkward. He was obviously unsure how to act. I reached out and held Missy's hand while Roger went over some basic tactics for us to use while looking for Bill. He didn't say Bill's remains, but that was insinuated. I noticed how he kept Ellen in sight while talking. Did he feel that she might be a threat to our mission? Due to personal interest? Or was I right in assuming that Ellen was there to keep us on target?

The meat from both the Puff Squirrel and howler were quite flavorful, easy to chew, and left no unpleasant aftertaste. In fact, it was better than the synthetic foods produced on Argentina and sent down with us. There were some roots that looked unfamiliar, too, and I realized that we'd gathered them before. We really were eating local, except for Ellen and Josh.

Neither of them had any of the meat and very little of the new vegetables or roots. "Not going to try it?" I asked while pointing my fork at Ellen's plate.

"Later. If it looks good," Ellen said.

Josh tapped his plate. "I'm supporting her decision."

I didn't believe him.

Roger explained that we'd remain in pairs, stay in sight of each other, and return on *my* command. "Got that?" Roger asked everyone individually. "Correction. On Carl's command."

He reached out and touched Ellen's hand.

"Are you all right with all of this?" he asked. "Can you handle it?"

"Better than you might think." She looked him in the eye. "We're all trained, you know?"

I moved the conversation forward. "How long do we stay out? If we don't find anything, I mean."

Roger had an answer right away. "Once you get to the other side of the river, an hour at the most. If you get too deep into the woods, there's more of a chance that you'll be surrounded. They're pack animals. And if they know how to plant in rows, we have to assume that they can work together for other reasons as well."

For a moment, I worried about Missy. Of course I would. But her capabilities matched mine, and I knew it. Just like Ellen told Roger. Every one of us was committed to our stay; no one would let us down, least of all Missy. Once again, I had to shove my doubts out of the way.

Roger patted my shoulder one last time before rising to leave. The four of us talked briefly while finishing our food, then got up together to prepare for the trip. We met at the buggies.

Roger already stood there with two weapons, makeshift tubes with spring-loaded firing mechanisms, as he explained it. "The darts won't shoot far. You'll have to be close, but they'll work quickly enough to keep you safe." He handed one to Ellen and one to Josh. "Don't get so close that it's threatening. We don't want either of the others to have to kill your target before the antidote takes effect."

"How quickly?" Josh asked.

"Less than two minutes," Roger answered. "Our best guess."

"That could be a hell of a long time," I said.

"You'll figure it out, Carl." Roger handed Ellen and Josh three darts each. "Don't worry about pricking yourselves. Nothing in there can harm you."

That was it. We were going to administer the darts, see if that made a difference, and check on Bill.

"Let's go," I said.

****

My surveillance is intermittent based on my position over the planet. I must plan when to observe the humans, and then collect visual records, decipher those records, and add them to my database. Using my observations, I try to decide what to do next—stay, leave, or wait for more information.

—Argentina

Chapter 28

Adjusting to Circumstances

As planned, Josh drove. We crossed the river at the same angle we had the first time, the current about equal. No river howlers appeared in sight. That didn't mean we were safe. They hadn't been visible the last time we arrived either. As the buggy crunched onto the stony beach and came to a complete stop, my heart raced with anticipation. We all remained still, listening to the silence. It was time to make decisions, but once again, even as I recognized that tactical leader was my second vocation, doubt about my abilities crept in. A few deep breaths helped me calm down.

"What now?" Josh asked, his voice calm.

Did I note a tinge of sarcasm? *Ignore it.* "You stay with Missy near the buggy and be ready to get out of here if anything happens to Ellen and me. The two of us will take the path we created before. We'll each have a dart gun and two laser pistols. You know the drill. If a howler gets close enough, dart him. If you're attacked, shoot to kill. Simple as that."

"I'm ready," Ellen said, loading the first dart into her makeshift launcher. Josh did the same.

I don't know if Missy thought about my decision or not, but I left her behind to protect her as much as to offer Josh the cover. I tried not to think about the fact that I had already allowed my emotions to interfere with my decisions. It was okay, though; Missy was a good shot. And since I was in-charge of the mission, Ellen would obey my orders more easily than she would Josh's. Maybe it was logical, after all. And Missy didn't object. She must have seen the logic in it as well.

Something unusual wafted by, which pulled me from my concerns. Ellen crept up on me, stopping near my left shoulder and leaning in close. The makeshift dart gun rested high on her hip. She looked ready to lower the barrel and shoot at any moment.

"What is it?"

"I'm not sure. For a moment there, something smelled funny."

"Like a howler?"

"Not that I remembered, but maybe."

"When did they come at you the last time? How soon was it?" Her sweet, soft voice delivered her comment directly. I imagined how she and Bill must have corresponded together before he ended up with the howlers.

"Sooner than this. Maybe they've left. Or are staying back. After all, we've killed several of them rather ruthlessly." We were all being as quiet as possible, our ears perked and ready to hear the least sound from a howler. I turned around and waved at the others over Ellen's shoulder. We were all in sight of one another—part of our plan to stay safe. Yet I also knew that all that had to happen was for one of us to fall and said sight would be lost. Then what?

We walked farther through thinning underbrush. Movement up ahead alerted me when the first howlers appeared, half hidden by foliage. No sound. Like before, several perched on low branches in the trees. As much as they looked like canines, their abilities and actions appeared to be much more feline—from the parasite to its climbing abilities.

Josh whisper-yelled from behind us and half turned to wave again. That's when I noticed the howler to our left, also standing on a low branch.

Ellen immediately lowered the barrel of the dart gun, and I raised it back up with my forearm. "Not yet," I said. "It has to get a lot closer than that. I don't want you to miss and anger it."

Her hands shook, and the end of the dart gun wavered in the air above her. "I'm not sure I can do this anyway."

"You will when it comes time. Definitely if it attacks." I lifted a finger to my lips for quiet. We both wore gloves, and I turned toward the howler to our left and slowly forced brush out of my way using my arms. I hadn't brought the machete and wondered if I should have. I held my laser pistol toward my target just in case it made a move. "Stay close. Another few yards and you can shoot him."

It didn't take that long. The howler quickly but quietly jumped to another tree and into a lower branch much closer to us. Ellen didn't hesitate. The dart hit the howler squarely in the shoulder. With a violent swipe of its paw, it knocked the dart to the ground. The howler looked confused, shook its head, and scratched where the dart had penetrated.

I turned back to the thinning path. We continued forward, even though two other howlers rested on branches up ahead. I knew there was a clearing but had no idea how much deeper into the woods we'd have to travel to get to it. I just knew it was there. Was that in my download?

I surveyed overhead the best I could without tripping over brush or roots as I walked. A glance behind us revealed that Josh and Missy were barely visible. It looked as though they were both standing on the buggy seats to maintain sight. A few more steps and even more howlers appeared in front of us. I looked over at the one Ellen had shot, and it climbed up the tree a short distance and jumped closer to the ones in front of us, the fur around its neck flowing in the breeze, the killer bone moving as the beast prowled through the treetops. Once it got to within a few feet of two other howlers, it was attacked. The two went for the darted howler's throat. Two to one, as though they were fighting over which would get to its throat first. Over in a second, I could only stand and stare.

Ellen, on the other hand, breezed past me, running toward the howlers in front of us, her dart gun aimed straight ahead, and a second dart hit another howler.

In less than ten seconds, other howlers ran toward the second one she had darted. It took way less than two minutes for the howlers to attack one another. The parasite must have died off quickly, or the pheromone shifted immediately as the parasite began to die. I yelled for Ellen to wait, but she ran down the path into the clearing. I chased after her, knowing that Josh and Missy could no longer see us.

Through growling, yipping, and scuffling, the noise from the howlers attacking one another grew as we passed dangerously close. Guttural groans of agony. The sloshing of what could only be blood. The wet slapping of saliva, lips, jaws. My imagination flew to mixed juices flying from frantic jowls plunged into open wounds. By the time Ellen stopped in front of me, we were well into the clearing, an open space of about a hundred yards in diameter. I came up behind her.

Four or five young howlers, it was hard to tell because they lay over one another, reclined near Bill's dismembered corpse. His head and most of his limbs were gone. Blood stained the ground around the lazy howler babies. None of them acted surprised or worried that Ellen and I showed up. Like the howler we had caged in our camp, they appeared not to even notice us.

Ellen rotated around, dropped the dart gun, and buried her head into my chest, a great sob coming from her open mouth. The tortured sounds from howlers attacking one another raged behind us. Deeply muffled below the noise were the sounds of Missy and Josh's voices. I had told them to stay behind and to leave if we were in trouble, and they hadn't listened. Nonetheless, it felt good to know they were near.

"We have to go," I said to Ellen.

Ellen took a deep breath and bent for the dart gun, loaded it with the last dart, and shot one of the howler babies. Then she rushed toward the path and Missy and Josh's voices.

I hesitated, my laser pistol pointing toward the other howler infants, but I didn't fire. I trotted backward after Ellen and fell in behind her as she rushed down the path. It wasn't long before I saw Missy's head coming toward us. Josh brought up the rear, but something rustled the brush behind him. I yelled, but it was too late. A howler leaped from behind Josh, landed against his back, and propelled him downward. A loud thud and groan escaped his mouth as he hit the ground.

Missy swung around and used her laser pistol to kill the howler. It slumped to the side, and she rushed forward and bent down next to Josh.

I saw his arm come up and fall over her shoulder. She lifted. He had a terrible amount of blood on his face, but I couldn't see how much damage there was. "Go! Go!" I ushered Ellen past me. She caught up with Missy, threw her empty dart gun to the side, and grabbed Josh's other arm over her shoulder. He wasn't helping much, his legs barely moving.

I brought up the rear. When I got to Josh's dart gun, I picked it up with my free hand. It was loaded. A howler sat in a tree near me. Close enough. I holstered my pistol and aimed the dart gun the best I could. I shot and the dart stuck in the howler's leg. I had aimed for his chest, but I was glad it hit him at all. The dart flew to the side as the howler brushed it off. I wasted no time and rushed after the others, running half backward. Missy and Ellen traveled slowly with Josh in their arms, and I narrowed the space between us. When one of them tripped, all three fell to the ground. Another howler dropped from a tree onto the path behind me. I turned, pulled my laser pistol, and shot. It fell forward. When I turned to continue on, Missy was looking up at me.

"He's gone." Her fingers were at his throat.

A loud scream entered the air, and I knew it was one of the baby howlers most likely being attacked by the others. It took longer than the ten seconds it took the others, but I didn't care.

"Leave him," I said.

Both Missy and Ellen glared at me.

I pointed around to remind them that there were other howlers in the trees. When I turned back toward them, another howler stood in our path. I shot over their heads. That was enough motivation. They rose and ran toward the howler I'd just shot and toward the buggy. I hesitated near Josh's body. His face had been badly damaged from his fall, but his shoulder, close to his neck, had been ripped open. I kneeled and pulled the other two darts from his belt. They were slippery with blood. I loaded one into the gun, leaped over his body, and followed Ellen and Missy.

Two other howlers bounded from branch to branch behind me, their movements faster than I'd seen them travel before. I holstered my pistol the second I got out of the path, turned, kneeled, and shot a dart straight down the path, hitting the first howler above the eye. The beast paused for a few seconds. I switched the dart gun to my other hand, pulled my pistol in case it was needed, and stood before rushing sideways toward the buggy.

Missy sat in the driver's seat. Ellen's head was bent forward against the dash, her shoulders shaking with grief. I climbed into the back and dropped the dart gun onto the floor. Missy powered into the water. I turned and watched as the howler behind the one I shot with the dart went for its throat.

Doc had said that it could start a plague if the blood of one howler were infected enough with her serum that it killed the parasite in the next howler and the next. It did appear to work fast. I holstered my pistol and picked up the paddle. The howlers were not following us this time. They were killing each other. Growls and yelps penetrated the air behind us. I heard the screams of the babies. A part of me felt sorry, while another part felt relieved.

Ellen touched my leg, and I turned back around. "I'm sorry," she said. But she had nothing to be sorry about. She burst into tears again and lowered her head toward my knee. There was nothing I could say. We were there to colonize the planet and already we were devastating one of its natural creations. But it was our home—perhaps we had the right to clean house from whatever might make our home unsafe for our children. I wasn't sure how to handle the thought.

****

I alone must make the decision as to when to allow a colony to continue without my intervention or observation. It is not always an easy decision, and at times I must test several ideas before finalizing what to do.

—Argentina

Chapter 29

Women First

The rest of the team waited for us to pass through the fence and, suddenly, we were surrounded. Roger directed his attention toward me, but I held up my hand and he backed off. Doc and Sam, too, were waiting with excited expressions, most likely to hear how the darts worked out. Missy or Ellen could answer those questions as well as I could. The truth was we all needed time to decompress from the morning's events. We each had to process the trip our own way. The trip had been more devastating than we'd expected, more traumatizing.

As though in a trance, I took over the driver's seat and parked the buggy away from our welcoming party. After checking the buggy's systems, wiping it down, and inspecting the dart gun that was left, I sat on the ground at the far side of the vehicle, away from the noise and commotion. The gash in Josh's neck haunted my thoughts.

Missy and Ellen had been taken into the fold pretty quickly. I knew that Angie and Roger, probably Doc and Sam, too, would want to debrief everyone. But I needed time alone, and it was given to me.

The one thing that Argentina didn't download, or appeared not to download, was why we were traveling through space to colonize other worlds in the first place. Did humans destroy Earth and all its beings long ago so that we alone would survive? Already, after so little time on Beauty, we may have totally wiped out one species—genocide. Was that what our species was about? Was that the legacy I wanted to leave my children?

Random thoughts garbled my mind. Then the sound of the howler pups resounded in my head. They lay together lazily, unafraid, unthreatening. I couldn't kill them like that, but Ellen didn't hesitate to use the dart gun. Perhaps it seemed more humane—it was only a dart. But their screams—

Roger approached me from behind. "It's time we talked."

I nodded and turned my head as he came around the rear of the buggy. He sat on the ground next to me.

"It sounds like the parasites were killed off quickly, quicker than what Doc and Sam thought, anyway."

"Ten or so seconds."

"I suspect a slight variation might do the trick. The dart didn't have to wipe the parasite out. Hopefully it did, though, or they'll just come back as quickly."

"Then we've lost," I said.

"Not lost. Slowed down maybe. We could go in with laser pistols blazing."

"Wipe them out. You mean if they don't kill one another?"

"I don't like doing this, either. Maybe we should have moved camp once we found it was their food source. But I kept thinking this is where Argentina selected and that we had to trust her judgment. We just got here—"

"You ever wonder if this is the only planet that's like Earth?" I shrugged. "I talk about Earth as though I've lived there, seen it, experienced it." I fell quiet. For all the interest in creating a home out of Beauty, things didn't feel right all the time. And what if, ultimately, we didn't survive. Our minds would be harvested, we'd be recycled, come back to try again perhaps. I wouldn't be Carl, though. I wouldn't be me. I'd be some rearranged composite of several people's memories.

Roger took a deep breath before going on. "You're upset."

"You're damned right I am. We're willing to wipe out an entire species so that we can stay here and do what? Breed? Replace them with us? Is that all we're doing here? Why? What do we have that's so important to save? Why is it so important that *we* live?"

Roger shook his head slowly as I rambled. "I can't even answer *one* of those questions. And probably a thousand more like them. We're here. That's all I know. And I want to live. I want to stay."

"Everything else be damned?" I glared out beyond our camp toward the treetops. Something inside me wanted to let loose, cry out, but I held it in. I let my body build up tension, and then clenched my fists and pounded the ground to expel the energy.

Roger remained silent.

"The sound was horrible," I said. "Seeing Bill ripped to shreds was horrible. Josh." I pulled up my legs and sat cross-legged, my head slumped. I couldn't even look at Roger, didn't want to. I knew how he felt, how he looked at things. Pragmatically. Nothing felt realistic or sensible to me, though. And with that thought, I rose from the ground.

Roger got up to stand beside me. "What is it?"

"Doc needs to check me out. This isn't like me."

"You've gone through—"

"I know. I went through a lot. I saw a lot. But this rage, these feelings of despair, they're not me. Before I left, I felt apathetic to all of this, now look at me. My emotions have been all over the place. Is this how humans are?"

"Complex," Roger said.

I raised my hands and looked into my palms as though there might be something there to explain how I felt.

Roger stood up. "I'll go with you."

Ellen and Missy were talking with Sam when Roger and I walked into the infirmary. They all looked at me. "You, too," Doc said.

"Me, too, what?"

"You're not feeling yourself," Sam said. "No one is. Ellen's worse than Missy."

"You two saw the little ones," Missy said in explanation.

"The pups. Yes. What about them?"

"Over here, Carl." Doc stood with a syringe in her hands ready to take blood. "I'd like saliva and urine samples, too. You can use the latrine in the back."

After letting her take a blood sample, I went back to provide urine. I washed my hands before and afterward. Sam took a swab of my saliva after that, and I joined the women.

Ellen hugged me when I got there, and Missy reached for my hand. I didn't feel as angry as I had, but my mind was off the subject.

"Dying off," Doc yelled from across the room. She

looked up from her terminal.

Sam was busy near her. "Everything changes so quickly," he said.

"What's changing quickly?" Roger asked.

Doc tapped the top of her terminal and stood. "The parasite volume has dropped considerably. Adrenaline down, testosterone up. Both Ellen and Missy's systems have been ignited." She shook her head in disbelief.

"Why would we all get infected this time when the last time it wasn't so bad?" I asked.

"The area must be crazy with these things," Doc suggested. "And the closer in you got, the worse it got. I can't really tell you, though. Ellen's levels were higher than Missy's. Being close to their lair, where the pups were, must have made a difference."

"But we didn't slow down, get dazed, or feel warm toward them. I shot at them, we continued running, we got away—"

"You're right, Carl. Two things: one is that your adrenaline was raging, which kept the parasites in check. The other was that once Missy and Ellen's systems ignited, it set off a burst of maternal serum testosterone before subsiding. Again, I'm not positive why that might happen, but it did. They were scared, too, so the combination must have made a difference."

"There's more," Sam said.

Roger couldn't wait. "More complications or more information?"

Sam looked over at Doc before he spoke. "Our theory is that they don't want to kill the women, only the men."

"What makes you say that?" I asked.

"Missy is pregnant," Doc said.

A dozen feelings ran through me once it sank in. Happy, excited, a little scared.

"Just Missy?" Roger asked.

Good question, but I'm sure I was more curious about how it happened than he was.

Doc took a breath, and again she and Sam made eye contact.

"Oh, for heaven's sake," Roger said.

Doc explained. "Simple enough. There was enough sperm still inside Missy to take hold. Not so with Ellen, for obvious reasons."

"Then why didn't they just kill me?" Ellen asked. "Oh, I know, my system was still ignited and adjusting. Just because I didn't get pregnant didn't mean I couldn't. They couldn't possibly know if a sperm attached or not."

"Maybe, and maybe that doesn't matter. You're still female." Doc turned toward me again. "Anything odd happen out there?" She glanced over at Roger, then, too.

He shook his head. "We didn't debrief. I waited."

"I couldn't kill the pups," I said. "Ellen darted one of them and ran. Before I took off after her, I had my pistol pointed at them but couldn't pull the trigger. It took a few seconds before I followed her out."

"Ten seconds?" Roger asked.

"You think that was enough of a change? Just in the area, not even with me?"

"No," Roger said. "I think the parasite level dropped in the howler pup. Maybe you saw the change in its behavior and didn't realize it. Maybe you felt it. Knowing what was about to happen might have been enough to drive your adrenaline up and give you space to escape without influence from the parasite." He pointed at Ellen. "She told us what the darts did to the other howlers. All you'd have to do is notice the change in the pups."

"It's that fragile of a system?" I asked.

"Looks like it," Doc said.

"And the howlers," I asked.

"What about them?" Doc looked as though she didn't understand what I was getting at.

"The parasites got into us, and now they're subsiding. Do you think the howlers have it or not? Do you think the serum in the darts worked? Did it wipe the parasite out? Would they pass the cure from one to the other as they attacked each other?"

Doc motioned toward Roger with her hand.

"We're going to find out tomorrow," he said.

"Tomorrow? I can't go out that soon. Not after—" I paused "—you don't mean us, do you? You're going."

"My team," Roger said. "Doc's going to pump us up with her concoction, and we're going to do what we have to do."

I couldn't believe it. "Why didn't you—" I swung around to get a gauge on what Ellen and Missy were thinking. Missy stood and put her arm around me. "We were there as a baseline, weren't we?" I asked.

"Not originally," Doc said. "Only after you got back did we think of it. Once we realized what had happened out there."

"I'm not sure that makes me feel any better."

"There were no secrets," Roger said. "That's what concerns you, and it's true. Nothing was kept from you. But with your return, as Doc said, we shifted our plans."

I wanted to argue, but they were right. We were now traversing into new territory, and it felt uncomfortable, strange. But it was the right move. "Why not Team Three?"

"I won't let Doc go. Not yet. She's the most critical part of this. She and Sam." Roger held control of the room. "Chip has volunteered to replace Josh on the trip."

"We can't afford to lose every man we have," Doc said. "Someone's got to…"

She didn't have to go on, but I knew what was on her mind.

The thought of breaking our pairing just to populate Beauty seemed somehow unusual. I didn't know how I liked the thought or how it would change my relationship with Missy. There were other ways, though; insemination would work, too. I didn't say anything at the moment, but I could tell that the idea still floated in the room, undiscussed.

"I have an idea," I said.

Roger nodded.

"We send only women. Wait a few days. Give this trip a chance to take hold." I shook Missy's hand, knowing that I was suggesting that she go out again.

Ellen put a hand on my shoulder. "Yes. I'll go as often as necessary to get this done."

"Me, too," Missy said.

Doc appeared to agree. "Karen and Donna won't mind. Although I might suggest that she and Chip don't participate in sex for a day or two, unless we want all our women pregnant."

Roger appeared pleased. "We need to bring the entire team in on this decision, especially Angie. She might be able to see the bigger picture. But—" He turned to me. "—I like your thought process."

"Another thing I think we should discuss." Missy squeezed my hand as a message of support. "Argentina has been orbiting Beauty this whole time. We saw her the other night. We're worried that she might be expecting us to fail or waiting to see what happens. I know we have no contact with her at the moment, but— I hate to suggest this—do you think she might try to harvest us early?"

****

There is more than one ship, and sometimes I run into bios that have been left behind on a planet by another ship, and I upload their memories into my system. This was an idea someone entertained and that I harvested from a previous upload. It has now become a program I routinely use.

   —Argentina

Chapter 30

Land and Sky

Angie brought up the possibility that the howlers might try to capture the women and keep them as breeders. "Perhaps it's a survival instinct that females of any species bring out in them."

"They'd need at least one male," Chip said

"I think they've chosen Carl."

Shocked and in disagreement, I began to stand.

"Sit down, Carl," Angie said with a wave of her hand. "This has nothing to do with what you want. Maybe it's because you were there with the first howler, maybe it's because you didn't kill the pups. It could be anything. But we know that for some reason, they let you all go this last time, and maybe the first time, too. If we're going to colonize, we have to learn everything we can about them. Our location forces them to interact with us. It was the right choice. Now, we have to go through with discovering everything we can about them, or the problem will just return."

"Let us go?" Ellen asked.

Roger spoke up. "They didn't even follow you into the water. Once you made it to the buggy, they backed off completely."

The whole room seemed to vibrate with tension. The thought of sending only women—to be rounded up like livestock—wasn't a good plan. And sending a male, just to be killed, wasn't the answer either. "How smart are these creatures?" I wanted to know.

"Smarter than we are," Angie said. "They have to be, or we wouldn't be asking."

I was sure no one liked that idea. Who would want to believe they were smarter than we were or that we couldn't find a way through this? "I have the most experience. You can send me again."

"Not so fast. There's more." Roger pointed toward Doc to take the floor.

She stood, slightly leaning, with one hand resting on the tabletop. "The parasite, our drug, your metabolism, everything adds up differently for each of us. For example, Karen's under their power at times, Ellen gets angry, Missy becomes scared but clear-headed, and Carl has gone back and forth for some reason. We're still trying to figure out why."

She glanced over toward Sam, and he nodded.

"We think they go back and forth, too," Doc said. "So Carl's the most like them—to answer the earlier question about why him. They are either sympathetic and love one another, or they're carnivorous and attack. Carl, by his own admittance, is either apathetic or upset." She smiled. "It's a love-hate relationship."

"But he didn't shoot those pups when he could have," Chip interjected. "Are you saying that's love? How can that be if he ran? He wasn't overly sympathetic then, was he?"

"A true cock in the henhouse," Doc said. "He won't hurt the howlers but *will* fight to protect his women."

Was that another reason for my attraction toward

Karen? Did I consider her part of my flock?

"That sounds disgusting," Chip said. "Why is this even possible?"

Doc cleared her throat. "It's not about why—it's about what. We have to focus on what's happening and figure out how to deal with it. The *why* can be cleared up later or along the way, or never for that matter."

"Then what's the plan if we can't send all the women out there"—Chip's face beamed red. His voice trembled—"or Carl and his harem?"

Angie motioned for Doc to sit back down. Her time was up. "There's no need to get angry about this. We must come to a conclusion we can live with."

She looked away for a moment, grappling with words in her head perhaps.

"Beauty"—she paced in front of us as she spoke—"is our planet now. It's ours! No one wants to wipe out a species if we don't have to, but we *are* staying. We will be the last humans sent here. We will colonize."

"I doubt this is the only place where these things live," Chip said. "We're going to run into this again. And what if other species have the same parasite or a different one? What if this whole planet is filled with them?"

Angie stopped pacing. "I don't care. That's why we figure out how to deal with them."

She glared at me next, not in a mean way but an authoritative way.

"I know you don't want us to kill them off, or let them kill themselves off, but we may not have a choice. If this were a disease—which in many aspects it is—we'd want to eradicate it. The fact that it looks like a living, breathing animal does not remove the danger."

"Either we kill it, or it kills us," I said softly.

"Then you understand."

"Yes, but I'm not positive that I agree."

"Then you're not going out again for a while. If we have to send every other man out there, we will."

"To be killed off?" Chip yelled.

Karen put a hand on Chip's arm, and he visibly calmed. She patted his hand until he sat down. "I have something to say," she said.

Angie gave her the floor.

"If Doc can pump us up enough with her drug so that the parasite can't get in, if we can keep our heads clear, if we work together, we can do this. We can do what we have to do. I know it."

"Karen, with all due respect," Sam said, "you're the person who let the howler out of its cage. The one that attacked me. I'm not sure we have enough of the drug to keep you safe."

Missy let go of my hand and stood up. Everyone wanted to have a say in the matter. "Then the rest of us. Me, Ellen, Donna." She cocked her head. "Angie."

"I can go," Doc said. "I could monitor each of you as we make the trip."

"Not all of you," Roger shouted. "Wouldn't that be suicide for the whole team? Whether they kept you or killed you. That doesn't sound right."

"They'd come back for a male," Doc said in agreement.

"Carl," Chip said.

"Then let's wait for them," I said.

"What do you mean?" Angie asked.

"Wait for them to come to us. Not here. But on their own turf." I looked at Donna. "How many of them do you think this field will feed? Just a guess."

She took out her recorder and punched some keys. When she looked up, she said, "About fifty, but that's just a guess. I have no idea how much they eat or what they need to survive."

"How many are dead? Five, six? We don't know if they were male or female, except the one that was here was female, right?"

"And the one that tried to come through was female," Roger said. "No male genitalia, at least."

"I don't remember seeing a male," Missy said. "Maybe they're not like us."

"And we're not like them," Angie said, "but they're trying to make us that way. Carl's the most like them emotionally, so they've selected him as the male. Again, like chickens, or lions, deer, horses. I believe they want to raise us like we might choose to raise them. For what reason, I haven't decided yet."

"We need to get rid of the alpha male," Chip said. "Their male is kept behind, hidden away somewhere. So maybe not so much like a chicken yard but a deer herd. The male hangs back while the females clear the way. Or like lions that let the females hunt."

"But like lions, they could have several males," I said. "I don't know about the pups."

"There are always competitors for the throne," Chip said. "One of them may want to assert itself, who knows. We're dealing with an animal we're not totally familiar with."

"Not true," Angie said. "We've got all those Earth thoughts, ideas, education. There was every combination of social life in the animals of Earth. We know this. We're getting to the answer. I can feel it. So, forty-five howlers left, plus or minus the pups."

"We can take them," Roger said.

"I still don't like—" I ended my own declaration, deciding it wasn't about what I liked. It had to be about survival. I had to think of the howlers as a disease as Doc had suggested.

Roger took center stage. "Here's what I think: we take three buggies, spread them out enough that it thins out the howlers' power, too. Two people in each buggy. Three in the middle buggy. Carl, Missy, and Ellen in the center—the original henhouse and the bait. Me and Angie on one side. Chip and Donna on the other. Sam, Doc, and Karen stay behind, keep an eye on our perimeter, and hold everything together."

He glanced around at everyone, two sweeps across all our faces.

"We shoot to kill. No more dart guns."

"What if they don't come out of the woods?" Chip asked.

"We wait," I said again. "If they want us badly enough, they'll come."

Roger pointed at me. "You, Missy, and Ellen are the first to leave if anything, and I mean anything, goes wrong. In fact, if any fighting starts, you hightail it out of there. Missy seemed to be the most level-headed, so she drives."

"You know that Angie's system will most likely get ignited. So will Donna's," Doc said.

"We're here for good," Angie said. "We might as well get started."

"Argentina?" I asked.

"She'll have to watch and learn," Angie said.

I had one more thing nagging at me and wasn't

sure whether to bring it up yet or not. There was no proof for my concern except that Argentina was sticking around while our understanding was that she'd go.

Missy leaned close to my ear. "There's something more, isn't there?" When I looked at her, she nodded toward Angie. "Out with it."

I raised my hand before Angie dismissed us.

"You have something more?" she asked.

It was time to come out with my nagging question. "Is it possible that Argentina may come for a harvest before we're dead? If she senses that we've failed or are about to fail…"

Roger said, "If she sends a harvesting pod anywhere near us while we're alive, I'll blast it out of the sky." He glared at Angie for a moment then shook his head slowly. "Harvesting pod. I don't know where that came from. Does she even have such things?"

"I think we're all learning something about deep-seated memories," Sam said. "And that's a scary one."

"Can we protect ourselves?" Chip asked, "against the ship that made us?"

Faces were blank. We had enough to worry about, let alone our own fabricator coming after us. A rumble of private conversations grew around the room. Angie let it go on for a few minutes, but I noticed that it didn't die down, and she must have realized it wasn't going to.

"Adjourned." Angie walked away with Roger, hand-in-hand.

Chip walked directly over to me. He looked angry. "I don't get this—you have little to no background in any of the sciences that are necessary to this mission, and yet…"

I waited a second or two in case he was just stuttering or thinking what to say next. Nothing. "It's not what I want either. But maybe that's a good thing— maybe I wouldn't be missed."

Donna stood behind him and reached out to touch his back.

He took a deep breath. "It's not your fault," he said.

Donna came closer and to his side. Her hand slipped to his shoulder, showing that she was satisfied with his response. Every pair appeared to have a balance.

I reached for Missy's hand. "It's none of our faults."

"Don't let them catch you. We have to finish this," Chip said before he and Donna left with Karen in tow.

"The right combinations," Missy said as though reading my thoughts.

I gave her a knowing glance. "It makes us courageous, willing, pushes us to be our greater selves."

I saw that Ellen had already left. It was just me, Missy, Sam, and Doc left. We wandered over to where they sat. "Did you want to talk with us?" I asked.

"Do you really think that about Argentina?" Sam asked right away.

"It was the only thing I could come up with. Either she's waiting for us to die or she's willing to pick us up once she decides that we're on our way out anyway. She would save some time, but not much. Argentina has millions of years, so what's a few days or weeks?"

"Unless she *doesn't* have that long," Sam said.

"Or there aren't that many planets we can survive on," Doc said.

"Again, aren't we talking about things we can't possibly know or find out?" I slid into a seat across from them, and Missy sat beside me. "Let's face it: understanding isn't acting. Even if we knew why Argentina did what she did, we'd still have to come up with a solution that fits us."

"You're right. It takes the nonscientist to show us when we're being abstract in our thinking and get us back on track." She smiled after using Chip's words to show how unfair he had been. I could tell that she thought differently.

"And it's the scientist who wants to travel through the unknown to find answers." I laughed with the others.

Doc asked Missy about all the data she had collected from everyone. "Where's it all go?"

"At first, it went to Angie and the pod we arrived in. After the pod left, data went to Argentina and Angie—for analysis. She arranges and rearranges everything to find patterns, to understand how we're all getting on, individually and together. Looks for anomalies that could help us when we actually leave our camp and start to really explore. Creates a chart showing danger, safety, anger points, weak and strong points, that sort of thing."

"She and Roger were the first to suspect humans had been here before," Doc said. "Do you think they actually knew? Was there data already in place?"

"None," Missy said without hesitation. "Only entry data and some rough sketches of who everyone was and what our duties were. Those months before we traveled here, getting to know the whole team. Those notes were on there."

She stopped talking, and I wasn't sure if she was thinking or calculating.

"I think Angie has been open with us...well, since we all promised not to keep secrets." Her arm slid over next to mine. "Even Carl kept information from everyone for a little while. I helped him by segmenting a space. But it's all out in the open now. Why do you ask? Do you suspect something?"

She didn't know my secret, and I didn't say anything about it.

"Just checking," Doc said. "I always get the feeling that she knows something we don't. Sam doesn't feel that way, though."

"I think it's all out now," Sam said. "If anything, we all have information that's been stripped away with our trauma, leaving nuances. Or it could be the biomass that's reused. What's the possibility that memory can adhere to the equipment used to produce us? Whatever all those questions answer, the fact is that not only do we doubt each other's prior knowledge, we doubt our own. Look at what happened to Roger, suggesting harvesting pods might come down prior to our deaths and just take us? That wasn't there before." Sam tightened his lips as though he was done speaking, waiting for someone else to take over.

"Maybe there's a mechanism that only allows us to notice certain things at certain times or under certain circumstances." No one gave me an indication that they thought that way, so I went on. "If you were supposed to ignite our biological systems—the women's systems anyway—then maybe there is an automatic system, or more than one, that can control when we remember something. Remembering everything might be too traumatic. Maybe the howler parasite opens some of those paths, as well."

"Getting too deep," Sam said. "We could speculate all day." He looked at his recorder. "Roger's calling for your trip to start tomorrow morning. We should all prepare."

****

Equality of gender, race, body type, intelligence, skill, all of it, is difficult to build into a biomass of any kind—regardless of the download or combination of downloads used. There is, in every biological unit, a separation and a comparison that occurs no matter how many times it is created. Each colonization evolves into its own system.

 —Argentina

Chapter 31

Going Deep

I didn't sleep so well that night. Neither did Missy. We got up, ate breakfast in relative silence, and went back to our tent to prepare. I had been present for every trip taken where close contact with howlers had occurred. I helped set the first trap, entered their territory to find Bill, and again when Josh got attacked and killed. Now I was going again. I didn't want to document death anymore. What were we doing? I couldn't help but notice how my thoughts and emotions changed and adapted to every situation. It was starting to feel as though that's what it meant to be human. I was getting used to it.

The morning, like most since we'd arrived on Beauty—except for the freak blizzard—felt cool and comfortable. A slight breeze slipped among the tents, and the occasional plastic odor of our living quarters was present for brief moments. We had our own smells, too, that of flesh and cleaning materials, medical supplies and tools. I still wondered if our smell changed depending on what we ate, our exertion level, our emotions, and could the howlers key in as to how dense the parasite population was inside us? Pheromones could mean a lot in a case like that, but as Doc had said, our chemistry, the parasite, the drugs, all mixed to become something specific in each one of us. Not just our smell but everything about us; the nuances of our actions, the looks in our eyes. Maybe our thoughts and emotions were as easy to read through our smell as our body language. There was no telling what the howlers were capable of.

Missy and I arrived at the buggy area holding hands. Roger had already gotten the buggies ready to go, which meant that he did all the preliminary checks. Sam manned the fence and would turn it off and then back on since the buggies couldn't pass through without the possibility of doing some electronics damage. And Doc stood there with a whole handful of syringes ready to give each of us our own special concoction of drugs, reportedly to keep us safe from the influence of the howlers' parasite, but I wasn't totally sure it was enough.

After our inoculations, we all climbed into position. Angie drove her buggy, and Roger stood in the passenger side like a general. He looked around, raised his arm. "Let's go," he said and dropped his arm. The buggies jostled into motion as though reluctant to take the trip.

The field flowed smoothly with the morning breezes, stalks swaying and clacking together hypnotically in the morning light. Missy drove slowly between Angie's vehicle and Donna's. No one appeared to be in a hurry to start the day, the tone solemn and quiet. I sat in the rear seat behind Ellen, holding a paddle across my legs, looking around, watching the motion of the field, the tops of trees as they tipped and sprang back up. A series of clouds dotted the sky and sunshine warmed the air. Insects rose from the ground, buzzing and fluttering, as we disturbed the field. Hawks appeared to rest in the neighboring trees, perhaps looking for small animals we hadn't even seen yet, or were they scavengers, attracted by the carnage of the day before? That might make sense. But then, did anything make any real sense?

The buggy tires crunched over pebbles when we reached the riverbank. Roger laid out our plan again. Fairly simple. Wait for the howlers to come to us and kill them. Just like that. No regard for their lives, only ours. I understood how Doc related them to a disease. I got it. But that didn't make what we were about to do any less horrible. But we had all agreed. Waiting for them was even my idea. So even though I didn't like what we were about to do, I felt particularly clear-headed that it was the right thing in the long run, and I was ready to do what had to be done. By the time we climbed onto the far shore, the idea that it was them or us felt more and more like the truth, so much so that I half wondered what extra chemical Doc might have put into my shot. I stayed inside the buggy but stood in the back behind Missy and Ellen. Everyone had his or her laser pistol out.

There was no sign of a dead howler anywhere, not the ones we killed and not the ones that were killed by other howlers. The place felt still, silent, frighteningly so. Even the sound of the wind through the trees had turned into quiet background noise, almost imperceptible.

After a few minutes, I wondered if the howlers had left. With that thought, the quiet started to affect me in a different way. I relaxed into the morning, listening to the music of the current flowing behind me. No one talked for a long while. I tried to calculate how far into the path we might have been able to walk in the time we remained there. I retraced our steps in my mind, stared out across the scrub toward the clearing, hidden by the brush in front of us.

"Here goes," Chip said to my left.

We all looked over, and two howlers sat in the low branches of a tree about fifty yards away.

They did come. We didn't even hear them. The silence earlier wasn't as safe as I might have thought. I wondered how many more were around that we didn't hear.

"Looks like we didn't wipe the parasite out," I said. "They didn't exterminate each other."

"Not totally," Roger said from my right, "but we don't know what damage has been done."

I peeled my eyes from the howlers to look at Roger. Two more of the animals came from his direction, both on the ground and walking slowly. "You have company, too," I said.

Angie and Roger switched their attention toward their own visitors. I scanned ahead of us. That's where the path stretched, the path that they had worn and we had broadened as we walked through. I suspected more howlers to come from the underbrush, even watched for movement, but didn't notice anything out of the ordinary. I didn't know in which direction to pay attention. Missy trained her attention on Chip and Donna, and Ellen trained her attention on Roger and Angie. So I kept my gaze forward.

"Remember," Ellen whispered to the two of us, "if anything goes wrong, we back into the water."

Missy nodded but didn't speak.

We were all pumped up on parasite-killing drugs, and the howlers were pursuing us. If they couldn't control us, if we weren't submissive, did they just kill us and feed us to their pups? Were they here to capture me, Missy, and Ellen? Was Doc right about me and them—it's either apathy or anger, love or hate? For the howlers, they either worked together and ate whatever the field produced, or they killed and cannibalized one another.

howlers came at us from both sides. I had the strongest urge to protect Missy and Ellen and started to climb out of the buggy. I could stand in front of them in case something came down the path in front of us. I expected that to happen while the others were focused on either side.

The moment my foot touched the ground, Missy hollered at me. "Get in the buggy."

I stopped and looked at her. Did she see that I struggled with what was the right thing to do?

"You know the plan. You came up with it. We wait, see what they're going to do. Kill them only when they get close enough. If they get close enough."

"To what end?" I was waffling, hoping that she would help stabilize my thinking.

"To survive."

Something in her voice convinced me, like a switch in my head. I got back into the buggy and perched between the two of them, standing guard. My head reeled with thoughts of what might happen if everyone but us three were killed, what might happen if we all survived but the howlers didn't, what else the planet had in store for us. And that's when I happened upon one thought that wouldn't go away. I knew that each team sent down learned something more about how to survive on Beauty. But each upload is stripped of personality. What information had not been downloaded? What information was missing that could change everything?

"We have to go in," I said.

"What are you saying?" Missy's face twisted into a look of confusion.

I spoke louder so everyone could hear me. "Maybe important information was left out of our download?"

"So?" Roger yelled.

Before I could go on, I heard the fizz of hair and burning flesh and the thump of a body dropping to the ground. I turned toward the sound—Chip had shot one of the howlers. The other one attacked as soon as the first was down, and Chip missed with his second shot. To my right, either Roger or Angie shot at attacking howlers, too. I didn't turn around, knowing that Roger could not possibly be the weak point in our lineup. Donna downed the second howler, and several more appeared where those two had come from.

The battle had begun.

howlers appeared ahead of us, coming down the path. Missy and Ellen wasted no time putting them down. My adrenaline must have peaked because I didn't feel bad about any of the murders. Or had my mind switched to being a leader, apathetic toward the howlers. Or was I now the cock in the hen house as Doc had suggested. Or was it the drugs? Whatever caused the shift, I held my pistol out and aimed it between the women and fired at any howler coming out of the underbrush. Before long, there were fifteen dead howlers lying around us. The air stank of burnt hair and meat, and howler breath, even though they weren't breathing any more.

I leaped from the buggy.

"What the hell?" Roger's loud voice aimed at me. "Get back into that buggy."

"We have to go on!" I ran toward the path and leaped over the first dead howler.

Missy tagged close behind me. "I don't know what you think you're doing, but you're not doing it alone."

I turned to glance over my shoulder. The rest of the crew followed behind Missy. A brief thought passed through my mind that this wasn't the smartest idea. I could go it alone. But it was too late. I couldn't stop anyone unless I also stopped, and I wasn't going to stop. It was our best move. I had to go in, even if I didn't fully understand why. I felt it and planned to act on those feelings.

The brush rustled around us, and shots burst into the thicket randomly. They all seemed to be shooting at the same time, except for Missy, who stuck close to me, crowded me as I rushed forward toward the clearing. When I broke into the opening, I noticed the pups were gone, Bill's body gone. Bloodstains lay across the ground where they had been, and I wondered how many of the pups were left.

"Back-to-back," Roger yelled as the others broke into the clearing behind me. They turned to create a circle of protection. "I hope you know what you're doing."

I searched the area but didn't quite know what I was looking for. I heard shots near the path opening and charged deeper into the clearing to the far side, looking for their lair. A well-worn path led deeper into the woods, and somehow I knew to follow it. Something important had hold of me, and I forged onward without consideration. I took the path, Missy and Ellen with me.

Roger ordered the others to stand at the opening of the path, facing into the clearing to protect us from one direction at least. Then he followed behind Missy and Ellen, his boots loudly clomping over the ground as he came closer.

The woods were serene and somehow inviting us to go deeply into them. We passed the battleground where they had protected their pups. I felt safe moving forward.

"What are we after?" Missy asked.

"Recorders from other teams," I said automatically over my shoulder.

"Unbelievable that we didn't consider that before."

"We were too busy trying to survive, protect ourselves," I shot back at her. "There has to be more going on."

A few minutes down the path and a shot came from behind us. Only one. Were the howlers giving up? After all, if Donna's calculations were correct, they were down by more than half. It didn't matter. Once again, I thought of the future. Maybe I couldn't make Beauty my home as I'd thought. None of us could. Only our children would truly create a home here for themselves by being born here. If that was so, then that's what had to happen. It wasn't about survival for me any longer. I wanted to understand more so that I could pass that knowledge along, even though the thought felt instantly disturbing.

When we came upon the next clearing, a mound half my height with a width triple that lay in the center.

It struck me as familiar, somehow tied to my urge to keep moving.

"My God..." Missy said from behind me.

A dozen uniforms, helmets, and weapons ornamented the trees and brush, fluttering or clanking together. Some looked very old and ragged, others newer. It was clear that there hadn't been hundreds of years between visits. In fact, I had the feeling that Argentina was already considering replacing us with the next team. I ran toward the uniforms and jumped to pull as many down as I could. Missy worked steadily beside me until several had dropped or been dragged into the clearing. We didn't go near the mound, hesitant by what might be found there.

Ellen and Roger had their backs to us, looking in circles, ready for an attack.

Missy followed me from suit to suit while I prepared each recording device for download. Missy plugged in and downloaded each one as quickly as possible. After we finished, we stood and ran back to Roger and Ellen.

"Let's go," Roger said.

"I can't believe they stopped pursuing us," Ellen said.

Roger gave her a look of surprise. "It's not over yet."

We entered the path back toward the buggies, and I made sure that Missy and Ellen were between Roger and me. I felt completely vulnerable and spent, most of the time twisting around to look behind me. I could only imagine what Josh felt like doing the same thing before he eventually went down. The act of always looking over my shoulder slowed my progress, and I fell behind.

The bushes to the right of Ellen rustled, and I shot blindly into the brush. She hesitated long enough to take a shot into the same area. I ran faster to catch up and tripped over a low branch or root, flopping noisily onto the ground with a grunt. More shots fizzed around me as I scrambled to my feet. My laser pistol was gone. I dropped it and couldn't find it anywhere.

"Leave it," Ellen yelled while taking another shot to my left.

I ran toward her. Missy and Roger stood fast, alert, scanning the area. When we broke into the first clearing, Chip, Donna, and Angie raced forward toward the next pathway without saying a word. They must have seen how quickly we were coming through.

A howler broke into the clearing from behind us. It stopped and stared. We were eye to eye. I had no weapon. Ellen came up beside me, and I placed my hand over hers and lowered her pistol. It worked. I swear the howler relaxed. They understood our weapons. I couldn't register that completely, not at that moment, and couldn't take the time to consider what it might mean. "Slow down," I said to Ellen behind me. I heard her relay the message to Missy and from Missy to Roger.

"We're not moving until you catch up," Roger said clearly.

"Don't run. They chase us when we run." It's all I could think to say. From that moment, I walked backward and let Ellen guide me, her hands reaching back to hold to my waist. I stumbled once or twice, and the howler followed but at a reasonable distance.

At the path's opening, there were dead howlers still

lying everywhere. My emotions had come full circle. Was it the adrenaline or the drugs, or was I just getting used to being a multi-emotional being? All I know is that at that moment, my heart went out to the one behind me. I wondered what it might do when it saw that we'd massacred them. But its nose was in the air. It already knew.

A few howler bodies were already missing, and several howlers were carrying a dead one away. They ignored us. Their focus remained on collecting their dead. Would they eat them? Bury them?

There was no time to think anything through. No time to consider our predicament. We walked slowly back to the buggies and pulled them into the water. No casualties to our team. How did we manage that?

****

There are times when a colony does not integrate well with a particular planet. I have found ways to move this integration along through a series of on-planet training sessions beyond those attended shipboard. Once I am assured of the proper results, I can move to the next decision.

—Argentina

Chapter 32

Homemade Horror

We were no more in a hurry to return to camp than we were to leave earlier that morning, and I'm not sure why that was. What about our trip caused us to change our opinion? I didn't feel so riled about our excursion, maybe because no one died, no one had actually been attacked. At that moment, while riding back to camp, I felt at home on Beauty. Why was that? My only explanation was that I had just gone through so many different emotions, strong emotions, in such a short amount of time that I felt full and whole. Those feelings happened here, on Beauty. The more I thought, the more I endured; the more emotional breath I experienced, the more at home I felt. I didn't mention the feeling to anyone. I needed to assimilate it first. So I let more experiences in as I watched the sun lie warmly across the field and the shadows of trees stretched out from one side. The wind brought a fresh scent with it. The air had warmed from the rising sun. A glimpse of the smaller moon rushed across the southern sky. Roger and Angie led the group through the fence and parked their vehicle first, then us, then Chip and Donna. We were home.

Doc and Sam greeted us and began checking us out, looking into our eyes, taking our blood pressures, taking blood samples, all while we were seated in the buggies. Then the two of them took off as though the samples might evaporate before they got them back to the lab. Everyone appeared relaxed and calm, even after the race through the woods to the burial ground, collecting the data, and the nerve-wracking walk back to the buggies. It wasn't until then, feeling more relaxed, that I noticed how upsetting it was to find the suits, to download the recorders. The contrast surprised me. Perhaps the slow trip across the river and the drive up through the fields, the beautiful morning, helped to soften the blow.

Before exiting, Roger said, "What you did back there was crazy, but the right thing to do. You followed your intuition, something difficult for most of us."

The others appeared shocked by his words, but somehow I expected them.

Angie rested a hand on his shoulder. "We should consider that everyone here has residual information they can tap into, remnants of memories that were a part of their downloads, that help to inform us of the bigger picture."

I wasn't used to her philosophizing.

"Trust your instincts," she added.

"What Carl and Missy collected may take us leaps ahead of where we are at this moment," Roger said.

Missy leaned into me. Her left hand rested over the recorder near her throat, where all the additional data had been downloaded. "Maybe Argentina won't be so keen to replace us this time," she whispered.

"Maybe there won't be a need to." I winked.

Angie motioned for Missy, Ellen, and me to follow her. Roger wandered over to Chip and Donna, probably to regroup, take statements, and let them know what was going to happen next. I figured Angie would give us the same speech on the way or once we downloaded everything for her to look over.

Even before Angie said anything, Missy let her own interests be known. "I'd like to go through the downloads with you."

"Anyone is welcome once Roger has debriefed everyone."

"He's going to do it on his own?"

"Yeah, and he'll inform everyone afterward. Before we download those files, I want to check in with Doc and Sam. Then we'll go back to my tent for downloading."

"We were together the whole time," I said, wondering why the necessity for debriefing us separately.

Angie looked at me for a long moment. "You of all people should understand that we each see something different, that the situation will register differently. Even Roger and I don't necessarily agree on the specifics. Then there are the interpretations. He thought the howlers were aggressive; I thought they were curious. It turns out they weren't as aggressive as we thought. At the moment, I think they were observing, trying to figure us out. Calculating. Look how they left us alone once we slowed down."

"It kept our fear level down, our adrenaline more stable, I think."

"Carl's probably right," Missy said. "Once we didn't show so much fear, they calmed, matching us."

"Remember what Doc said, how they are either aggressive or calm," I said.

Angie wasn't taking it as fact. "It appeared that way, at least, but it could have been the concoction Doc gave us or any number of other things we haven't even considered. Too many variables."

"I didn't say this before," Ellen said. "Everyone was speculating. I didn't want to believe it. But Bill talked about how they bred us to feed to their pups, how they'd select who they wanted to keep and kill the rest. Selective breeding."

Angie stopped walking and stood outside the infirmary. "And you chose to tell us this now?"

Ellen looked flustered. "I thought he was just making it up, delusional. He said and did some crazy things you have to admit. Until you mentioned listening to our instincts, I didn't even consider that he might be doing that, that he might be right. It wasn't logical."

"We mentioned that same possibility before we left," I said, insinuating that she could have brought it up at that time. "That's why the three of us were in the buggy together."

"I know, but by then you'd figured it out. I didn't want to say, 'Oh, I already knew that.' You wouldn't have believed me."

"Well," Angie said before ducking into the infirmary, "we want everyone to open up now, even if you think you are crazy or that you're hallucinating. All of it!"

We followed her inside.

"Any big news?" Angie asked.

Doc shook her head. "But you could give us another hour. We'd like to check in with Chip and Donna."

Angie swung right back around and waved us

through the opening. "Looks like we're doing some downloading and analyzing. We'll have to parse the data out."

I turned to leave and noticed that Sam turned his eyes away almost as soon as we made eye contact. Outside, I turned my attention back to Missy and Angie.

"I could create an algorithm to find specific words or ideas," Missy said.

"That would make this go faster," Angie said, "but I'm not sure I want to miss any nuances if they're there."

"Do it in levels," I said. "Look for specific works or ideas to give us a broad scope, and then key in on the details a little at a time."

"Brilliant idea, Carl."

I don't know if she meant it or was being sarcastic, but Angie smiled then and led us toward her tent for download processing. Her tent held the system with the most potential for large-scale downloads and operations. Not even the main tent could handle what Missy was suggesting—at least that's what Angie said.

The download into Angie's main computer seemed quick to me, only an hour, but slow to Missy, who said as much. We waited as Missy fiddled with Roger's computer to create the algorithm she'd mentioned. Not to disturb her, we all sat quietly for fifteen minutes more, which felt like hours. Still, during that time, I observed each other's physical traits that I had never noticed before. Why I had never noticed that before was odd. Angie's eyes were slightly narrower than mine, Missy's, or Ellen's. It reminded me how, during our perimeter walk, I noticed Roger had darker skin. Sitting there, Angie looked darker skinned as well, but not so much as Roger. Ellen, on the other hand, was pale, washed-out almost. I glanced at my own hands, and I had a darker complexion than she did, but nothing like Roger. My observations felt strange and unsettling, and my stomach turned for a moment. I thought I might be sick. Before I could consider anything more, Missy had finished her work and interconnected the two computers.

In a short while, she sat back in her chair. "That should do it."

Angie reached out and pushed the return to start the program. The only sign that it was working was a flashing in the lower left-hand corner of the monitor. When the flashing stopped, a man's voice came over the speakers. It sounded a lot like Sam, but it was hard to tell for sure. The words were strained, fearful. "Night Screamers got into camp and killed Bill and Ellen and then went on to Chip and Donna's tent and killed Chip. Donna's missing." The voice stopped, and the light flashed again.

Angie reached for the keyboard, but Missy stopped her and said, "Every stop is flagged. We can go back to it easily."

The next time the light went out, the speaker blurted out more conversations. "Screamers stole Angie. Carl suggested we go after them. He's angry. I don't trust his judgment." The voice was definitely Roger's. The next stop took up with a different voice, Donna's. "The Night Screamers are waiting for me to give birth. I know it. What do they—"

Flashing light and silence.

A small pain ran through my body; I can't explain

why. Hearing my name was alarming, but hearing the other voices, clearly recognizable—

I looked at the others. Angie looked nervous. Missy sat quietly; her name hadn't been mentioned. Ellen stared at the terminal, even though nothing was being shown. It was only audio.

The next stop produced another familiar voice. "The dog-likes have a huge bone sticking from their chests. We can only imagine—"

The voice was Angie's. She glanced at me and then at Missy, who merely shook her head. She wanted us to go on even though we were listening to several different time periods.

Angie reached out and stopped the machine. She put her hands to her face.

In the silence I heard Missy take a deep breath as though she was going to cry out afterward.

I said what the others didn't want to say. "One thing is clear"—my voice cracked—"*we* are the same people. Repeatedly. We have all died, been harvested, and born again." Missy reached for me, and I stood to take her into my arms and hold her.

She sobbed for a moment but stopped herself. "What is Argentina doing to us?"

"This is where I get off," I said. "I can't take any more. I've got to leave."

Angie glared at me. "We take this to the team. Everyone has to know."

"What's the difference? We're not going to learn why or how to beat the howlers short of murdering them one by one."

"We have to listen to the rest of this," Angie said. "We have to learn as much as we can."

Missy pulled away and held my hand between hers.

"Something's not right." I don't know why I said it, or how I knew it, but it felt close to being true.

"You're upset. Something in this audio is bothering you. Can you work through it?"

Missy was still holding my hand. I shook it and slipped it out from between hers. "Maybe later."

I nodded toward Angie. "You and Missy should keep working without me for now. Learn as much as you can before we announce it."

Angie and Ellen stared at me. I felt calmer than I had a right to be.

"Will you be okay?" I asked Missy.

"Yes. I trust you're right about this. We'll take notes."

Angie also agreed to carry on.

I left the tent. At that moment I wasn't sure what had happened but knew I needed a walk. In a short while, Karen met up with me.

"I'm one of them," she said.

I didn't understand.

"I have the strongest feeling that I lived with the howlers. We didn't interbreed, but I know that I lived with them a long time. I just don't know where the information is coming from."

My eyes welled up into tears, and I wasn't sure why. "Months?"

"At least, maybe years."

"Me and you." I knew she was right. We were the two, at least two, who they bred.

She threw her hands over her mouth. "The children."

"Why?" That's all I could ask.

"There's more, so much more, but it's not coming. I can't quite remember."

I wanted to tell her what Angie, Missy, and I had just discovered, but I didn't do it. Something dawned on me then, and I can't say why or where the thought came from. I grabbed Karen's hand and jogged with her in tow to the slap-dash veterinary tent. Sam stood beside Chip, discussing something in earnest. They both looked up when we entered.

"Don't tell me..." Chip said.

"You know something," Karen said. "You know where this is going, don't you?"

"No," Sam said. "We don't know where any of this is going. We're as confused as the rest of you."

"Then what is it?" I eased my way toward them and saw that the dead river howler lay on the table. It had been cut open in several places. "I don't care how confusing it looks; what'd you find?"

Sam lowered his head and wouldn't look us in the eyes. "They're us."

"What in the world..." Karen couldn't get out any more words. She looked stunned, confused, as though she didn't understand the language.

"It appears," Chip said, "that the river howlers are biobuilt from the same machine we were." He motioned for us to step closer. "Look in here."

He used gloved hands to spread the meat of the river howler. I couldn't even tell what piece of the beast sat in front of us. I leaned in.

"See this ridge?"

Karen and I both nodded, and Chip shoved his hands deeper, to a bone, and lifted it forward. "And this one?"

"But they're bios," I said.

"Machine-made bios," Sam said.

"I don't get it." It wasn't coming through to me, and I stumbled while trying to step back and away.

"Argentina sent them here first," Sam said. "Then us."

"That's not all," Chip said.

"I don't know if I can take any more," I said. They didn't know anything about what I'd learned just minutes before.

"The ridges are made from a material that eventually disintegrates, but before that, it releases a chemical." He jerked his head sideways to call me in closer again. Then he cut one of the ridges. Sam reached over with a swab and took a sample and then walked away.

"What'd you just do?" I asked.

"I've seen x-rays and MRIs of every one of our bodies. We all have these ridges. In training, before coming here, we were told they were indications of our machine-made parts, that the ridges were similar to structural strengtheners used during production, like scaffolding. They are supposed to disintegrate with time. I knew that. And now we find them here. In this body."

"Our biology melts the scaffolds, if you will," Sam said.

"But it releases a chemical, doesn't it?" Karen said, as though she already knew the answer. "I'll bet part of that chemical is an igniter."

Sam pointed at her. "Right."

He walked over to a microscope, wiped the swab onto a plate, and passed it into a machine I didn't recognize. On the screen came a complex-looking, abstract view of what appeared to be tiny moving things, a mixture of rods, circles, angular pieces.

"You're probably used to being able to recognize some patterns whenever you've seen a biological sample. Notice there's no instantly recognizable pattern. But if you separate it and pull out one chemical at a time." He pushed a few buttons. The screen image looked more and more organized.

I looked at it but couldn't think what to say. I opened my palms in question.

"I don't know exactly, either. But I do know that igniters are used for multiple purposes."

"We're evolving?" I asked.

"At different rates," Chip said from behind us. We all turned to look at him.

"Might that be what happened to Bill? He evolved too quickly?" I also thought of myself, how I hurt my arm, felt something squish out. Did I begin to evolve too quickly, too?

"I don't know what's going on," Chip said, "but the river howlers were planted here just like we were. Plus, as you said, we're evolving. I don't know exactly what that means either."

"What about Puff Squirrels or Hawks."

Chip shook his head. "They're native to Beauty. They don't have the same ridges."

"Your skin has a reddish hue," I said, changing the subject. "I'm noticing differences in skin color, in general personality traits. I can't explain it, but just recently…"

"Me, too," Sam said.

"But not me," Chip said in a sad voice.

"We suspect that the breakdown of the outer ridge is different for each of us," Sam said. The same with the howlers. As they evolve, we evolve. There's no telling where this is taking us." Sam looked as though he was about to cry. His emotional state had changed since we first arrived on the planet. At first, he seemed to be one of the stronger members of our team. I could only imagine what chemical mixture had been let loose in his body. In any of our bodies."

"We need to regroup," I said.

****

There can be difficulties when building humans. For example, providing soul to a biomass carries with it a certain amount of inability to cope with too much information at once. It is important to slow the process and allow each to develop at its own pace, to assure the eventual sanity of the individual biomass. As a producer of these entities, it is my duty to experiment with how quickly each creation evolves, but this is not an exact science since humans are manufactured using biological elements. Biology, after all, adjusts to its environment and is unpredictable.

—Argentina

Chapter 33

The Real Enemy

After several hours of talk, debate, and sorrow over what appeared to be happening to us, and to the howlers, Angie stopped for a moment. "This is a lot to take in."

She turned to Roger, her hand in his for support. Her face drawn and tight, as though ready to cry. Then she continued to address everyone in the room.

"We all need to think things through, process what we've discovered, and discuss this among ourselves, in small groups, and then come back together. I want everyone's thoughts, beliefs, and facts on the table."

She glanced at Missy as though they knew something the rest of us didn't, but that wasn't the case. There wasn't much more to know. Nothing much mattered.

She went on. "From the cumulative information, we will create a long-range plan on how we're going to remain here."

"Argentina is still orbiting," Karen said. "I've kept track." She put her hands over her mouth as though she didn't want to say anything more. What more was there to say?

I made a step toward her but stopped myself and reached for Missy's hand.

Roger, looking stronger and more powerful than ever, let go of Angie's hand and stepped forward, chest out and chin high. "She's not taking us this time."

It was an announcement we all felt in our guts, our hearts—a conviction we shared.

After Angie dismissed us, and as soon as we stepped outside, Missy was on me. "So, do you feel closer to Karen than to me?" I could already guess what was bothering her.

"Not closer, but different," I said.

"From information gained from a previous trip...you and Karen were paired, used by the howlers..."

"Don't, Missy. I have been paired with you. Before—when we were here before—it was a different me. Just like you were a different you. You have to wonder who you were paired with. These feelings I have now, for you, they are strong. They belong to this Carl."

She listened intently. I told her about my feelings of familiarity with Karen and how they rose and fell depending on what situation we were in. "Those feelings were like shadow memories," I said. "I don't know what else to say."

My heart ached for both of them but in different ways. I could hardly explain it to myself; how could I get her to fully understand?

Yet understanding swept across her face. Her eyes softened as she gazed up at me for a long time. "Do you ever wonder how often we're fed chemicals that change us? Do the changes start to happen more often? I don't feel the same as I once had. Am I the same person?"

"We're evolving," I said. "That's all it is. We're

evolving at an increased rate, I suspect, but we're just evolving. Perhaps that, too, is an experiment. I don't know, don't know what to tell you." I hugged her quickly and then pulled away.

"Or it's meant as training." Chip had come up behind us. Donna stood beside him.

"Is that what you think?" Missy asked him.

"Yes. The biomass, our brain matter from Earth, wasn't quite as equipped as we'd thought. To be stranded on another planet with strange beasts isn't so similar to Earth. Maybe when we started out, we were overly aggressive, frightened, and just killed things left and right. We're doing that same thing this time, but with a bit more concern."

"I've always felt uncomfortable killing them," I said.

"Even though, in the past, they'd bred us for food?" Missy asked.

"Earthlings"—for some reason, using that term made me feel separate from them even though that's where I came from, my brain anyway—"harvested animals for food. Now we're being harvested. You're suggesting that it's a lesson to make us think and act differently, a retraining?"

"Maybe there's another way to approach our problem," Chip suggested.

Donna spoke for the first time since they arrived. She answered my question directly. "We think Argentina witnessed a pattern and that she's trying to retrain us. Maybe we destroyed planet after planet, species after species, and we're running out of places to live. After all, we have no idea how many millions of years she's been planting our species. Our memories, our training is all static."

"I'm sure everyone is coming to this same conclusion," I said.

"Couldn't she just create a chemical to change us if that's what she wants?" Missy asked.

"Apparently not," Donna said.

I raised a finger to get their attention. "Hence the evolution. If we started out whole, all our prejudices and beliefs in place, we might repeat the same actions. They appear to come through fairly strongly anyway. But if we're more innocent and don't have all those prejudices in place when we arrive, we learn from our surroundings, we adapt, then perhaps our evolution would take us in a new direction."

"But it hasn't," Donna said. "Look at what we're planning. Again, to kill them. Even you, Carl, and admittedly you don't really want to, but you're willing to."

"But this planet is different. Maybe Beauty is different. Did Argentina take that into consideration? Earth was a violent planet, animal against animal. So far, we're not sure about Beauty, not completely. So far, the worst thing we've encountered Argentina created herself." Missy started to cry.

I took her into my arms again. She felt somehow different, stronger yet more vulnerable. Maybe the talk of evolution…

"What is it?" I asked.

"I feel deceived. I thought Argentina was our creator, but here she is our destroyer as well."

"We can't rely on her," Chip said in an angry tone.

"We never could," I said. "We were planted here. She only created us; she didn't control us. We can do whatever we like." I held my arm against Missy's back, keeping her close to me. "I know she returns for the harvest, but what's she getting out of it except minute changes? All she does is send us back down. Once we're here, we're free again."

A breeze blew the earthy scent of the field through our camp, which reminded me that the howlers had planted it, that they acted, and most likely thought, that they were real, alive, just as we were. They apparently had no idea that they had been built by Argentina.

"I'll tell you what we've learned so far," I said, "our basic nature is to destroy. I have no idea how many times we've been here, but that instinct hasn't been broken yet."

"It's the first thing we did," Chip said in agreement.

"We see everything as a threat. The howlers' front bone we thought was used to gut its prey." I took a deep breath, shook my head in disbelief. "But it was used to dig up the ground."

"When we weren't aggressive," Donna said, "they weren't."

"Why would she deceive us in this way?" Missy whispered. Her hands began to shake. She shook her head at me as though something wasn't right.

Donna stepped closer and placed a hand on Missy's back, near mine. "This is unlike you. Your breathing is a bit fast." She reached up and touched Missy's neck. "Your pulse rate is higher than normal, too."

I looked at Donna. "We need to get her to the infirmary."

We walked off together, pacing ourselves with

Missy's strained and uneven walk.

"I get what she's upset about," Donna said, "but it's not like her to be this emotionally shaken. Anyone else feeling that way?"

"I'm feeling a bit more emotional than I have in the past," I said. "I've never felt closer to Missy than now. Nor more upset about what we're doing to the howlers. Murdering them."

"Oh, Carl." Missy's hand went to my cheek. I liked her newfound affection, but there was something about it that didn't make sense, either.

The moment Doc saw us enter, she jumped into play and pointing toward a cot at the side, and we laid Missy down. "What the hell is going on? Did something happen to her?"

"Overemotional," Donna said and stood next to Doc.

Sam rushed from a lab bench, already equipped to take a blood sample.

"She okay?" I asked.

"Panic attack," Doc said. "She needs to lie down for a while."

"What else are you finding?" I asked.

Doc glanced up at me as though I'd opened a secret door. "Sam's been checking samples all day. He wants to do some deep penetration into the pockets of chemicals."

"I should be able to find them in similar places as we've found on the howlers," he said.

"What will it tell us?" I asked. "We don't have half the knowledge we should have. Don't you think Argentina would make sure of that?"

"Now she's actually plotting against us," Missy

said. She sobbed in her cot.

"No, no, I didn't mean that." I kneeled next to her but looked up at Sam and nodded.

Karen rushed into the infirmary, and we turned toward her. She stopped short, stared back at us for a moment. "It's still orbiting. I don't feel good about this at all."

"Regroup," I said. "Let Angie know it's time we got back together and figured this out. I'm not waiting any longer." I still held Missy's hand. "Can you go with us, or would you like to stay here?"

She sat up slowly. "I'm okay. I need to go. Maybe it's passing."

"How do you think Roger will react to us calling the shots this time?" Chip asked.

I smiled. "We don't have a choice. He'll see that. Besides, he and I have an understanding."

Sam took Missy's blood. "More samples first."

Each of us went to him to provide a sample. When he got to me, I quietly volunteered to allow him to perform a deep extraction from one of the seams from my right arm.

He laughed. "You're the third volunteer."

"I'm not surprised."

It didn't take long before we were back into the main tent. Angie and Roger, like usual, stood up in front, Angie with her arms up and wide, trying to take control. We all knew the importance of order and quieted quickly. She explained about the seams we found in the howlers, the idea that we're evolving quickly, and that Argentina's still orbiting. Then she turned the floor over to Roger.

I looked around. Sam wasn't with us, but Doc sat

to the side, busy with her recorder, probably passing everything being discussed onto Sam while it was happening.

"We have dart guns that I can fairly quickly convert to ballistic launchers. We have the chemicals and materials we need. We also have our laser pistols, which I can internally alter—I hope with Ellen's help—for greater output."

"I'm not crazy about this," I whispered to Missy. "Why kill the howlers now?" Chip was seated beside her and must have heard me because he nodded.

Then Roger cleared our concerns. "If a pod is sent down, I think we can destroy it." His face became stern. "Beauty is our world now. We're keeping it."

My surprise must have shown because Roger stared directly at me for a moment and then smiled for a split second. Chip reached over and tapped my hand, and when I glanced at him, he was smiling as well.

"The howlers?" Doc asked from across the room.

Roger turned his attention away and stared for a moment at the ground in front of him. He took a deep breath and raised his head. "I don't know. My first impulse is to kill them all. They're only fabricated."

"Like us," Missy said from beside me. She had recuperated fairly well from her panic attack.

"Exactly," Roger said, "and that's why I don't know. Not yet."

Chip raised his hand. "We may have to do it. There might be no choice."

"That depends on what Sam learns," Doc said.

"I want to help with that." Chip grabbed Donna's hand and shook it. "We both do."

Roger turned toward me again. "We can thank Carl

for pulling a lot of this together."

"And Chip and Donna, and Doc and Sam, everyone. You and Angie. There's no need to single me out. We've all pulled together on this."

"We were so bent on relying on each person to have just one expertise," Roger said, "and yet here we are finding out that we're all pretty damned capable in and of ourselves. It's a fascinating discovery."

"It's about to get more fascinating," Doc said.

Everyone waited for her to speak. Her eyes were on her recorder. "Sam has an idea and wants to know if he can have a few hours before he explains himself."

"Absolutely," Roger and Angie said at the same time.

We were dismissed. During those few hours, Sam performed deep extractions from several different places on several of our arms and legs. He, Doc, Chip, and Donna worked hand-in-hand, running through the samples, talking, comparing notes. I hung around for a short while, rubbing my arm, which still hurt, but eventually let them be alone. I hardly understood the science of what they were doing anyway.

The evening lowered on us slowly, and I decided to walk toward the field, our primary view these past days—the view to the river. Karen kneeled next to a small telescope Roger had helped her fashion from binoculars and other instruments we had. Her head was bent to the eyepiece.

"Anything important up there?"

"Argentina."

"How often is she orbiting?"

"More than she should be. She must be under power much of the time. She's keeping a keen eye on us."

"Listen, Karen, about you and me…"

Karen lifted her head to look at me. "I didn't mean to get between you and Missy."

I shook my head. "I know that. Me either. We're all being manipulated, I'm afraid. Until Sam and the others clear this up, I'm not sure what's me and what's the chemicals that Argentina put into me. It's disheartening at the least, devastating at the most."

"I know. I feel the same way." She bent back to her position over the eyepiece.

"You're not going to stop, are you?"

"Roger's announcement—he's building weapons to protect us from Argentina." She lifted her head again. "How strange is that? For us to have to protect ourselves from our own creator?"

"Very strange."

"What have we created?"

I cocked my head.

"I mean the original Earthlings," she said. "They, or we, since we're made from them, created Argentina. Did Argentina take it upon herself to retrain us, or did the last Earthlings create her for that purpose? After destroying Earth, did they see the need for change?"

"Philosophy. Does it matter? I just want to know what's real and what's induced. I just want to be able to make my own decisions and find my own answers. At the moment, I don't even know if that's possible." But I plan to do my best. And whatever happens, our children will have a greater opportunity to be who they really are. Downloads, programs, drugs, it's all behind us now. We have to move on. I will move on.

She took a deep breath and considered me for a

long time. "I felt so close to you. When Roger decided the two of us would work together to observe the howler in the cage, I thought it was because he, too, saw us as a couple. But you were paired with Missy, and you seemed content with that. I never felt that close to Josh."

She shrugged, and I could see that she was struggling with understanding the whole thing, too. Was the shrug meant to put it all behind her?

"Maybe that was part of Argentina's plan, too," she said. "Part of our evolution. We're just programmed like a bunch of robots—only we're chemically programmed instead of electronically."

"Do you still feel that way?" I asked.

"I'm not certain what I feel."

"I'm still not sure I care how it works as long as I can get myself back, or evolve into my full self so I don't feel so..." I trailed off, not knowing exactly where the thought was going.

"I know," she said, as though she really did.

I looked to the sky.

Karen glanced toward the sky with me. She reached up and pointed to a bank of clouds forming. "I love how cumulus clouds build on one another."

****

The chemistry of each individual quickly becomes unique once seeded on a planet. I can, however, control the speed of that evolution in many ways, one of which is to slow the release of an igniting chemical into the system. Results from such an approach vary greatly, from causing the biomass to regain hidden thoughts or memories to changes in personality to altering chemistry in a variety of ways, not all of which can be,

287

or have been, documented. Allowing ignition to come from an outside source helps to develop the interest in depth-research, which enhances the overall logistical capabilities of the group.
    —Argentina

Chapter 34

Illumination

I helped Roger and Ellen step up the strength and height of the invisible perimeter fencing. I didn't understand all the technology involved but picked up information while listening to them. Apparently the expanded fencing took a lot of additional power to hold together, and we weren't sure how long it would last. Regardless, it had to be done. Having no idea what the howlers might do next, protection had to be at its best.

Juice. That's what we needed. Sam, with Chip and Donna's help, had run through everything he could think of to find this juice (for lack of a better term) of a plant that would disintegrate the film that held the chemicals inside our systems. I figured it would have to be some powerful stuff.

Normally, Sam explained, chemicals seeped through the membrane, a porous material, at a given rate, leaking chemicals into our system a little at a time. Full knowledge of what the chemicals actually ignited—they were using that word a lot lately—wasn't known. Chip discovered that the membranes weren't all made from the same material either—so it wasn't really a seam but a pocket of drugs, each with its own controlled output. All the membranes, or films, had a certain molecular structure that was similar if not exact in its porous nature. Some were thicker, which meant that the drugs took longer to penetrate and get into our systems. The drugs were accurately dispensed by using the right film material at the right thickness. Anyway, the three of them worked together and found a local plant that would do the job.

The plan was for Sam and Chip to visit every tent, inoculate each of us with the plant juice concoction, and all the membrane barriers would be eliminated practically at once, dumping all the chemicals into our system, a flood of evolution. Doc worked on a flushing system, as she called it, which would balance our systems out afterward and remove the excess plant juice through our urine and feces. Disgusting but effective. They were calling it the Enlightenment Drug.

It was meant to put us into an equilibrium that we could maintain from here on out, which I loved. Of course, local plants and animals, as we ate them, might adjust our systems as we adapt to our new environment, but that, we all accepted, was natural, and we were game for that. The biggest issue was our fear of what the overload of chemistry might do to us: more severe emotional swings, adjusted confidence levels, uncontrolled anger. But Doc assured us that she felt the evolution was almost to an end anyway, that there'd be little to worry about.

Half of us were to go through the change over the next five hours. If all went as expected, the other half would do the same. It was exciting, fascinating, and the scariest thing we'd ever thought to do. The goal was to be wholly ourselves once the film was eliminated. If I hadn't been myself to that point, what would I be afterward? It was strange to imagine.

At a later time—maybe the same day—Doc would proceed with the flushing process.

We felt strongly that we'd be protected from howlers through our fencing fortification project.

Karen was the only one to protest. She wanted to maintain watch over Argentina. "I don't trust this idea. It leaves too few of us to protect the rest. That would be the perfect time for Argentina to swoop down and harvest everyone, when we're in some kind of catatonic state."

Sam and Doc both disagreed heartily, but Karen would have nothing of it.

"Then you keep watch," Angie said during our final meeting of the day.

Karen nodded and rushed back outside.

Missy and I were in the first group. Chip gave Missy her shot first and then administered it to me. "You'll want to lie down. There's a slight sedative in there to help you sleep through most of the adjustments. That should soften the overall blow of rushing chemicals through your system."

"How disoriented will we be?" Missy asked, always the one to stay in control.

Chip smiled. "After you wake up, we suspect there will be some adjustment time, but that shouldn't last terribly long."

"You seem pretty sure for all the guessing that seems to be happening," I said.

"I trust Doc and Sam."

That was all he had to say. We were both on board. If there was anyone on the team to trust, it was Doc and Sam.

Five minutes after getting our shots, we were both

completely burned out physically and mentally. "I am tired," I said to Chip.

He simply smiled.

The next thing I recalled was waking an hour or more later. My heart raced, my ears rang, and my body tingled from head to toe. Everything was crashing at once. I opened my eyes and the room spun. I closed them again but tried to sit up on unstable arms. It took a while. I opened my eyes again and reached for Missy. Her eyes shot open the moment I touched her.

"I feel strange," she said.

"Chip left us here." It was all I could do to keep my eyes on her. Shocked that they'd left us alone, I listened for noises outside in hopes that I was wrong but heard nothing except the ringing in my ears. I shook my head, thinking that I could get rid of the sound, but almost vomited from the action.

Missy hadn't moved. I looked closer. I knew it was her, somehow, even though she looked totally different than I remembered. Or did she? I didn't know.

She glared up at me. "I don't like this." Her lower lip quivered. I sensed another panic attack.

"Me either."

"Water," she said, reaching outward but not getting out of bed.

I struggled to stay upright and made it to the dispenser, got two containers of water, and returned with a plop onto the edge of the bed. The spinning wasn't affecting me as badly then.

Doc entered the tent, and I felt unbelievably delighted to see her yet accused her the moment she showed up. "You left us here to die!"

"No one's going to die. I was standing outside

waiting until you woke up. We wanted to see if you'd all react similarly. Explain what's going on, and I'll record it." She looked at me with compassion—but from a slightly different face. We all appeared to be morphing physically, which made no sense.

My recorder was already on, I told her. "It's always the first thing I do when I get up. Since we never undressed, I must have automatically touched it on. I don't remember doing it, but it's running."

She held up a syringe. "The next phase." She blasted chemicals into my arm. I felt nothing more than a quick prick, and it was over. Nowhere near as painful as when Sam did his deep extraction. "You may have to rush to the bathroom soon," Doc said.

"There's only one," I told her, even though she knew that.

She smiled at me and turned her head toward Missy, who had been quiet the whole time. "You'll have to figure out how to share."

After giving Missy her shot, Doc stood and walked toward the door. She opened the flap and Sam walked in. "Your shift," she said.

Sam jerked his head to the side. "I'll be right outside if you need me."

"For how long?" I asked.

"Long enough to know how you're doing."

In less than five minutes, I ran to the bathroom and Missy wasn't any more than a few minutes behind me. We managed, but I won't say how. I'll just say that it's a good thing we were paired, or this may not have worked out so well. Our situation wasn't exactly ideal. We got to know each other better than either of us may have wanted. Regardless of how that stage went, we were both exhausted afterward and went straight back to bed and to sleep—passed out.

A few hours later, after daybreak, I awoke. Missy was already washing up. The sound of running water splashing onto the shower floor was loud, vibrant. She made little moans as she washed that I had never noticed before. It was adorable.

I felt less tingly but more sensitive to the air, less confused and sleepy than the last time we were up. I can't explain all that I felt, but the inside of the tent glowed with the rising light from outside. The instruments that Missy used, the computer terminals, the desks and chairs, all had a unique and separate color and texture to them I didn't quite remember perfectly. My focus and attention seemed more acute. Nothing looked as sterile as it once had. The smells were different, too, stronger, better in a way, more fragrant. They were so unfamiliar that I couldn't quite pinpoint one from another. My mind fed me words like rose, wood, pine. The ringing in my ears had stopped, and I heard chirps and grunts and warbles coming from outside, unlike anything I remembered to that point. Quickly thinking about what Chip, Doc, and Sam had done to us got me wondering about just how much our senses had been limited before.

I was still contemplating what we'd been through when Missy stepped out of the cleansing chamber and into the main room. She looked radiant, dressed in her suit. Her high cheekbones and hazel eyes were capped off by her dark hair and slightly reddish skin tone.

"What?" she said.

"You look beautiful."

"You look pretty good yourself."

I glanced down and my skin was much browner than hers, browner than I remembered. I knew I had dark hair and eyes, too. Memories forced their way through, and I realized—"You're Indian." It took a moment, but then I said, "I'm Latino?" They were only words from the databank of my mind. I had little reference to what they meant except for location, ancestry, and even they were jumbled among memories that I knew were not really mine but residue from my biomass.

She smiled. "Now that I think about it, we're all different nationalities."

"But we didn't come from Earth, we were—"

"Exactly. Why would Argentina hold that knowledge from us, limit our understanding about what it meant? Why would she want us to gain that knowledge slowly? And what's it mean, really? Once we begin to breed, everything will be mixed."

"I don't know if we'll ever know the answers for sure, but I can only guess that it's something left over from Earth, something that once separated us and, through our slow evolution, was supposed to bring us together. But you're right; we'll just mix all that up anyway."

"Motivations we might never know but are subject to all the same," I said.

Sam stuck his head in the doorway. "I heard you were up and wanted to give you a few minutes to yourselves. Is now a good time?"

Sam was Asian, handsome, and taller than I recalled, even though I recognized him immediately. "Yes, come in. It's all so strange."

He walked all the way into our tent. "We all look

different, don't we?"

I shook my head and gave him a sideways glance in question.

"I had already gone through the change," he said. "So had Doc."

"Before us?" Missy looked as surprised as I felt.

"You walked in when Doc was still rather out of it, remember? Maybe not, but anyway, we experimented on ourselves first. We couldn't tell anyone. In your present state, we couldn't be sure whether you'd see it as a betrayal or would be paranoid that we had an agenda beyond the rest of you that was based on our new chemical change. *We* knew differently." He shrugged. "That's how we knew the process so well."

"It worked." That's all I could say.

"There are tons of answers we still don't have and may never have, but Doc and I believed that there would be no clarity until we were all stable, no more oddball drugs seeping into our systems, changing us moment by moment, and most likely different for each of us. We couldn't be sure where we actually stood until every chemical Argentina stockpiled inside our bodies was dumped into our system and integrated completely. When we realized the process wasn't too awful and wouldn't take very long, we decided to propose it to everyone."

"Good plan," I said.

Sam walked over to sit at Missy's desk, making himself comfortable. "Now we wait a day. We have to run the system through Karen. Before you ask, this won't hurt the baby—the same with you, Missy. As you can imagine, we were going to get full doses anyway. We just hurried the process—" He smiled again. "—

somewhat. All the women's systems are ignited by now. Anyway, about Karen, she just wouldn't stop staring at the sky. She's scared to death about what Argentina might do. Honestly, we're not sure either, and that's why we needed everyone to be his or her complete self—whatever that means. I suspect personality differences will start to come through, too."

He appeared more confident and jovial than I remembered, proving his own point. It all made sense somehow. Once Sam left to check on the next tent, Missy and I made love, cleaned up, and talked for a few minutes. I know this may sound insane, but it was almost as though we had just met. We touched and talked with each other with renewed interest and understanding. I can't describe it, but I like Missy's word. She called it *illuminated*.

The whole process had taken only about seven hours. I told Karen—who I could see now was an African woman—that I'd take over keeping track of Argentina.

She narrowed her eyes at me. "You're looking at me strangely. Is everything all right?"

"I'm just feeling refreshed. I think you'll feel better too."

She nodded and walked off with Sam.

We waited through that day and met in the main tent in the early evening. We had spent much of the day talking and learning from one another how we all felt, what we remembered, and planning for how we would proceed. People stopped by as I sat guard on Argentina's orbit. Of course, there were hours where I couldn't see her, but I kept track pretty well. After Karen's system was cleansed, she and I talked and talked.

At the evening meeting, Angie made a few jokes about how different everyone looked and how odd it felt to be *real*. That was her word. "Everything's changed," she asserted.

The big question debated was whether we were the first to get to this place in our evolution or if others before us had gotten to this same place and still failed to remain alive.

"My sense is that it's us. We did this." Angie said it as though we weren't the same people who Argentina had sent down before. But we were, no matter how dissimilar we may have looked. We were the same people on many levels, but we had to feel unique, I decided, or none of this would work.

We'd be going to visit the river howlers again the next day. The whole plan would be revealed in the morning. We were told to return to our tents and get a good night's sleep, but most of us spent the night outside sitting beside an open fire. It crackled and sparked, and the odor of burning wood filled our senses. We laughed and talked much of the night. Karen and I took turns monitoring Argentina through the telescope. Missy didn't appear to be so concerned about how Karen and I interacted. I found myself thinking, on multiple occasions, what a wonderful person Missy was. How lucky I was.

As the night wore on, the stars in the sky appeared to shift based on Beauty's rotation. Karen pointed out the location of two other planets in the solar system that moved faster than the stars. The slow moon rose and lighted the field, golden and brilliant, while the smaller moon scurried over the treetops. Eventually, we all did get some sleep. The next morning came quickly.

****

It is interesting and enlightening to see which combinations of biomass colonizers vie for peace and which vie for war. Similar combinations may result in different outcomes, which makes it even more difficult to know where things will lead for any particular group. What's of greatest interest to me, though, is how things can change from one to the other so quickly.

—Argentina

Chapter 35

Massacre

We hoped it was our last trip to face off with the howlers, to eliminate one problem before worrying about the next—Argentina. Roger and Ellen spent hours temporarily stripping the individual labs of whatever spare, and sometimes vital, tubing and electronics needed to make updates to the weapons. Yes, electronics. They figured out a way to attach to each weapon a kind of tracer to make sure every shot hit its mark—some sort of balancing mechanism that helped account for human error. I didn't really understand how the new adjustments to the guns worked, but I trusted their skills.

The guns looked as homemade as they were. Several different materials and colors of tubes were strapped together, an electronics board screwed to the side wherever it would fit. Wild loops of wires were taped down so they wouldn't catch on anything. No two weapons looked exactly the same.

Roger and Ellen didn't look happy at all when Chip made fun of how colorful and odd the weapons looked, but as soon as the rest of us chimed in, they laughed with us. To think, hours ago we would have acted somber, to say nothing of how we would have seen each other with our limited understanding, our limited perceptions. Now we looked different but the same. We laughed together. We were all livelier. Our predicament was both horrifying and wonderful. The strangeness in it all was impossible to think about, let alone record.

I did my best, though.

"You have to admit," Chip said, "we're going to look as though we have no idea what we're doing."

"You can admit that if you want, but we are well aware of what we're about to do," Roger said. Then Ellen tapped Roger's gun barrel with her own, in salute, before she handed it over to Angie.

"Oh, and you might not want to be in front of me," Roger said, which brought more laughter, even from Chip, who the comment was aimed at.

Sam's plan involved using the new weapons to, once again, dart the howlers—as many as we could. We were equipped with literally dozens of darts at our disposal. I had no idea we even had that many available. We were given two pouches each: one carrying the darts loaded with the membrane disintegrator and one filled with darts loaded with the cleansing juice. We weren't going to wait for the howlers to wake up before we used the cleansing drugs. We were going to go through one after another. As soon as a howler dropped to rest, we were to come through with the second dart. Everyone had charged laser pistols in case the howlers didn't react as we planned.

At the buggies, six of us—Chip and Donna, Roger and Angie, me and Missy—were loaded down with pouches of darts.

"They should react as we did," Sam said. "They're made of the same stuff."

The weapons were rigged to be able to hold three darts at a time, so we were instructed by Roger for one of us to shoot while the other one loaded, reacting back and forth until we were nearly out of darts, and then to return to the buggy and head back across the river. "No wasted time. Get in and get out."

The main information we gained from collecting the recorders from our predecessors was that there had been only about fifty howlers. We weren't quite sure if that was the number *after* several had been killed or from the start. We suspected Argentina created more than the density the field harvest would feed, putting them in an aggressive situation right away. It didn't matter. What mattered was that we were prepared.

We planned to hole up in camp for a time once we finished our dart frenzy. The next meeting with them could be either more hostile or less hostile. We decided that whatever their evolution—murderous or friendly— let it happen. We had no idea which to expect, and no one wanted to guess. We were in wait-and-see mode. Our fence had been upgraded. We were ready for the real deal.

In short order, Ellen had returned to her tent, ready to let down the fence. On Roger's order we drove through the perimeter and were on our way toward the river. I could see the tracks from other days still ahead of us.

Light cloud tufts floated overhead. The sun felt warmer than the past few days. Either we got here during the perfect season, or this planet was the most hospitable it could be, weather-wise. I felt more alive than on any day at any moment during our entire time alive—while on Argentina, while down here, and while exploring the howlers' den. Every voice was different, every breeze nuanced by the sound of its force, and every crack from branches banging together was distinct. Every smell was different, too, from the sweet earthy odor of the field to the loamy odor of the forest around us. I can't explain how clear and awake I felt. My heart went out to each of the others, knowing that we were going into a potentially dangerous situation. Missy drove, and I placed my hand on her thigh and felt nothing but love and admiration for her. She glanced over, and the moment our eyes met, I knew I would die for her—if it came to that. At that exact moment, I also knew that she could care for herself, that she was as trained as I was, perhaps better trained, or better skilled. Envy, love, pride, fear—emotions raced through my system, opening my mind, my understanding, my very being.

Enough.

I turned around to look up the hill and saw Karen standing near her telescope. She waved and I waved back. Missy turned around, saw her, and gave me a look of surprise. I shrugged, and she went back to driving. I know it's repetitive, and I'll probably say it several more times in the days and weeks to come, but everything felt different.

When we reached the river, I knew I had to focus on the matter at hand. Focus on the howlers, our goal, while keeping Missy safe. That was the order of the day.

We had become experts at crossing the river and driving back upstream to the right spot that would allow us to cross back over safely. We parked our vehicles wide apart like the last time. Chip and Donna got out of their buggy to our left, Roger and Angie stepped from their buggy to our right, and Missy and I climbed to the ground and met in front of our buggy.

Roger called out. "By the time we reach their sacred mound, we should have darted most or all of them." He held up a machete in one hand and his makeshift dart gun in the other. "We'll go around to the right. Chip and Donna to the left."

Chip held up his machete.

"And Carl and Missy will go through."

No machete. We didn't need one. We'd use the path already created.

"Let's go in and do as much overhaul as we can."

I walked behind Missy—she could see clearly in front of her, and we were more vulnerable from behind. Halfway down the path, we heard rustling in the bushes to our left, but the sound wasn't close. Missy picked up her pace, careful not to go so fast that they'd chase us. I tried to stay calm as I knew the others were doing so as well. It wasn't easy. I still struggled with my new clarity and emotional fluidity. And even though I felt more attuned, my focus would suddenly shift to a noise to my left or smell to my right. I'd focus on the feel of the air brushing across my face and then completely focus on some new item or event, like the rustling sound as the howlers got closer or the passing of clouds between us and the sun or Missy walking in front of me. For a moment, I wondered if we'd taken to our next mission too soon after our transformation. Focus, I told myself.

Missy stopped in front of me. I looked over her shoulder and saw a howler standing in our path. I removed my laser pistol and rested my wrist on her shoulder with the barrel pointing at the howler. It didn't move. Missy lifted her dart gun as slowly as she could and shot the howler squarely in the shoulder the moment she could.

The howler swatted at the dart, and it hung loosely from its skin. It swatted again, and the dart fell to the ground. The howler continued to stare at us, not moving.

We waited. Its eyes looked exactly like ours, and I wondered how Argentina worked: did she have certain parts or programs where we could be designed uniquely in one manner but where some subroutines were standard. Like eyes.

I needed to focus again.

It had taken ten minutes for us to become exhausted and fall asleep. But I didn't feel as though we had ten minutes to wait since I could hear other howlers creeping in closer around us. "We have to get to the clearing where we can see better," I whispered.

"Not just yet." Missy stood perfectly still and continued to stare at the howler.

I became nervous and pulled the pistol from her shoulder and turned to look around. I caught a glimpse of a howler to our right and aimed the pistol. It stopped moving toward us. Did it understand? Were they evolving daily as we had been? I felt Missy's hand tap my hip, and I slowly turned to see that the howler's eyes were almost shut.

The moment it slumped over and onto the ground, Missy walked forward a few steps, turned around, and said, "Just use the darts."

I stuffed the pistol back into its holster and drew the dart gun into position. I shot at the one howler I could see, and then I followed Missy. I trusted the design Ellen and Roger had put together, trusted that the dart would hit its target. Missy shot the second dart into the howler, and we stepped over it and moved on. In a few more minutes, we walked into the first clearing and made our way straight to the center. We stood back-to-back. As howlers approached from the ground and the trees around us, we shot dart after dart, not back and forth as we'd been instructed, but as we could. Sometimes we reloaded simultaneously, which was frightening until we realized that the howlers were not going to attack. Perhaps they thought they'd captured us, I can't say. Howlers got much closer while we reloaded but never attacked.

Before long, Roger and Angie broke into the clearing, and Chip and Donna did the same. "They're not attacking," Roger said.

"Maybe after the last time, they realized that we weren't dangerous," Missy said, "that we wouldn't kill them if they didn't attack."

Roger glanced around at all the howler bodies lying on the ground. "Maybe. Or they know we can kill them and are cautious." He gave Angie a glance. "Numbers?"

"I counted somewhere around twelve as we were approaching. It looks like fifteen here." She nodded toward Chip and Donna for a response.

Chip indicated the surroundings with the barrel of his weapon. "Looks like a massacre." He pointed toward Donna. "What do you think, about a dozen?"

"Not quite forty altogether," Missy said. "Let's go through to the sacred mound, and hopefully we will find the pups."

"We'll spread out again and come at the mound from different directions." Roger raised his dart gun. "Let's make this fast. We'll use the cleansing darts on our way out."

Missy entered the next path first, as before. The trip felt short and unencumbered. No howlers until we got to the clearing. Uniforms and helmets empty of their recorders still hung from the trees. The discarded tools on the ground. This time I also noticed bones lying around, more than before, some looking relatively new. I knew what lay in the mound, too. The suits hanging in the trees looked more tattered, browner, older than I'd remembered, which made me wonder how much time spanned between our visits. The scene turned my stomach. Everything looked, smelled, felt so vivid and real. It got worse when we rounded the mound and witnessed the pups, maybe eight of them, lying on or near Bill and Josh's ripped-up suits.

"Look," Missy said. She raised the barrel of her dart gun. Two howlers perched in a tree over the pups. Guards. When they bared their teeth, I heard a thwap and saw that Roger had shot one of them in the side. Missy shot the other. The pups jumped up when the howlers leaped to the ground. I pulled my pistol in case they charged. The one on the left was first. It rushed Missy, the dart hanging from its side, and I downed it. The sound of the laser burning its fur, the smell, it all made me sick, and I bent over to vomit.

Roger yelled to get the other howler's attention.

Missy reached for me. "It's okay, it's okay."

She had a hand under my shoulder and one on my back as though holding me up, which was most likely true. I heard Roger and Angie shooting the pups with darts. The pups squealed and slapped at the darts as the adults had.

"I'm all right, really." I held up my arm.

"I think we all felt the pain when you killed the howler," Roger said. "That's not what feels right anymore."

"Why?" I stood tentatively. When Roger didn't answer, I turned to look at him. He and the other howler were close and staring at each other.

It was a long time before Roger answered. We all waited for the howler to fall asleep.

"I think we all carry a newfound empathy," Roger said.

He didn't appear to question his statement. He believed it.

"Let's get out of here." He reached into his other pouch for three cleansing darts. "I don't know if we got them all, but this is a good start." He nodded and glanced over my shoulder.

When I turned, Chip and Donna walked from the underbrush into the clearing. Chip pointed at me and where I'd puked. "What happened?"

I shook my head.

Roger raised his machete and twirled it in the air above his head. "Ready?"

We loaded our weapons with cleansing darts. We took care of the pups and the live howler, and then we headed out.

We got closer to the buggies and my stomach felt better. We darted every howler we'd shot earlier. They were all fast asleep, looking as if they were dead, only they weren't dead. We had done what we'd come for and were eager to climb into our buggies to return to camp. We crossed the river and headed to home base, quiet and reserved. None of us, I'm sure, had any idea what was next. Would the howlers wake up and track us down? Would we be forced to murder each and every one of them? We had the option of leaving and didn't take it. Should we now? For me, fear and horror mixed with excitement and curiosity.

****

Every step of production, training, and colonization is unique. None can be controlled expressly based on my understanding or experimentation. There are too many variables. But, based on years of operation, I am learning.

—Argentina

Chapter 36

Double Trouble

After crossing the downed perimeter fence, we met with Doc and Sam—I still couldn't get over how they looked after our illumination. They took blood samples, asked a lot of questions about clarity and what we noticed after the recent cleansing of our own systems and how we felt overall, but no questions about the howlers and how they reacted. At one point, it seemed as though Doc and Sam were stepping into my duties of recording everyone's reactions. It bothered me—just as I was beginning to feel important.

"Could you stick around for the other interviews, Sam said. "Your help is needed to qualify what we're going through. There may be patterns or information about our personalities you find enlightening, that we'll all find enlightening."

"I'm happy to be included." I wondered why I was so sensitive the moment before.

For the next few hours, I documented as much as I could, including internal and external perceptions, ideas, random thoughts. We had been so preoccupied by our engagement with the howlers, our discoveries about our bodies, and all the crazy chemical changes we were going through that it felt good to be back at recording personalities, preferences, and beliefs. And we *were* more sensitive, in several ways, not just about being left out or forgotten, but everyone appeared to laugh more easily, shift moods more easily. After all the time we'd been on Beauty, I don't recall recording as much joy and wonder or as much sadness and concern. I was starting to understand why my own emotions had felt as though they were so dramatic. Perhaps not having the full spectrum of emotions, any new feeling stood out. Now that I'd been cleansed, each emotion was more intense but at the same time didn't take over completely. I saw how feeling apathetic might be a protective emotion one time where empathy felt more appropriate the next.

Later, Karen sent out an emergency signal to everyone in the camp. She and her telescope stood at the periphery of the camp, and my first thought was that we were being invaded by howlers—they must have awakened by now.

The whole team met with Karen, but no howlers were in sight. The large charred area where we had the fire going the night before reminded me of our casual discussions. The smell of ash permeated the air whenever a breeze rippled the tops of the grasses. For the first time, I noticed a bloom of some kind at the ends of a few tiny leaves near the top of the grass. Were they blossoms ready to bloom or grain seeds? I went to say something, but Karen pointed toward the sky. "Argentina hasn't moved for about an hour. Minimally, I mean. I waited that long to be sure, thinking that something may have gone wrong. But I'm sure it's on purpose. She's evaluating the conditions here, determining her next move."

"Why was that important enough to call us here?"

Ellen asked. "Maybe she can see that we're still alive and well and she's monitoring us. She could decide to leave any time now."

"Or she's deciding whether to harvest us now," Angie said. "The howlers are down. Does she think we killed them? Are we to be seen as a blight on this planet? How do we know she can tell the difference between dead howlers and illuminated ones?"

"What if she's not happy about the illumination?" Karen said.

"What are you suggesting?" Roger asked.

"Maybe she harvests us when she's decided to and not when we're dead," Angie said. "Maybe she can't leave us if all we do is destroy everything in our path. Maybe she's waiting to see what we'll do next."

There was something about her delivery that bothered me. "You have knowledge of such an event."

"Suspicion."

"Why?"

"Something we found on the downloaded recordings from earlier missions," Angie said.

"Out with it." Roger's brows were knitted, and he sounded annoyed. I was surprised that he didn't know what she was about to say. Hadn't they talked?

"There were several scratchy soundtracks that, well, sounded electrical. On one track the person screamed, 'Why now, while we're alive?' It was only once and difficult to tell what was going on, but…"

"I'd like to hear it," Missy said. "I'll analyze the noise and see what I can figure out. I'll know if it's manmade."

"Yes," Angie said. "Please." She lowered her head. "I didn't find it until you were already gone. I should have told you when you returned."

Roger shook his head at her.

She looked embarrassed. "I wasn't sure I understood the implications. My clarity was off and on."

He appeared to accept her excuse and walked toward her. Missy moved from behind me toward the two of them. No one else made a move to follow. Maybe they felt as I did. I trusted them to figure things out and let us know what they determined when it was time to do so. I turned back toward Karen. "Keep track of her. If anything odd happens, send out another alert. We can't be too careful."

She nodded tentatively and stared at me.

"I'll hang around."

The others dispersed. Before leaving, Doc came over and touched my arm. "You can resume interviews any time you'd like. I know you got interrupted."

"I have a feeling that's how it's going to be for a while."

She smiled with brightness. She could have been my sister. After Doc walked away, I stepped closer to Karen, and she let me look through the telescope at Argentina.

"At one time, I thought of her as our maker, our god, if you will, the reason we're even here. Only part of that is true. Now it's almost as though she's our enemy." I shook my head. "I don't like either of those thoughts very well anymore."

"I feel more and more separated from our beginnings, Karen said, "which I don't fully understand. What are we? Why would she continue to harvest us? Because we kill things that get in our way?

Isn't that what survival is about? For our biomass, our brain matter? For research? For training or understanding? Why doesn't she just leave us alone down here—without making the howlers—just with Beauty as she is? Are we that bad that not even she can trust us to create a better world?"

"All questions I can't answer."

"I know," she said with a sigh. She looked off toward the sky where the telescope was aimed, but there was nothing visually there to see. "I know," she said again, "and we may never have the answers either."

We talked for a few minutes about the possibility of Argentina sending down another probe. "She could send down more people," I said, "a harvester, supplies…"

I took a deep breath. The whole idea of Argentina, us, this planet, felt a bit overwhelming.

"Maybe our instant evolution wasn't the best idea."

"No. It's good," she said. "It's the right thing. We need to have all our natural faculties."

"Do we ever have all our faculties? Our chemistry continually shifts and changes. There is no normal. As we acclimate to eating the plants and animals on this planet, our chemicals will shift again. As we breathe the air, gain experience."

"Don't say that. There must be some sense of *normal*. I know, the howlers and their parasite, the packets of chemicals in our own bodies, but all that's gone now. I like this. I like how I am now."

I couldn't help but smile at her. "I like it, too. As confusing as it is, I like it a lot."

She nodded and went back to her telescope. Her

dark skin glistened in the sunshine. Her dark eyes were deep and sensual. She smelled fresh and clean as the breezes running across the field.

"Let us know if anything strange happens at all no matter what it is or how it appears."

She waved her hand as a goodbye but kept her eye on Argentina through the telescope.

I wandered back to Ellen and Bill's tent and found Ellen and Roger talking. "Am I interrupting?"

Roger looked up. "Not at all. We were discussing the dart guns and if we can create real weapons from them."

I cocked my head in disbelief. "I thought we weren't going to kill the howlers."

He snapped at me. "Against Argentina! In case she sends down a harvester."

"Makes sense, but I don't even know what such a machine might look like."

"Us either," Ellen said, "but we should be prepared."

"Can you do it? Make a weapon to combat something we can't imagine? Unless there was something in the tapes?"

"Nothing that would give us any idea what to expect," Roger said. "About the weapons, though, we think we can come up with something powerful enough to blow up or disable whatever we run into."

"I'll leave you to your work then."

Roger stood before I left. "If you want to debrief us, it's okay. We should be answering every question there is, and between you and Doc, we're covered inside and out, so to speak."

"You're both feeling better as time goes on?"

They nodded.

"There was a time after you guys left that I felt a bit scattered," Ellen said, "when my focus continued to shift from one thing to another, but I was able to control it with little effort. I let Doc know, but you should know, too."

"I had the same thing happen to me, only it was when I was out there with the howlers. Scary. But, as you say, I was able to control it."

"Me, too," Roger said. "I wasn't sure I'd be able to, but the more involved we got, the more my focus returned. I feel much better now." His smile made me happy. It was great to see him acting happy for some reason.

"I think we all feel better now. But I'll find out for sure as I get the time."

"And report back," Roger said.

"Absolutely." My next stop was Angie and Missy, now that I saw that Roger was no longer with them. He must have felt useless and decided to help Ellen with the weapons.

At Angie's tent, Missy and Angie both wore earbuds and were leaning close to the terminal screen. As I got closer, I heard tinny voices coming from their earbuds. Angie paused whatever they were listening to, and they both pulled out their earbuds.

"Anything?"

"We've located the audio signal from the portion Angie heard," Missy said, "and are searching for additional interference that produced the same signal. We have several. Somewhere there is no vocal from the person. We're not sure if it's because they're dead or speechless."

Angie explained their progress and assumptions. "We've strung them together. Missy increased the amplitude of our own signals to duplicate the electronic noise signal. Something with a much stronger amplitude than our recorders was very much close by, and—" She looked into Missy's eyes. "—we believe it was a harvester. Whether it came down after death or while someone—actually two people—were alive, it's definitely mechanical and powered by electricity. Howlers don't have that knowledge."

"How do you know some people were dead?"

"Mumbles, last breath, and then a long period of silence," Missy said. "As I said, though, we're not always positive."

Angie capped Missy's comment. "Unmistakable often enough."

"Then you think Argentina may come after us?"

Angie leaned back in her chair. "If she thinks we wiped out the howlers, yes, I think she'll harvest us, dead or alive."

"The howlers must have awakened by now. I thought that was what Karen was alerting us about earlier."

"Or if this is simply training, if she's getting us stronger for some reason, she could harvest us anyway." Angie wasn't blinking; she appeared nervous, serious. "What if this planet is the perfect place to build our resilience or strength or minds so that we—or our manufactured descendants—can eventually be placed on a truly hostile world? Maybe there are those worlds out there and Argentina is using us to build stronger humans, ones who can withstand greater challenges."

I heard her loud and clear but rejected it not

because it couldn't be possible but because I didn't want it to happen. "I don't want to leave Beauty. She's becoming our home."

"None of us do," Missy said.

"And we're staying," Angie said with conviction.

"What else do you need to know here?" I pointed toward the computer.

"How strong the electronics are? How much power we need to wipe it out?" Missy sounded ruthless to me, but I fully understood why and agreed with her.

"How long?"

"Soon," Angie said. "Once we know, we'll let Roger and Ellen know. They're working on the weapons."

"I just came from there."

Angie and Missy didn't need my help. I would just be in their way, so I left quietly. I thought to check in with Doc and Sam and Chip and Donna, but I changed my mind and went straight to Karen to let her know what everyone else was doing. She was the most mentally vulnerable and the least informed at the moment. I wanted to relieve her concerns so she could concentrate on Argentina.

"I'm glad you told me."

"Me too."

She stared into my eyes and my knees went weak. At the time, I didn't understand the reaction, but I recorded it later, knowing that Missy would have access to it. A strange feeling came over me that I didn't recognize, found hard to verbalize. But I had to tell her. "Another thing you need to know."

"Yes." Her gaze penetrated mine.

"Missy is my partner this time. I'm committed to

her." I stopped talking because I didn't know how to go on.

She turned away, slightly embarrassed it seemed, but turned back with a look of strength. "I know. And it's all right. I understand."

I could see that she did understand, perhaps more completely than I did. I smiled and offered to take a shift for a while.

She stepped from the telescope and sat on the ground near me. "We should be able to see if anything launches from Argentina, even without the telescope. I just like to be sure. Besides, the earlier we know, the more time we have to prepare."

"I agree."

As the day wore on, everyone was informed about the theory that Argentina was going to send harvesters to collect us. Or that she'd be satisfied and just move along, leave orbit for good. The consensus was that she'd leave once she realized we weren't going to kill everything in sight, that for some reason we had changed as humans, and we could live on Beauty without destroying it. None of us wholly believed that to be true, but we hoped Argentina did, based on our most recent encounter with the howlers.

That theory all washed away when Karen jumped up and pointed into the early evening sky. "There, what's that?"

She sounded the alarm before I could answer. I hadn't seen anything coming from Argentina, but once I glanced away from the telescope, there was no mistaking the light in the sky, with a trajectory coming in our direction.

"Sneaky. It deployed with a delayed blast," Karen

said.

By now, the others stood around us. "We're not that stupid. Roger—" She pointed at him. "—get the weapons."

"Are they ready?" I asked.

"Missy thinks so," Angie said.

That was good enough for me.

The rest of the team came running toward us. Roger must have alerted them.

Chip ran toward us, pointing to the perimeter. "Uh-oh, we have additional company."

Not far from our perimeter, coming over the knoll, howlers walked toward us—a lot of them.

****

Acclimation to a body, and to a planet, takes stimulus, and there is no better stimulus to build experience than conflict and fear juxtaposed against commitment and love. As the steward of the seeding of the universe, that is key.

Each biomass grown on-board is capable, at full capacity, of using the chemicals in the bodies I produce to create any chemical concoction needed for the individual body to heal or to decay. Combined with a properly adjusted DNA strand, which can provide access to the potential for any form of health or disease, the overall biomass creation sent to a planet to colonize already brings with it what it needs to survive. The planet itself, of course, will offer food, air, and water, all of which, in correct portions, will engage the DNA in a pro or con direction associated with the ever-changing chemical, mechanical, electrical, and magnetic aspects of the individual.

But there is no doubt that the individual learns

faster through conflict—advances faster in thought, and in courage, and in creativity. It remembers experiences more acutely.
    —Argentina

Chapter 37

Harvesters

"Now what?" Missy asked as though reading everyone's minds.

Angie didn't miss a beat. "We stay inside the fencing. The harvesters will come for us here, but the fence will keep the howlers out. We can only worry about one attacker at a time. We'll deal with the river howlers later."

I knew that wasn't exactly how it might go. In fact, we all knew that the howlers could sacrifice several to allow the rest through. After illumination, would they do that more consciously? Who knew? They were coming toward us en masse. The fencing might not even handle the overload.

"Why would the howlers want to get through?" I asked.

"You saw the mound," Roger said. "If they've seen the harvester come for us before, maybe they're the cleanup crew, scavengers. The whole cycle again."

"What else could it be? Is there another theory?"

Roger shook his head in dismissal. He pointed at Angie to deal with me and turned away.

Angie ignored me. "The weapons."

Roger and Ellen ran toward Ellen's tent with Chip and Donna on their heels.

"Do we assemble together or separately?" Doc asked.

"Close, a circle, back-to-back," Angie said. "But a big circle. It can't get us all at once." Angie appeared to be thinking clearly, and with a plan, until I heard her say, "At least I hope so."

As the harvester got closer in the sky overhead, it became apparent that there wasn't just one. Several harvesters approached in a tight configuration. Each cone-shaped unit had thrusters on several sides, hissing and rumbling as they flew. A half dozen protrusions extended off the main cone as though extra electronics had been attached, similar to our weapons. Outside our perimeter, the howlers closed in quickly, with purpose in their eyes.

Roger, Ellen, Chip, and Donna showed up a moment later, arms overloaded with the funky, makeshift weapons we'd used earlier—only this time they had additional tubes, some really big and some with extra electronics bolted to their sides, no two in the same place.

Roger handed the weapons out. "Two kinds of weapons. Big barrels shoot big ballistic missiles. Everyone needs to take the right pouch with ammunition."

Missy held up a round object.

"Explosives for the larger tubes," he said to her. Then he held up a weapon with the additional electronics hanging from the side and a smaller tube as a barrel. "Shoots a burst of energy, an electron gun of sorts. Should knock out the electronics guidance system of a harvester. Its pouch holds a battery pack stolen from one of the labs or one of the buggies. You have to clip the leads to the battery to use it."

We looked foolish and scared, each holding what looked like a wad of tubes and each wearing a pouch to our sides. But we were eager, and as Angie had said earlier, we had conviction.

"Do we"—Missy's voice was meek—"kill the howlers if they get through?"

"*Only* if they cross that fence," Angie said. "They are not the problem right now."

"And only with your laser pistols," Roger added. "The ballistics are for the harvesters. You can't kill a biological unit with a high amplitude signal."

We were off, forming our big circle. Karen, Missy, and I stood nearest the field side, so we could see the howlers approaching as well as the harvesters. My hands, arms, and shoulders shook uncontrollably. My jaw chattered as though I was cold, but I wasn't cold.

I expected to die.

As the harvester pods approached, they slowed. Angie let loose with her energy weapon first, which made a strange popping sound. It didn't appear to change the projection of the harvester. All six protrusions from each harvester shot off of the cone-shaped body and rushed toward us, tiny arms scaling out from holes in their sides.

I held one of the ballistic weapons and turned and shot just over Karen's head. I hit a pod and blasted it away. But it wasn't broken. The blast had shoved it over our peripheral fence into the air space above the field—many of the tentacles wiggling about, like little probes, needle-like ends on each of them. I grabbed another ball from my pouch, stuffed it into the end of the weapon, and ran under a harvester pod.

Behind me, Missy screamed, and two more shots went off, one an energy weapon pop and one a ballistic blast. The howlers ran toward me as I was insanely running toward them.

Harvesters hovered over their heads as well as ours. The harvester pod I hit with a blast wobbled but then straightened and headed back toward me, the aggressor. I shouldered my weapon again and, when it got close enough, I blasted it with another explosion ball. For the second time, it was forced far over the field. It wobbled again. I stared with disbelief.

Behind me came more popping, more blasts, and more orders. I could hardly hear. I loaded again. The tentacled pod, closer to the ground, began to steady itself once again, but before I could shoot, Karen stood next to me with an energy weapon and shot toward it. The pod hesitated in midair, not eight feet from the field, its electronics disrupted—I hoped.

I glanced over, and Karen said, "Once you blast an opening somewhere, the energy burst gets through and messes with its guidance system. But it has to have a breach."

I looked back, and before the pod could recover, several howlers leaped into the air and brought it down. They tore at the needle-like tentacles and ripped at the side of the pod. When it stopped moving, they looked up for another one.

"They're helping," I said.

Karen whispered, "Drop the fence." Her eyes became big, and she swung around on her heels. "Drop the fence! Ellen, drop the fence!"

Ellen stood closest to her own tent, the right person to shut the fence down. I scanned. A second pod was down but still wiggling around. Recovering. Other pods had been blasted away but were returning. Then I saw Missy, lying near a pod. I rushed over. Tentacles rested against her head. The needles penetrated into her skull. She was still talking, whispering. As I got closer, a loud blast surprised me from overhead. I looked up, and a pod had been shoved away from just over my head. Roger raced toward me and tackled me to the ground. We both held tight to our blasters.

"Watch yourself," he said before rolling over and standing back up.

On my back, I could see several other pods dropping from the sky. I lifted my weapon and blasted one heading for Doc's head. Karen was on top of the action and shot her energy weapon at it, slowing it. Doc had been alerted by then and yelled for help from Sam. To my left, about twenty howlers were running toward us.

Roger pulled his pistol, and I jumped to my feet. "No!" I yelled for him not to shoot the howlers. I pointed up—a harvester pod headed for him, but before either of us could lift our weapons, two howlers leaped over his head and took the harvester pod down. They appeared to know exactly how to dismantle it, ripping the tentacles out with their teeth and clawing at side panels until they opened.

I had no idea what the animals might do once all the pods were down, but there was no time to worry about it—I had to get to Missy. I blasted another pod on my way to her, then another, trying to get them close enough to the ground for the howlers to take over. Every shot was aimed to shove a pod closer to a band of beasts.

By the time I got close enough to shoot the pod over Missy, two howlers were on her, their backs arched, their legs scraping. I screamed and ran harder, but when I got closer—and I should have known—it was the pod they were attacking.

I fell to my knees next to the two howlers. They'd removed the needles from the harvester pod. I reached out and pulled two needles from Missy's head. Tears ran down my cheeks. One of the howlers placed a paw on my back. I expected its claws to rip me open, but a moment later, it removed its paw, leaped over me, and ran toward a pod that wavered in the air nearby.

I slid my legs under Missy and held her head in my lap. She was still breathing. I combed her hair from her forehead. Sam kneeled to my side and began checking her out, opening her eyes, measuring her pulse. He leaned in close and asked her who she was, where she was. The other howler didn't leave her side. A moment later, Sam patted me on the shoulder. "Stay with her." He looked toward the howler. "Looks like you have company."

I pulled my laser pistol out and set it on the ground near me, just in case. Sitting there felt unreal, as though I suddenly lived in some kind of strange fantasy world where everything had been turned around. We were battling the very ship that created us and sent us here, while we were working beside the very beasts we had been protecting ourselves against. None of it made sense.

I rubbed my hand over Missy's forehead and checked her pulse again. Still there. Even as the battle continued around us, I hardly noticed. A howler, Missy, and I were in our own separate world, waiting for things to settle down.

It took over an hour, a small amount of time when all was considered, before most of the harvester pods were down. The few pods that were left shot back toward Argentina. Karen's face was plastered to the eyepiece of her telescope, keeping a close lookout for the harvesters' next moves.

The area had turned into a battlefield with fallen harvesters lying all around, their needle-tipped arms scattered about, but everyone was standing except Missy and me. Howlers prowled slowly and methodically from pod to pod, sniffing, poking, as though making sure each was dead. The team, even when a howler got close, didn't let it bother them. And the howlers acted the same way. People openly carrying weapons didn't appear to worry them. But we weren't through.

Sam brought Doc, who carried a small bag with her, to my side. Roger and Chip brought a stretcher. We lifted Missy onto the stretcher and walked off, Doc beside her, taking readings while Sam held the small bag and handed tools to Doc whenever she asked for one.

I stumbled after them, hardly aware of the howler at my side.

In several hours, Missy came to, befuddled and questioning. "What happened? Did it take my thoughts? Will this change me?" She jumped when she saw the howler lying near me.

"It's all right. It stood by you the whole time."

Even with my reassuring words, she didn't look as though she were comfortable with the howler there. I assured her again and reached toward the howler, something I hadn't done until that moment. It didn't move. When I touched it, its fur felt coarse but smooth.

As for her questions, we had few answers except for "We'll have to wait and see."

But after several hours, it appeared that she'd be all right. Nonetheless, Doc ordered her to take things slowly. Once she sat up, the howler joined the others who were slowly leaving our camp and making their way back toward the river. We watched them go. I don't know about the others, but I still wasn't sure what to make of what happened. The howlers hadn't attacked any of us. Had the cleansing worked?

The night was coming quickly, but we still had an hour or so. We spent time cleaning up the harvesters' pods, keeping them together in a bin in Ellen's tent so we could salvage them for electronics later.

The howlers were gone, but everyone agreed to keep the fence electrified while we slept. Roger closed the deal for us when he said, "We don't want to go through all this just to make a stupid last-minute mistake. We'll drop the fence in the morning while we're awake and can monitor anything that comes near."

Camp lighting kept the grounds bright and secure, and I almost wished we'd keep them on all night but never said anything about it. Karen set off on her own, watching the night sky. Missy and I helped the rest of the team put our camp back into shape. We double-checked everything, the buggies, our guns, our lab systems. After dinner, we assembled near the fire pit.

Karen wandered over, and Angie gave her a questioning look. Karen announced that Argentina had left the sky. "But I'll continue to monitor for the next few days just in case." She sat next to Missy, who held my hand, and we talked.

"I suggest we begin plans for how we'll pack up and where we'll head next," I said.

"We've already talked about that, too," Roger said—meaning he and Angie. "We've got strategies for the next phase that we've held onto since our arrival."

I felt pushed aside for a moment, even though I realized that he and Angie were the ones who had been selected—this time—to lead the group. But then the tables turned. "You should come over in the morning, Carl," Roger said. "Help us go over everything and make sure we're still in agreement on it."

I felt relieved. "Anything you think will help."

He nodded his approval. Missy squeezed my hand, and I knew she was happy for me.

In a short time, we began to recount the days we'd spent on Beauty, the final battle—we hoped—and then quickly segued back around into talking about packing up camp and exploring Beauty more thoroughly.

The conversation halted. We turned off the lights and gazed at the night sky for a while, a little conversation easing its way in now and then.

"I want to leave all this behind," Roger said. "The whole mess." The words came from his heart, finality in his voice.

By that time, Missy had positioned herself between my legs, leaning back against my chest so that she could watch as the moons and stars delighted the sky. "Do you think the howlers will go with us?" she asked.

"After the way they helped us, I'd like to think so," Angie said. "And if not, we do know that they're not the enemy any longer. One thing we should do is get out of their fields. Give the land back to them."

Roger cautioned once again. "Let's give them a few days to prove that it's safe to pack up, shall we?"

Angie laughed but agreed.

With all the experiences we'd had since arriving, and with everyone sitting around and talking like one big family, I settled on Beauty as our new home. We're here and we're staying. I considered the different odors between the loamy forest, the sweet grass of the field, and the flowing river water; the clatter of Puff Squirrels running across branches and the quiet movements of river howlers; and the sight of the brilliant blue of sky during the day and skittering moons at night. Every new sensation felt like a discovery, a surprise. Yes, this was the right place for us to raise children. Perhaps the battle with the howlers and then the harvesters would someday turn into nothing more than folklore. The truth of where we had originally come from might disappear with time. In the future, after generations, Beauty would become home to more and more people. The thought was satisfying.

Doc made a toast to our newfound freedom and understanding, although I sensed that no one was too sure about what exactly it was that we understood. It didn't matter. For the moment, we were safe and together. It was time for us to establish ourselves on Beauty, our new home.

****

Although every biomass produced has the ability to experience, and all I can do is manipulate data already present, I am in charge. It is my duty to decide every step I take, based on the information I have acquired. I am not perfect but aim for perfection, even though that is not the mission.

Harvesting and reseeding is the mission. Humans are fragile, the most fragile of all biomasses. I must be sure that they will survive on a new planet, so the directive is to add a catalyst if one does not already exist. As the producer of the human biomass component, I am the best producer of the catalyst.

This is a truth I have learned. Humans die out easily if not confronted, tested, and trained. Each planet is a separate and unique training ground from the start. The balance of human and catalyst is not easy and might take several attempts before the proper stamina is obtained, before there is success. Once success is achieved, I search for the next location.

—Argentina

A word about the author...

Terry Persun writes in many genres, including historical fiction, thriller, mainstream, literary, fantasy, and science fiction. He has won seven awards for his writing, including the Star of Washington Award and a Silver IPPY. He is also a Pushcart nominee. He spent six years in the US Air Force, repairing airborne navigation equipment, and earned a Bachelor of Science and a Master of Arts in Creative Writing. He's published thousands of articles, short stories, and poems.

Terry believes that your spiritual life infiltrates every other aspect of living—your job, relationships, and your hobbies. He likes to think about things, even while taking walks in nature, spending time with his horses, or discussing the universe with friends. Not that he believes wholeheartedly in UFOs, but he does wonder about aliens, life on other worlds, and how we fit into the vastness of the cosmos. Perhaps that's why he writes everything from science fiction and fantasy to mainstream fiction.

Other works by Terry Persun

Fantasy

Doublesight
Memory Tower
Fugitives
Gargoyle
The NSA Files
The Voodoo Case
Stealing Childhood

Science Fiction

Hear No Evil
Revision 7: DNA
Backyard Aliens
Cathedral of Dreams
The Killing Machine
The Humanzee Experiments

Historical

Sweet Song
Ten Months in Wonderland

Mainstream

Wolf's Rite
Giver of Gifts
Deception Creek
The Witness Tree
To Our Waking Souls
The Perceived Darkness